WALTER FALLS

WALTER FALLS

Steven Gillis

brook street press

SAINT SIMONS ISLAND

Brook Street Press
www.brookstreetpress.com

Brook Street Press is a trademark of Brook Street Press LLC

Grateful acknowledgment is made for permission to reprint the excerpt from "Before the Deluge" by Jackson Browne. Copyright © 1974 Swallow Turn Music. All rights reserved. Used by permission of Warner Bros. Publications U.S. Inc., Miami, Florida 33014.

First Paperback Edition 2004

Library of Congress Cataloging-in-Publication Data

Gillis, Steven.
     Walter Falls / Steven Gillis.
          p. cm.
     ISBN 0-9724295-0-6
     1.   Middle aged men—Fiction. 2.   Failure (Psychology)—Fiction. 3. Midlife crisis—Fiction.   I. Title.

PS3607.I446W35 2003
813'.6—dc21

                                                                        2002154540

ISBN 0-9724295-6-5 (pbk.)

Book design by Kerry Dennehy

Printed in the United States of America

10   9   8   7   6   5   4   3   2   1

For Mary

WALTER FALLS

PART I

"Where were the trout streams of my youth, and other innocent pleasures?"

JOHN CHEEVER
The Housebreaker of Shady Hill

CHAPTER 1

ᘛᘚ

I screw things up sometimes.

My wife, Geni Sharre, lovely Gee of the long-legged and red-haired Boston Sharres, professor of sociology and writer of many exemplary articles published in a host of scholarly reviews, used to provide my gaffes with liberal excuse. (She doesn't anymore.) When I stumble now—at work or play—and make an ass of myself, offering up some unintended imperfection, a careless malapropism, inappropriate sentiment or unsound judgement, injecting the wrong name into a conversation, investing client's funds into stocks I researched as thoroughly as any senior account executive at Porter and Evans only to have my forecast fall short of expectation—or blow up in my face—she no longer musses my hair and laughs in the same way she used to, but simply sighs, fatigued, and lets me know what once amused her fails to do so as before.

My doctors at Renton General are all well-intentioned specialists in long white coats and deep winter tans who come separately and together to steal a peek at me; shining flashlights into my eyes and ears, jabbing sticks down my throat, pricking and poking me in the legs and arms and up the ass. They occupy my time yet dismiss all symptoms that don't emerge for their convenience from my blood work, a sampling of my stool or scraping of my colon. After lengthy consultation, they insist my condition is a severe bout of asthenia. (Extreme exhaustion is how they refer to my collapse.) I'm too weak to protest, and while I endure their exams as best I'm able, I know their findings are false, and eventually implore them to, "Please! Forget about my blood and stool, my liver and kidneys and other tender viscera, and ask about my heart!"

They refuse me this, however.

Laid out on my bed, a flaccid stain of lumpy pudding, I try and diagnose the revolt of my once healthy constitution. Those who know me are surprised by my breakdown. (Walter Brimm? No, not him!) As part of the modern pantheon, investing large sums of money for the movers and shakers, I've acquired a reasonable amount of success and—until now—a reliable reputation, and was not supposed to succumb in such an inglorious fashion. As a child, the conduct that brought me here had defense. As a boy there was always excuse, but as a man the consequence of my indiscretions—the betrayal of Philos and Eros, charity and integrity, with faith turned to fear and pettiness inviting false promise—all crashed down hard. Friends believe my breakdown was sudden, but they're mistaken. Few people ever collapse just like that—snap!—and more often than not we give way in stages, like stone worn by the lapping of the waves, or the outer shell of a once sturdy house deprived of bricks and wood, until slowly the walls become hollow and little of the original frame remains.

It is in this way the measure of my dissolve can be marked, by the faintest hints found in the briefest moments.

CHAPTER 2

The spring before it all began, Gee published her latest article in Tod Marcum's *Kerrytown Review* under the title "Deconstructing Middle-class Mores While Redefining the Family Unit in Terms of the New Millennium." (A mouthful to be sure, and enough to confuse me even after I read her treatise.) As owner of the *Review*, Tod met often with Gee on nights a new article was nearly complete, editing and advising, encouraging and cajoling until the work went to print. All such meetings were conducted downtown with my full knowledge, yet far from where I might otherwise observe them.

I'd not met Tod prior to then and was introduced for the first time at a party given by Jay and Andi Dunlap. Ordinarily, such an encounter would not have fazed me. I'm not by nature a jealous person and have met any number of Gee's male friends over the years: journalists and college professors, social activists and graduate students, politicians and writers, musicians and actors, doctors and lawyers, and occasionally a businessman or two like me. My wife's affinity for keeping a healthy stable of male friends as comrades and mentors, sparring partners and flirting companions, pedagogical and spiritual advisors, was something I'd grown used to and I rarely thought twice about it. (One such aged professor, a well-known scholar in the field of ancient aboriginal cultures, had taken Gee under his wing in the time just after we married and liked to sit beside her in his small apartment, stroking her neck and hair in something less than an avuncular fashion, while reading aloud from the early works of Margaret Mead as his wife cooked stuffed cabbage and lentil soup in the kitchen. The man is dead now and I mention him only as an extreme example.) My wife is a vibrant woman, entitled to her friends, and if I once wondered how she managed to settle into marriage when her younger days involved something else altogether, I avoided voicing my concern and evaded raising the issue with her.

Before Tod, that is.

More than once I was told what a keen and clever man he was, an inscrutable and enlightened presence, liberal in thought and deed, unpretentious, ambitious and enterprising, a rabble-rouser and social reformer, the author of several seminal essays and distinguished articles of his own which were anthologized and won awards. ("It would do you good to read them, Walter," my wife exhorted.) A supremely confident yet modest fellow, self motivated and plain spoken, amiable and warmhearted, possessed of wry humor and a sincerity of purpose. Two years ago, Tod wrote a piece criticizing the ineffectiveness of social services within Renton entitled "Lazy Fare and the Republic of Indifference," which won three prestigious prizes and led to the journal being sued for libel by six city officials. The complaint was subsequently dismissed—with cost to the plaintiffs—and Tod wrote a follow-up piece about the ordeal, which was made into a documentary and earned him $600.

Tod's one flaw—and Gee insisted there was but this—revealed a total lack of business savvy. Despite his talent as a publisher and writer and how well received his journal was in certain arcane circles, the *Kerrytown Review* spent the last ten years in a state of fiscal instability. Struggling to keep his journal solvent, Tod employed an intricate system of robbing Peter to pay Paul, borrowing against projected sales and the full extent of next month's earnings in order to pay his writers. And yet somehow, through a mix of luck and pluck and shrewdness, the *Review* survived.

Tod Marcum then. Let us praise his excellence and ambition, his sagacity and resourcefulness. There is a glorious sense of uniqueness about him—or so Gee is convinced—a way which suggests here is someone of significance, a decent and dependable fellow, noble in his pursuits and generous in his ideals. Over the years he's been an aggressive spokesman for the community, championing children's rights and women's shelters, health-care reform and Dr. Janus Kelly's free medical clinic. He organized marches protesting racist policies in the Renton police department, in favor of same sex marriages, against discriminatory housing practices, and advocating strict gun control. He promoted rallies for dozens of charitable causes, wrote and spoke on issues of education, AFDC and affirmative action, social accountability and political fraud, and was it any wonder then my wife found him so appealing? Weren't they though but birds of a feather?

As parties go, the Dunlaps supplied an evening of endless possibility. Jay Dunlap was a heavyset man with short quills of argent hair, wide eyes, and a defect in his left hip that corrupted his stride with imbalance. ("I was born to walk in circles," Jay made a habit of joking.) He owned a chain of dry cleaners, nine stores inherited from his maternal grandfather, all in and around Renton. Commercials ran on local radio and TV under the slogan "Drop 'em at Dunlap's where even the dirtiest come clean." Andi McMillun-Dunlap was a junior partner at Likmee and Benofer, a corporate firm of forty attorneys specializing in mergers and acquisitions. Blond and blue-eyed, tall and large-breasted, she embodied a Nordic preeminence; her well-toned arms and shoulders making her the sort of woman one could imagine being favorably crushed by in bed.

When we arrived Andi was circulating through the main room, directing the caterers toward whomever needed another drink. Trays appeared with stuffed artichokes, imported cheese, Atlantic shrimp, miniature crab cakes, and vegetarian egg rolls.

Gee went to say hello to our hosts while I moved to the bar and got myself a whiskey. Several people were out on the patio and I took my drink and followed after them. The night was warm, the scent of juniper and rosebud mixed with cigarette smoke, after-shave, perfume, and liquor. Gee had mentioned earlier that Tod planned to be at the party, his friendship with the Dunlaps dating back several years to when Andi first helped him iron out the purchase of his *Review*, and standing some twenty feet from the house, I surveyed the faces of men passing by, trying to spot some-one who fit Tod's description.

I looked for a man about my age, thirty-seven, with slightly long, raven-black hair—Gee's word—casually dressed in a T-shirt and jeans as contrasted to my neat slacks and a button-down collar. Where I have olive skin, Tod was said to be fair, and while I'm tall and almost broad through the chest, Tod was described as "willowy"—another word Gee chose which I found peculiar. I remained outside for several minutes, was twice approached by people I knew coming up for a quick chat—"Hello, Brimm." "Hello."—and with no sign of Tod, turned back in the direction of the house where I searched for Gee through the sliding glass door.

Perhaps it was all only nonsense, but I began fantasizing then about my wife. I've heard of men in party settings slipping their hands beneath the clothes of women, and where slightly drunk—and non-drunk—wives find stolen moments in darkened bed-rooms, bathrooms, and even closets, undoing belts and placing more than a Chekhovian kiss upon the quivering sex of some equally non-drunk other husband. Not that Gee ever would, but I quickly imagined her in compromising places and positions, in tenebrous rooms and strange apartments, in expensive hotel suites strapped down on hands and knees, or naked in some spe-cially equipped dungeon. I often like to visualize situations where she is a bad girl and I am the source of her fulfillment, and also to dream of watching her with different men, though the arousal I experience from this bewilders me, for such is without question my greatest fear and fills me with a sadness so sudden and devas-tating as to bring me immediately back to my senses.

All things told, I suspect my conduct is only natural and harmless, and believe there is something healthy and refreshing about a husband continuing to be aroused by his wife after nine years of marriage. I love Gee absolutely and have never once cheated on her, adore equally her physical strengths and weaknesses, her intellect and ambition, self-assuredness and emotional center. (Her heart is fearless while I tend to quiver at the slightest trace of doubt or challenge.) Aware of my needs, I've been known to suffer distraction when Gee comes home exhausted from work or slightly under the weather, when she's preoccupied or annoyed with me or Rea, our daughter, for whatever reason, and rather than help resolve the problem, I focus first on the prospect of being denied sex that night, or knowing I'll have to be extra clever to get some. I'm not proud to think this way—sex alters my rational core even when I realize it shouldn't—and I've tried more than once to improve my conduct, all with limited attainment.

I first met my wife several years ago when a client passed on an extra ticket to an exhibit of the Spanish painter Joan Miró at the Modern. I arrived late. (My ticket was good from eight until ten p.m. and I didn't reach the first painting until almost nine.) The exhibit was spread out through several rooms, and with the rest of the evening's crowd already far up the hall, I proceeded at a pace which brought me rapidly from the first room to the second, and from the second to the third. Despite such haste, I enjoyed myself a good deal, taken in by the playfulness, the inventiveness and sensuality of Miró's creations, the colors and shapes found in such beautiful works as "Portrait of Madame K.," "Blues I, II, and III," and "Birth of the World."

I had just entered the fourth room at the start of the second hall when I noticed a young woman sitting on a bench, staring quietly at a work entitled "The Beautiful Bird Revealing the Unknown to a Couple in Love." The canvas was large and filled over every inch with a series of intricate lines and shapes, abstract figures, floating eyes and faces. A brown and beige backdrop gave life to black spheres, triangles and stripes, ovals and dumbbells and hourglass patterns done up in yellows and blues, reds and green. I didn't plan to stay, but something about the woman and her attraction to the piece intrigued me, and I was still standing there at ten o'clock when a guard came and informed us it was time to close.

I smiled at the woman, thinking I should apologize for intruding on her moment alone, but could only manage to mumble some innocuous observation about the size of the canvas and the flight of the birds. "Miró saw them as he looked out the window of his train," Gee said, "on his way from Paris to Varengeville in the spring of 1940. He was going through a period of self-doubt, unsure about the direction of his art, and spotting the birds inspired him. He later wrote of the experience: 'Whatever happens, I will follow my own trajectory. No person or thing will cause me to lose my way. I am alone and mad, but only madness rings true. It links me to the cosmos.'" She returned my smile, and before I could speak—without missing a beat—added, "I appreciate the sentiment."

We became lovers soon enough and enjoyed an uncomplicated sort of courtship. Eventually our affair turned more serious and we monitored our involvement to make sure we could manage a prolonged commitment, gauged our fundamental differences and found we were nonetheless happy in one another's company. Our passion acquired a healthy permanence, our sex an earthy vitality which I tried to maintain over the years. I bought a print of "The Beautiful Bird..." for Gee's birthday which she hung in the front room of her apartment, and later in the main room of our house where we lived together for six months and married in the spring. Gee seemed to delight in our togetherness, and while her writing and teaching and volunteer work took up much of her time, she was still a patient and supportive spouse, and later a tender and giving mother to Rea. Her honesty, intelligence, and sensuality were all indivisible parts of her nature and I was convinced—as a consequence of ignorance and having never lived with a woman before—that the trajectory of our relationship was hale and sound and would continue on this way forever.

But who can know for sure what path a marriage will take, or predict when fissures will form and no particular act of healing will be enough? Having believed mine was a perfectly favorable union, I assumed the emotional lethargy which grew between us after those first few years was a momentary blip, a commonplace and transient condition bound to pass, though Gee's view was something entirely different. As a social scientist, my wife is a classical theorist, her opinions on the evolution of social behaviors rooted in Locke and Rousseau, Jeremy Bentham and John Stuart Mill, her office shelves stacked high with dog-eared copies of Margaret Mead, James Clifford, and Louis Dumont, along with Geoffrey Barraclough's *The Times Atlas of World History*, Barzun's *The Modern Researcher*, and Gould and Kolb's *UNESCO A Dictionary of the Social Sciences*. Her specialty is the social connectives in modern communities, and for a brief period last year she experienced a measure of notoriety when the *SubEcco Quarterly* published her article "The Normalization of Sociopathic Behaviors in Contemporary Teens."

On love, Gee borrowed liberally from the laws of physics to suggest, "All forces lose steam after a certain distance is traversed. Passion is all well and fine," she wrote in another article, "Debunking the Myth of the Modern Marriage in an Age of Social Disenfranchisement," "yet no relationship survives for long without a practical level of compromise and cooperation. Marriage succeeds or fails by the ability of each partner to pull their weight, to take phone messages and manage their dirty laundry, cook and shop, balance the bank accounts, wash the windows, and service the car. Punctuality and the proper positioning of the toilet seat, agreements over what to eat, when to retire, and when to wake are all important to how spouses establish and maintain lines of intimacy, and it's this very sense of contentment and order which we eventually come to confuse as love."

I remember reading the piece with some anxiety and being left to feel puzzled about the underlying implication of Gee's thesis. I appreciated her rational assessment of how relationships required a balance of sensibility and similitude in order to sur-

vive, and was also impressed by how artfully she delineated between the pure spectacle of romance—Venus in the moonlight
dancing naked for Eros's pleasure—and the more efficient and
economical love between a husband and wife, and still the up-
shot did not seem promising. I tried to ignore my concerns, but
couldn't help sense in Gee's writing more than a measure of skep-
ticism, how extracting passion from the equation allowed her to
call attention to love's absence; the efficiency she wrote about in
the marital mix a convenient front. "What are you saying?" I
asked her one night in bed. "Are you suggesting couples gravitate
toward efficiency at the expense of actual emotion?"

"It's a natural occurrence."

"And yet the trend is ruinous to most relationships, is that it?"

"I didn't say efficiency and passion were mutually exclusive."

"Then what?" I was being defensive, was slightly unnerved
and couldn't help but feel there was an allegation looming.

"Cooperation," she quoted me then the three Cs, "comfort,
and compromise."

"Yes, but it isn't love. Isn't that what you're saying?" I wanted
her to tell me otherwise, to point out—as I was prepared to do if
she refused—that a love that had already lasted nearly ten years
was clearly immune to such challenges, that our efficiency was
not simply the deceit of a mortician prettying up a cold, dead
corpse but a purposeful part of our existence together, only Gee
fell silent and left me to ask once more, "All this talk of comfort
and efficiency avoids the question of love, no? Passion wears thin
and indifference wills out. What happens to the hunger then,
Gee? To the feelings your theory suggests are both lacking and
required in marriage? If it's a matter of physics, it can't just disappear. Where does it go then when it's no longer there?"

She considered as much—I could tell—and yet after a long
pause, this, too, she chose not to answer.

A few weeks before I first met Tod Marcum, at a time when Gee and I seemed happy enough and occasionally still sparked by passions—cooperative if somewhat compromised by wear—we rented an oceanfront bungalow along the southernmost side of Virginia Beach and took a family vacation. Our week together was something I looked forward to, and was disappointed then as the evening prior to our departure, Ed Porter came into my office and announced, "Congratulations, Brimm! I've something for you."

Even after all these years, I became instantly awkward and tongue-tied in Ed Porter's presence. His control over my career was distressing, and while I tried hard to please him and gave him leads on several stocks and complex deals which made money for his A-list clients, he extended little thanks and took full credit for my effort while only occasionally throwing me a bone. I am by all counts a diligent and dedicated worker, a meticulous and— at times—clever investor and financial advisor, thoroughly en- grossed by the theories and nuance of my profession, and still such competence was never enough for Ed who, at age sixty- seven, continued to rule the roost at Porter and Evans and ac- knowledged no achievements save his own.

Ed was not an especially tall man, though he projected a cer- tain largeness, his appearance imperial. Dressed in a royal blue suit of European cut, double-breasted, with a wide red tie and gold cuff links, his white hair was fine and meticulously combed, sprayed in place by an expensive hydrolyzed soy protein product. I felt my shoulders sink and roll passively forward as Ed stood over me. He had a low voice which rumbled inside his throat like a distilled sort of thunder, and dropping two heavy files down on my desk, said "I'm offering you a chance to take the lead on one of my deals, Brimm. It's a career maker!"

I stared at the files for several seconds, certain Ed knew of my vacation. He was a manipulative SOB, ever eager to test the loyalty of his staff by disrupting their plans to celebrate anni- versaries, birthdays, trips, and holidays, and however much I resented his hold over me, I knew—as did he—that under any

other circumstance I'd have jumped at the chance to work up one
of his projects. "I'm afraid I'm leaving for the beach in a matter
of hours, Ed," I decided to proceed with candor. "The family and
I haven't been away in over a year. I haven't taken a day off since
early last summer," I added for emphasis, a fact which didn't impress him in the least.

"Suit yourself," he frowned, the starched collar of his shirt
pinched up against the flesh of his neck. "If you can't handle the
job."

"It isn't that, Ed."

"And here I thought I was doing you a favor."

"You are."

"I'm sure I can find someone to replace you."

"I didn't say I couldn't handle it," I began to stutter, and insisted that I was simply concerned about the time frame and
whether the work was something I could do while I was on vacation or should I cancel the trip.

"You do it wherever you like, Brimm. You'll have the week to
pull things together. Check in with me then."

I took the files and put them in my briefcase.

We reached the beach early the next morning and I proceeded to spend most of that first day making and receiving
phone calls, studying the files Ed gave me, reviewing the market
on my portable computer, drafting reports, sending and receiving
faxes. I promised to work no later than noon, and planned to
enjoy the rest of the day with my family, but one thing led to another and it was nearly five o'clock before I came outside.

My daughter is a glorious child—I say this as objectively as
possible—nearly seven now and at the time of our vacation
just turned five, an intelligent, somewhat shy yet curious,
handsome, and polite little girl with her mother's green eyes and
sun-reddened hair worn somewhat long in thick waves and
curls, olive skin like mine, and a joyous sort of trusting spirit
which made me forever want to protect and guard her. I went
quickly to the water then, intent on making up for the hours
spent working, and finding Rea, asked her to come swim with me.

"Daddy wants to be with his girl. Are you ready to spend time with your father?"

Rea was excited by my arrival, and though the day had cooled a bit, hurried to slip off her shorts and T-shirt to reveal her pink and blue swimsuit. I scooped her up and ignoring Gee's warnings carried her out into the ocean where the water was, indeed, colder and rougher than I expected. Determined to make a go of it nonetheless—for we'd come to swim, after all!—I brought Rea out past the initial break and settled her into the tide. Twice I peeked over my shoulder to spot Gee on the shore, watching us anxiously as if my every effort was in error, and, annoyed, I allowed myself to be distracted for just a second, not noticing the next wave as it sprayed up to my chest and over Rea's head just as I was letting her go. She attempted at once to dive back toward me, but another swell caught her and pulled her under. The abruptness of her disappearance was shocking, but then the scene became worse, for when I reached down to grab her, the current had already altered her position, moving her left while I began flailing right.

Rea was under no more than a few seconds before I found her and scooped her up, but the time was immaterial; the look on her face a mix of injury and indictment that went well beyond mere childlike surprise. "There now. There." What could I do but clutch her against my chest and try to comfort her, even as she squirmed and fought through a series of coughs and gasps? "There, yes, Daddy." Her bright green eyes were darker, her gaze an ancient shade, as deep and knowing as the very waters of the ocean. She extended her arms away from me, wary of my hold while turning herself back toward the beach and her mother who was already halfway out into the water.

Later, and after much regret, I tried to put the incident behind me and prepared the evening's barbecue. I drank whiskey from a plastic 7-Eleven tumbler, grew slightly drunk, burned the burgers, and made a mess of the buns. The awkwardness of our togetherness became painfully clear, and after we'd eaten what could be salvaged for our meal, Rea grew tired and fell asleep in her mother's arms and was put to bed.

I waited for Gee in the front room, invited her to come sit beside me on the cabin's small sofa. I tried to be affectionate, and looking for forgiveness, said, "It's good to get away, don't you think?" I placed a hand on her arm, hoping she'd slide closer and allow me a kiss, but she moved from me at once and went out on the back porch to smoke. I followed her to the screen, where foolishly and in a tone of groundless self-pity, I complained, "What are you angry about?"

"I'm not angry, Walter."

"I already apologized for Rea."

"And I said I'm not angry."

"Then what?"

"Please."

"Tomorrow will be better."

"Are you planning to work all week?"

"Just an hour or two in the morning."

"Sure."

"Christ, Gee. What am I supposed to do?"

"I don't know, Walter," and here she was angry again. "You tell me."

"What about the work you brought?"

"I haven't even looked at it yet, and I won't if it interferes with Rea."

"Alright, I said I'm sorry. Why can't you appreciate my effort?"

"What are you talking about?"

"I'm here."

"Wonderful."

"Come inside," I resorted to pleading.

"In a minute."

"Let's not ruin our night."

"No, let's not."

"I'm going to bed."

"Fine."

"I want you."

"Charming."

"Are you coming?"

"I'm going to take a walk."

"I'll come with you then."

"No, you need to stay with Rea."

"Why are you acting like this?"

"I'm sorry, am I being selfish? You want me? Come on then. Come here. Let me just finish my cigarette, or maybe you don't mind if I smoke?"

"Hell."

"That's right," she turned and flicked her cigarette into the dark; I can still recall the spark from the ash as it hit the sand, the brief brilliance of color that flamed and was gone.

Later that night we lay in bed, separated by the pillow Gee brought from home and liked to wrap her legs around. I was a sound sleeper, though the events of the day left me restless, and at one point I rolled on my side, surprised to find Gee propped up on her elbow watching me, observing me intensely, her face illuminated by a single ray of moon passing through the window. Her look was serious, wishful and wondering, pained and forewarning, admonishing and imploring. Had I been but briefly sage—a desire forever cast by fools like me—I'd have heeded her gaze and realized what had to be done, but then I was careless and never so clever with love. Here was where I began to lose her, in failing to take from her eyes the notice she intended. ("It's now or never, Walter, do you understand?") I was tired, and rolling back over in an effort to find a comfortable spot on the bed, I yawned and whispered in a languid tone, "Go to sleep."

After a minute, I felt Gee turn away from me, and in time drift off.

The rest of the week passed more or less the same. I wound up working longer each day than expected, the deal Ed Porter gave me to pull together required serious attention, and I concluded, wisely or otherwise, that it would be absurd to ruin my vacation over a job performed half-assed. Gee remained annoyed with me, was distant when I sought her out before dinner, and colder still at night. Once we returned to the city, the detachment between us lingered, and even as things seemed to improve, I felt unsure. (It was as though I'd survived a terrible wreck only to have to deal now with residual scars.) When I walked into Ed Porter's office that first morning back and presented him with all the work I'd done, he looked up at me from behind his enormous teak desk and said, "Oh that, Brimm. Don't worry, we've plenty of time. There's no need to rush."

I dropped my head and returned down the hall.

CHAPTER 3

I stayed out on the patio a few minutes more, still hoping to catch a glimpse of Tod before Gee introduced us, and failing to accomplish this, I was just about to go inside and find my wife when a voice called, "Hey, Brimm," and I turned around.

The source of light out back was Japanese lanterns hung up in the low branches of two poplar trees, the blue patio tiles shimmering beneath as if the entire surface was liquid. Jack Gorne approached from between the trees, his right hand raised as he passed from the shadows in the rear of the yard and moved directly toward me. Nattily dressed in a beige cashmere sweater, pleated slacks, and Italian shoes, Jack was slightly taller than I, his face full and round, his hair thick and combed upward like an archetypal sort of gangster. With features near enough though not quite handsome, he had dark, deep-set eyes and a wide, up-turned mouth that cast his countenance into a bemused sort of dominance. I'd known Jack since my first days at Porter and Evans when he was a client, his portfolio flush with first-rate stocks and bonds and extensive holdings in real estate and companies in and around Renton. He recently removed his account from our care however, in order to manage his own money. ("There are things I'd like to try which you boys haven't the stomach for," he told Ed Porter.) For some reason he chose to retain me as an outside consultant, my fee kicked upstairs to the partners, and phoned every week or so to ask my opinion on specific investments. Most of my input on Jack's business was minimal, and yet he considered me essential. "I trust your instincts, Brimm. You're honest and I'm not. You're a talisman. A goddamn bunny's foot. You bring me luck!" I was credited with helping several of his deals turn a huge profit—such recognition was flattering while having Jack Gorne in my corner certainly didn't hurt my standing with Ed Porter—and last March I presented Jack with an idea Jay Dunlap had to open a facility that cleaned expensive rugs, furs, and sweaters. The venture was sound and recently the two became partners.

Jack slapped my shoulder, clicked his whiskey glass against mine, and asked, "How's it going, Walt?"

"Good, Jack. You?"

"Excellent, my friend," he glanced above the trees, then looked past me in order to survey the crowd. "I came for a drink," he smiled, "and maybe some party favors. Hell of a moon, eh, Brimm? And how about that Andi? Now there's a planet I'd like to orbit. She's alright, don't you think? Big women are a nice change of pace sometimes. They'll give you a bang for your buck." He raised his glass approvingly, then drank what remained in two swallows.

Although I'd had the same fantasy, I didn't feel comfortable joking about Andi and mentioned as much to Jack who dismissed my concern with a quick, "What's the matter, Brimm? Afraid to dream?"

"It isn't that. Andi and Jay are friends, that's all."

"So? Friends share, don't they? Besides, infidelity's overrated. It's barely a vice. If I'm attracted to a woman, and ask her to dinner and she agrees, why should I care if she's married? If I sleep with her, what's more important than my pleasure at that moment?"

I changed the subject and got Jack talking about work. He told me then about Atlantic Groceries and the rumor that had the chain about to go under. "A few months ago, remember, Brimm? Distributors were bailing left and right, settling their accounts for twenty cents on the dollar before Atlantic could tie them up in bankruptcy and pay no more than five percent of what they owed." Jack had an eighteen percent interest in Geotine Soaps and Salves which made thirty-five percent of its profits through sales at Atlantic stores. "Something didn't add up," he continued. "Atlantic was crying poor too fast and I didn't like it. I rejected all proposals to square Geotine's account, shouted down my partners until they agreed to not cut a deal. Fuck Atlantic! Why should we give them what they want? Something was rotten. I didn't trust them. It didn't make sense.

"I decided to place a few calls, and with the help of some people I knew, I tracked down the wives and lovers of executives at Atlantic. Getting them to talk was easy. I pretended we met at conventions and dinner parties, and after a bit of bullshit, had them tell me what was really going on. Hell," Jack clicked my whiskey glass again, "it wasn't as if they didn't want to give it all away. I barely had to pry."

It turned out Chapman Industries was secretly negotiating to take over Atlantic. "Here's why the bastards were so eager to open their books and expose serious financial troubles. By screaming bankruptcy and scaring companies into settling existing accounts, Atlantic could dump current debt and rid themselves of contracts useless to Chapman. At the same time, insider trading laws prevented officers at Atlantic from disclosing the impending takeover. They were protected from claims of fraud by distributors and conning everyone to cash out. A slick play, but now I had them by their balls.

"I got hold of Ed Fearn, CEO of Atlantic, and told him in exchange for keeping his secret, Atlantic would settle with Geotine for one hundred cents on the dollar. I then had Fearn arrange a meeting for me with Frederick Chapman, and I warned the old man if he didn't sell me 50,000 shares of Chapman stock before the merger, and expand the sale of Geotine products into his stores in New York, Pennsylvania, and Ohio, I'd start leaking what I knew to his distributors. Extortion? Fuck 'em! Who's to say what's legal and what's not? It's all in the cost of doing business, Brimm. Any fool knows this."

I relate the story about Jack as a means of illustrating the difference between us. While I was practical, fearful, and pragmatic, typically benign and nonthreatening, the sort of man people felt comfortable with at parties and conventions, Jack was combustible, opinionated, and quick to argue, a fierce force of nature who barrelled ahead without regard for whatever stood in his way. It was Jack's belief that the world was fundamentally amoral, the human spirit motivated by self-interest, and that the meek would not inherit the earth. "We're carnivores, Brimm, creatures influenced by personal needs, innately suited to Darwin's theory denoting survival of the fittest. It's the one law that matters, the only one we have to obey."

Of this, I wasn't as certain. I could accept intellectually that Man was not always gracious and kind, but the knowledge unnerved me. (If Gee was vested of both positive and negative impulses, the implication was that I'd reason to worry about her half the time.) I wanted to believe all people were inherently virtuous, but reality forbid me. (Lying here now in my bed at Renton General, the more I consider the complexity of human nature the louder I want to scream.) As an American male, corn fed and white of flesh, I was raised with certain predispositions and expectations, forever taught the world was my oyster and would always remain. Sadly, times are different now, the social order has been reshuffled and men such as myself—defined by the clumsiness of our forefathers, with all their sins and prejudice and crimes of self-interest—are treated with deserved suspicion and contempt. (The once golden child has dropped the ball, and threatened with obsolescence, stands haplessly confused.) One would think, after all these years, I'd have adjusted to how the world really is, but then love has a way of divesting the heart of its ability to react with reason, and in wondering how I got then from there to here, broken again and alone in the hospital flat on my ass, I simply have to remember earlier lessons somehow forgotten.

I was born in Palgree Falls, 300 miles west of Renton. My parents, Katherine and Charles, provided me with a pleasant childhood, were doting and protective, instructive and supportive; my days filled with football and paper routes, schoolwork and vacations, dates to dances, minor mischief and rites of passage marked by cigarettes, *Penthouse* magazine, and cans of Bud. I dated local girls, losing my virginity late one summer night hunkered down in a plush field of corn, as a classmate, more experienced than I, rode my hips while—for reasons never clear—singing the words to our high school fight song: "Oh hail to thee, oh hale perse knight of Palgree High!"

I was a good student—more sedulous than bright—and graduated near the top of my class. The genesis of my diligence was my parents, who in their work—my father was a banker, my mother a surgical nurse—adhered to a strict protestant ethic and instilled in me, their only child, a nose-to-the-grindstone orientation; the credo "Toil, Triumph, Rule!" introduced several generations before as the Brimm's family mantra and weaved its way deep into the pith and marrow of every heir.

I tried to take such familial cheers to heart, though the religion of my soul did not emerge from heeding any one particular hoot and whistle, but came instead as a consequence of bearing witness to my parents' conduct. I was inspired by their industry, their assiduity, and the intensity of their being, how well they displayed a willingness to follow their own personal ethic. My father's steady hand coupled with my mother's grace of spirit filled me with a firm sense of purpose, order, and focus, and imagine then my surprise when during my first semester of college my father was arrested on charges of fraud, his assets frozen, his bank put into receivership; photographs of his being booked at the county courthouse printed in large color shots on the front page of the *Palgree Gazette*.

The indictment, brought separately under State and Federal statutes, accused Charles Brimm of swindling hundreds of clients out of their life's savings through the sale of unsecured junk bonds. (Upon further investigation, my father was also found to have embezzled more than a million dollars from his own bank, syphoning off the interest from savings accounts while stashing the cash in overseas deposits.) As shocked as we were, everyone still expected my mother to stand steadfast at my father's side, but she surprised us and immediately distanced herself from her husband. With charges of complicity waved in her face, she pled ignorance to each illegal transaction, and on the advice of her lover, Dr. Mark Batelle (another bombshell exploding!), accepted an offer of immunity in exchange for testimony against my father.

Charles Brimm was sentenced to twelve years in prison. My mother filed for divorce, and working with several prominent attorneys to recoup what little was left of the family money—before civil suits drained every last dime—she lost the house and took an apartment near the hospital. Abandoned then by most of her friends, she relied on the help of barbiturates to sleep and amphetamines to wake, managing to get through her days with the solitary and sullen deportment of a proud queen cast into exile.

Life went on, though in a way which was so altogether altered and fundamentally foreign as to make even the simplest undertakings onerous. Six months after my father entered prison, my mother added morphine to her mix of drugs, and suffered a fatal coronary while assisting on the bile duct surgery of an overweight Armenian woman, dying instantly and with her face smeared and splattered atop a newly perforated duodenum.

I grieved each new disaster with disbelief, ruing the annihilation of my family with such initial horror that rallying myself from bed in the morning took all my strength. After missing a year of school, I transferred back in state to the University of Renton where I paid my way with student loans and the cash earned from an assortment of odd jobs, graduating four years later with a degree in business. I obtained my broker's license that summer, began taking classes two nights a week toward my Master's in finance, and was hired in the fall at Porter and Evans as a junior broker and financial advisor.

Clueless and with neither sufficient experience nor connections—hired because I seemed earnest and the sort of young associate Ed Porter could easily force to dance beneath his thumb—I chose to cut my teeth in uncharted fields, and invested in a series of upstart computer companies, privatized utility and telephone services, new biotechnology advances, wireless communication, and cable and Internet futures. Through a process of much hard work and a few missteps along the way, I parlayed my plan for favoring virgin firms into a doubling and redoubling of my assigned clients' funds. (My own portfolio now—and as given over to Gee—is three file cabinets thick and reeks of good fortune.) I was promoted two rungs up the ladder, invited to power lunches and a dinner given once a year where Ed Porter shook the hands of his minions and encouraged us to "Make me rich!"

A young man with money in his pockets is a particularly arrogant creature, and, filled with hubris, I thought about my parents and how far I'd come from the early shock of their betrayal. As a consequence of their crimes, I developed a severe distaste for the slightest form of deception. (Hyperbole, let alone prevarication, turned my normally kind eyes cold, while harmless charades brought me to the brink of choler.) I gained a reputation among clients, colleagues, and peers as a man of utmost honesty and frankness and, until the time I met Tod and all such virtue went to hell, maintained my rank with pride.

Shortly after my father was released from prison, he moved into a small apartment on the border between Palgree Falls and Shady Hill. We didn't speak often, though I sent him a monthly check, and he surprised me one night by calling, half drunk and alone in his room. "I owe you an explanation," he said, the only time he extended me such an offer. In trying to make sense of his crimes however, he wound up rambling about the vagaries of the human soul, denouncing avarice and envy, desire, susceptibility, and temptation, warning me ("You, too, Walter.") until I couldn't listen any more and hung up the phone.

I took a walk through the neighborhood and tried to dismiss my father's babble, only his caution stayed with me. The idea of the world laying traps to trip me up appealed to my vanity, the thought of snares set and lures unsprung, and how I might wake up tomorrow and be tested by what my father called "the chronic consequence of being as we are" aroused my interest. Convinced I was immune to my parents' nonsense, resilient to and stronger than whatever temptation caused them to crumble, I challenged the gods to "Come and get me!" and bayed at the moon, "The delusion that took down Katherine and Charles is in no way clever enough to cozen the son!"

For several weeks I dared fate to find me, eager to prove I was a firm and honest fellow. I concentrated in this way much more than I should, and when no cruel provocation overtook me, I beamed with conceit and great satisfaction, certain I'd won. So convinced was I, that in the middle of all such self-congratulatory hubbub and grand hurrah, I failed to heed the warning tick inside my head, as steady and foreboding as a bomb fused and set to go off.

Until eventually it did.

Jack finished his story about Atlantic Groceries, slapped me on the arm, and went off to freshen his drink. I turned toward the house and stared back through the sliding glass doors where I spotted Gee beside a man in jeans, a somewhat faded blue cotton shirt, and brown leather sandals. His face was narrow, his coloring fair, his features angular and finely drawn. His hair was dark and a bit long, his shoulders loose and legs straight, his mouth cast in the midst of a smile with lips roundly parted. He was sharing hors d'oeuvres with my wife from a single plate, Gee tossing her head back and laughing at something Tod said, turning further away from me and as she did so her body in the shadows was briefly lost.

I went inside. Gee glanced up as I drew near and said my name as if surprised to see me. I was introduced to Tod, "Pleased to..." "Delighted, sir..." shaking hands and all the rest. "We saw you outside," Gee noted, "talking to Jack Gorne."

"You should have come and said hello."

Gee looked at Tod. "Actually," she smiled.

"What?"

"Jack and Tod."

"What about them?"

"I understand you two are friends," Tod said.

"We're acquainted. I do some work for him from time to time."

"Involving Renton?"

"That's right, why?"

"Jack and I have had our differences over the years about what's best for Renton as a community."

"Anything specific?"

"Melstar Clinic."

"You mean Wintmore Towers?"

"That's right," Tod's eyes, a deep autumnal blue, opened wide as I mentioned Wintmore. "Are you familiar with the sale?"

"I reviewed the final papers." Two years ago, Jack purchased Wintmore Towers and forced the closing of Melstar, then a free mental health clinic on the north side. There was much to-do in the news for a time, before interest waned and the majority of complaints disappeared. I cleared my throat, and without thinking—an example of my clumsiness—fell at once into the enemy camp. "It seems the property Jack developed has worked out quite well."

"That's a matter of opinion," Tod shifted closer to Gee, his tone congenial enough, and yet there was an inflexibility about him, his casual appeal belying an intractable side. "The people who relied on Melstar feel differently. You say you reviewed the documents?"

"That's right."

"And Mr. Gorne's intentions didn't interest you?"

"I was paid to go over the papers, not impose social commentary." I meant my statement as harmless tripe. I was not confrontational as a rule and preferred to terminate all debate with a show of good will but something in my voice stiffened, and even as I tried to laugh the sound I made came out strained.

"Perhaps if you read Tod's article, Walter," Gee made reference to a piece Tod had written at the time.

"I'd be happy to." I tried to demonstrate my willingness to be accommodating, and in reference to Tod's article, said, "I'm sure there are points I've not considered."

Tod acknowledged my comment with a quick nod as Gee placed her right shoulder even closer to his. (I experienced my first real shock of jealousy—a jolt quite sharp and clear—altogether unlike me and yet the signals were all there.) "I appreciate that," Tod said, then added, "What troubles me is the way Jack thinks having enough money to buy a building automatically gives him the right to alter the landscape of an entire community."

"You object to how a man uses his own property?"

"I object to a man of wealth believing himself free to affect the interests of all."

"But what of capitalism, Tod?" I continued to suffer the physical challenge of his presence, the way Gee tilted her head nearer to his, her hip angled and right hand made available should he choose to reach for it. "As someone who owns a business," I found myself unable to resist, "how is it you feel Jack Gorne should not be permitted to operate Wintmore Towers as he sees fit? How would you react if someone came along and told you what pieces you could publish in your *Review?*"

Tod placed his drink down and folded his arms in front of him. More than I, he seemed to enjoy defending his views, though he didn't bother answering me directly. "I would like to think the rich recognize their responsibility to the community. Refusing to renew the lease of a mental health-care facility housed in Wintmore Towers for over twenty years, a clinic that served hundreds of patients in the neighborhood, the location of which these people depended upon for their very survival, represents a form of social genocide."

"You're being facetious, of course. Social genocide? Is that Lenin or Trotsky?"

"Trotsky rejected socialism, Walter," Gee pointed out to me. I pretended to remember as much, and replied, "That's right.

Universal revolution, a constant churning of the waters. It's important to keep the rich from consolidating too much of their power, is that it, Tod?"

"A society is judged by how it takes care of its less fortunate."

"But I disagree. A society is judged by how best it operates. If a society is inefficient, everyone suffers from bottom to top."

"Stalin was efficient."

"Stalin was myopic. His efficiency eventually collapsed. He was also a madman and a murderer, and certainly you aren't accusing Jack Gorne of committing these sort of crimes."

"You can't defend Gorne," Gee argued, "or even suggest that he was at all concerned about the people of Renton when he turned Wintmore Towers into exclusive condominiums and put hardworking lower middle-class families out on the street."

"I can, in fact, suggest just that when you look at the end result," I said with a certain confidence and leaned forward then in order to snatch the last eggroll from Gee's plate, a gesture intended to reestablish—in some ill-defined way—the connection between us, but to my surprise, Gee moved the plate out of reach. (A second later, she realized what she had done, and extended the dish back to me, but by then it was too late.) I withdrew my empty hand and shoved it deep into my pocket. Wounded, I said, "It's nonsense to judge a deal only by the minor inconvenience it caused while dismissing in turn its overall good. Sure, Jack was looking to make money when he converted Wintmore Towers into an expensive high-rise. And yes, a mental health clinic was closed, and it's true a handful of families had to find new accommodations, but let's examine things objectively. First, the city ran the clinic. The mayor's office had six months' notice of Jack's plans to not renew their lease, and yet the city failed to find a new space and let the clinic close. This is hardly Jack's fault."

"Objectively," Tod's voice remained calm, "everyone knew going in that the city was looking for an excuse to shut the clinic down. Jack Gorne took full advantage of this information when negotiating to purchase Wintmore Towers. He received preferential treatment from the city in their support of the deal. How hard would it have been for him to find another site for his project? Wintmore Towers wasn't the only property on the north side up for sale. By purchasing the building, Jack helped the city facilitate precisely what public policy would not have permitted them to do on their own."

I had no response to such an argument and could only shake my head. (Gee frowned as I did so and I felt instantly contrite.) For a moment I thought I might simply shrug my shoulders and let everything go with a submissive sort of laugh—for such was more in keeping with my nature—but even I could sense the situation demanded more, and I wound up countering with, "What about Jack being the only developer at the time willing to put his money into upscaling the north side of town? Look at the north side now. How many people do you think benefited from Jack's vision? The entire city was revitalized by his decision to renovate Wintmore Towers. Before there was no upper middle-class living downtown. Now everyone's hurrying back. A dozen buildings have been refurbished. Businesses are returning, restaurants and shops. There are new jobs and opportunities Jack Gorne's money helped seed. His effort should be applauded not condemned. A few people were displaced, it's true, and that's unfortunate, but a minor trade-off given how well things turned out."

"Even better," Tod wasted no time responding, "if Jack had purchased a different building and left Melstar alone."

"But why?" Once again, I shook my head. "What would you have Jack do, ignore the best deal available simply to forestall the inevitable and force the city to find another way to shut the clinic down?"

"That's right," Tod answered.

"I agree," Gee joined in, her elbow now in contact with the middle three fingers on Tod's right hand.

"Well then." We had crossed over into the sort of debate where everything rational was sacrificed and no clear victory could be had by either side without someone first committing a serious false step. "You'll have to excuse Walter," Gee chose to tease me then and hurried once more to Tod's defense. "It's part of his job. If Walter had his way, the entire world would be in a constant state of refurbishment and reinvestment," she smiled and squeezed Tod's arm.

The last vestiges of my composure collapsed on me, and even as I laughed at Gee's joke, I felt myself losing hold. For years I'd prided myself on maintaining a level of prudence and clearheadedness which kept me from making rash decisions, and—save for falling in love which I did hopelessly and totally, like a stone plunging downward into a warm puff of sand—I managed to keep my emotions in check. Here however, I was thrown off my mark, and the only thing worse than the way our conversation relegated me into the role of insensitive ass was witnessing my wife's determination to align herself with Tod. ("Come on, Brimm!" I heard Ed Porter's voice in my head, challenging me to "Get with it, man!") In my role as senior associate at Porter and Evans, I was required to think fast on my feet, to be agile and firm and shrewd enough to recover even when I blundered, but in my capacity as husband to Gee, I was never so clever nor confident. I tried to imagine myself at the office then, where the world was ever so much more finite and clear, and was able at last to say, "Tell me, Tod, do you own a house?"

"On Fetzer Street, yes. I inherited the property from my uncle several years ago."

"I see. And you've a mortgage?"

"I refinanced, and put the money back into the *Review*."

"And your *Review* has other loans, I imagine?"

Again, he answered, "Yes. Capital Financial and First National were recommended to me."

"Ah," giving what I hoped was not too telling a grin, "then I'm confused. You object to Jack Gorne's purchase of Wintmore Towers because it facilitated the city's closing of Melstar Clinic, and yet you're doing business with Capital Financial which holds the papers on some of the worst tenements in Renton and deals daily with the most notorious slumlords in the state. And First National, I happen to know, loans large sums of cash to companies such as Stenson Carbines and Dillar Chemical which you

vilify in your *Review*. This, of course, means the interest you pay
on your loans is being funnelled right back into the pockets of the
same firms you claim to oppose. Ironic, isn't it?" I glanced at Gee.
"And yet, business is business. You have your needs and Jack
Gorne has his needs, too."

I was full of myself, delighted to have put Tod in his place in
front of my wife. All this talk about Jack, and by inference me,
being pariahs devouring the city for our own personal gain had
hit a nerve and I wanted Gee to see what a hypocrite her friend
turned out to be, that in the grand scheme of things it was men
like Jack Gorne—and me!—who provided Renton with security
and structure, the fruits of our labor that helped people put
money in the bank, paid for food and mortgages, built houses and
bridges, allowed children to attend college, supported charities
and hospitals, and paid off debts. In contrast, Tod Marcum's
work—the essays published in his dyspeptic little review—consisted of nothing more than petty finger-pointing, griping and
whining, a tearing down of the world in worthless protest, super-
fluous and self-indulgent as he partnered himself with the very institutions he derided as avaricious and socially impure.

Tod ran his left hand back through his hair, somewhat coy,
and smiling as always, apologized then. "I'm sorry, Walter. I'm
afraid I've given you the wrong impression. I should have been
more clear. I meant that Capital and First National were recommended to me, but in doing my research, I came up with the same
information as you. You're right to think I'd be making a mistake
to secure my loans at those institutions. What money I borrowed
came through Berinfel Mutual."

"You know Berinfel, don't you, Walter?" Gee's tone departed
from its earlier tease, was less playful and more inculpating. "Or
doesn't Ed Porter allow you to deal with those sort of lenders?"

"But sure," I rallied clumsily to my own defense. (Berinfel
specialized in socially conscious investments, minority programs
and mutual funds which—in truth—I dealt with only sparingly
in all my years at P and E.) "Walter, Walter, Walter," Gee's voice
in my head. I was afraid to look at her just then, felt my face turn

red, yet did my best to pretend Tod's explanation impressed me, and went so far as to compliment him on his research. "It isn't often people are as thorough as you," I laughed nervously and a bit too loud, and without the slightest idea of what else to say, I offered, "If you ever want to make real money, Tod, you come and see me."

He considered my gesture, considered the source, then smiled again, and reaching over toward my wife, retrieved the final eggroll from Gee's plate, securing it like a ruby prize, like a lover's tit, the lush plump nipple of which he sampled first with his fingers, rolling the nub back and forth as if to savor the surface even more, before placing it on his lips, across his tongue, and into his mouth. "Thanks, Walter," he said. "That's mighty generous of you."

"Of course, of course, of course."

CHAPTER 4

"**W**hat a world, what a world!" in the immortal words of the slowly ablating Wicked Witch of the West, who pronounced with such exactitude from her hissing puddle the very axiom I now live by—"What a world, indeed." I also feel on the verge of melting, and looking about my room at Renton General can't help but blubber, "What a remarkable confusion."

I have at home—or more accurately what used to be home—a large collection of books and once enjoyed surrounding myself with works of poetry and fiction. I find the words upon the printed page provide a finite form of opinion, never changing, the consistency allowing me to believe the world reliable and coherent. Driving home with Gee from the Dunlaps' party, I recalled one such poem by Auden, who wrote about fresh love's betrayal, where every day over green horizons a new deserter rode away, while birds muttered of ambush and treason, and standing later at my bedroom window, I could hear the black crows cawing, "Tod, Tod, Tod!"

The events of that night at the party wore me down, and not used to feeling as I did, I experienced peculiar symptoms. My body became unreliable while my otherwise sound sleep was riddled with bad dreams. In the days that followed, as Tod phoned and

chatted with Gee as he always did about some such meeting, petition, or rally in support of a new liberal cause, I grew anxious and
alarmed. I'd hear Gee laugh at something Tod said and the sound
of her joy would chill me, her smile—too lovely!—making me desperate to feel her in my arms.

Two weeks after the party, Gee spent several afternoons
working with Tod on an article entitled "The Politics of Convenience: Big Business and the Subjugating of Community." Twice
I was phoned at my office and told by Gee that Rea was with
Sheri, our sitter, down the street. "Tod's ordered sandwiches. I'll
be home around eight."

As a rule, I try not to dwell on incidents which result in disappointment or otherwise rattle the foundation of my perceived
safe and infrangible world. Such a strategy, repressive in its ten-
dencies but self-protecting nonetheless, allows me to feel secure,
mistakes at work weathered with eyes closed, my greatest relief
coming when someone else screws up and earns Ed Porter's
vitriol. At home, quarrels with Gee are handled with equal denial, disputes dismissed as fast as I can manage. I am docile in
love, and remain always eager to end a fight by offering reconcil-
iation and compromise to my wife, and would have continued to
do so forever—I'm sure—were it not for Tod Marcum.

Peeved, I used Rea as the reason to register my first complaint
and suggested our daughter was being neglected, that her morn-
ings were already filled with school and then day care until Gee
picked her up. "And now you're gone past dinner." My tone was
pleading, my charge manipulative, inappropriate, and self-serving;
as a mother, Gee was otherwise above reproach.

"I'm trying to meet a deadline, Walter," she explained. "I
don't like it any more than you."

"All the same," I didn't retract a word, and the next afternoon—as a consequence of my disapproval—Gee took Rea with
her to the *Kerrytown Review*. That evening, my daughter came
home exclaiming the virtues of "Uncle Tod!" I went into my den
and closed the door where I searched long and hard for just the
right book.

Late that same July, Gee invited Tod to dinner.

"He likes you, Walter. I'm sure in time you two will become good friends." What reckless sort of wide-eyed fancy motivated my wife to think this way I didn't know and I approached the date with severe reservation.

Tod arrived just after six, dressed in his usual jeans, a pale green shirt, and old leather moccasins that looked for all the world like slippers. His hair was damp and brushed straight back, and eager to curry favor he came bearing gifts: a bottle of red wine and a small coloring book for Rea. My daughter is a bright, energetic child, intellectually curious yet shy around most adults, and it rankled me when she saw fit to move from behind her mother and offer Tod an embrace. I poured two glasses of wine, whiskey for me, and a bit of juice in a child's plastic cup.

Sheri came from down the street to watch Rea while we ate. Gee had chosen a spinach and cheese lasagna to serve, and while I wasn't a finicky eater and rarely cared what we had, seeing my wife so eager to please Tod—who didn't eat meat—put me in a mood to quarrel. In that moment food seemed to reveal the soul of all relationships, the conjoining of epicurean preferences symbolizing the health and commitment of a couple, bringing lovers closer together while giving them an opportunity to profess, "Oh yes, we like that." and "Why don't we try the new Korean restaurant tonight?" or "How about calf's liver and kugel?" Standing in the kitchen an hour before Tod arrived, I argued, "Wouldn't a sirloin be better? How about a barbecue? I know you'd prefer some potato salad to go with a nice fat steak."

"Not tonight."

"Why not?"

"I already told you. Tod's a vegetarian."

"Chicken's a good compromise," I sounded childish.

"Why are you bothering me about this?" Gee used the flat side of a knife to push carrots into the salad bowl. I watched the motion of her hand as if she was performing some remarkable task. She was wearing a pair of tan shorts which fit her a bit too nicely and flattered the length of her legs. Her hair was combed back and tied off by an orange sash, the top three buttons of her bone-colored shirt undone near her breast. "There's nothing wrong with vegetables," she said, and added without turning around, "we eat too much meat as it is."

"Really?" I looked at her with some surprise. "And when did you decide that?"

"Recently."

"I see."

The dining room table was set with maroon placemats and matching cloth napkins. I positioned myself at the head, with Gee and Tod on opposite sides. The arrangement seemed to favor me as I expected to direct the course of our conversation from my end, and only as we began to eat did I realize my error. Back and forth over servings of lasagna, salad, and bread, Tod and Gee chatted endlessly. I nodded when called upon to do so but otherwise said little, watching my wife in profile, her features sharp, her chin and cheeks, her mouth and the measure of her nose all lovely, yet bearing a certain inscrutability which softened when Tod made her laugh.

I continued to listen as they discussed a series of new essays and authors and matters involving the *Kerrytown Review*. They spoke about the recent slashing of Picasso's "Nude in Front of the Garden" at the Stedelijk Museum in Amsterdam, the petition of the Klan to march in New York City, and the current conflict in Renton involving the mayor's decision to crack down on the homeless and arrest all vagrants who violated the least letter of the law. "So, Walter," Tod reached forward and poured more wine into Gee's glass. (There was something familiar in his offering, a casualness which made it seem he'd extended the same gesture to my wife a hundred times before.) "What's your opinion on the mayor's decision to rid Renton of its homeless?"

I watched Gee sip her drink, then turned toward Tod and replied reflectively, careful with my answer. "I think the mayor's intentions are sound, but his policy is flawed."

"Then you don't feel homelessness should be treated as a crime?"

"No," this struck me as a safe response, but then I made the mistake of adding, "Of course, there are laws about vagrancy that must be enforced to keep our city inhabitable. The rights of all residents must be considered, not simply the homeless."

"And what exactly do you mean by inhabitable?"

"I mean no one is eager to shop or eat downtown when they know the panhandlers are out in force. Parts of the city are lost, restaurants and businesses suffer."

"Alright," he set down his fork, "and if not arresting the homeless and running them out of town, what would you suggest?"

"I don't know," I was afraid to be any more specific. "It's a difficult problem. What would you do?"

Tod pushed his right hand through his hair, his blue eyes passing once—a bit too cozily—onto Gee, before glancing back at me to answer, "I would build shelters. I would allocate resources and find ways to offer assistance. I would do whatever had to be done to provide these people with some sense of security and dignity in their life."

"That's a generous sentiment," I couldn't help myself, and felt a need to explain, "but a city's resources are limited. There's just so much that can be done."

"And spending money on people who are indigent and don't otherwise contribute to the city's coffers is unsound from a fiscal perspective?"

"That isn't what I said," I stopped Tod before he could back me completely into a corner. "All human beings deserve charity and kindness," I glanced toward my wife. "It's a question of what the city can afford."

"There are things the city can't afford to ignore, Walter," Gee rejoined. As lessons go, I should have learned something from our conversation at the Dunlaps and not allowed myself to be drawn in further, but here was Gee—the sash in her hair removed so that her red locks, lightened by the summer's sun, fell handsomely across her cheek—aligning herself again with Tod, and against all better judgement, I said, "It's a bit more complicated than that though, isn't it? Some of these people don't even want help. Some prefer to be on the street."

"That's an excuse," Gee shook her head. "It's always a strategy of the haves to find some measure of culpability within the have nots."

Sweet Gee! I slumped back in my chair, biting at my inner lip while trying to recall the last time I said something—said anything!—which she favored. (The other night in bed, I was in the middle of reading Jim Harrison's *The Road Home* and casually commented on what an excellent book I thought it was, to which Gee replied, "Harrison's a misogynist," as if the one word, whether true or not, summed up the whole of his parts and made me guilty by association.) I wanted to ask her then—as I thought to do at the Dunlaps—why she was so eager to attack me of late. (Where does love go, Gee? What does it turn into? Where were Cupid and Aphrodite when you needed them? Where was the bounty and mirth, the separation between amity and misanthropy? What was the matter, dear, and how could anyone ever feel safe?) Would it be too much for her to acknowledge that perhaps I had a point? "Christ," I said, but instead of continuing, fell silent again, and wished I never spoke.

"Walter's right," Tod raised his eyebrows suddenly and extended me the sort of look that said, "There, you see? Even your wife disagrees," while pretending nonetheless to come to my defense. "The issue is quite complicated and we can't expect to resolve as much over dinner. In the meantime, everyone's entitled to their opinion."

At the very least, I should have gone into the kitchen then and poured myself another drink, but I was frustrated and unwilling to accept Tod's assistance, and so I blurted out, "It's more than my opinion though, Tod. I'm trying to be reasonable here. I'm grounding my views in reality while you're tossing out this idea of allocating funds to build shelters as if laying one's hands on that kind of resource can be grabbed out of thin air."

"Any worthwhile vision must begin with bold ideas," Tod maintained his cool.

"That's a luxury of your profession," I tapped my middle fingers on the table. "All you journalists and writers love to bandy about your ideas. You make the most untenable arguments while treating reasonableness and practicality as dirty words. I'm sorry," I said, and found the nerve to look at Gee, "but you're like that guy on television who twirls plates atop broomsticks, waiting to see what will stay and what will crash. The truth doesn't matter as long as you can keep the trick going. You writers," I said again, only here Gee cut me off.

"We writers present truths that enable the reader to draw their own conclusions," she responded with her voice pitched across the word "we" as deliberately as if she'd gotten up and thrown her arms around Tod.

"But that's just it," I had no choice but to continue, "you don't present the truth. You present what you want the reader to believe."

"The goal of any good writer is to establish his position in the best possible way while staying true to the facts," Tod said, to which I countered at once, "And what does that mean, true to the facts? Your *Review* is politically left of center. This is an editorial choice. Everything you print is slanted by design, all the social commentaries, essays, and articles you print are influenced by how you want a set of circumstances to be interpreted. You adopt a perspective, manipulate and massage it until it shines and what could be easier than that?"

"Presenting personal convictions in a public forum is not as easy as you think," he remained still calm, as if my outburst amused him.

"No?" I was less composed. "Try doing what I do. Try working with the facts and figures as they exist. Try presenting your ideas when your resources are finite and subjectivity is not an option. People in business have to play the hand that's dealt them, Tod. We don't have the luxury of casting about for quixotic ideals. There's no personal perspective for us. The market is cast in stone. Each investment and the consequence that follows is absolute. I can't hide behind philosophical mumbo jumbo when a client loses cash. I can't resort to platitudes when the economy is off. Imagine if you had to write a piece using no verbs or words beginning with the letter T. Think how limited you'd be in what you could do. Those are the conditions I have to deal with every day."

"And yet," Tod seemed not at all fazed by what I said, "at least in your profession there's the finality of a specific tally. There's a sense of security in knowing exactly what you're dealing with, the numbers not being able to lie as the expression goes. You have the luxury," he winked at me then, "of operating from a point of certainty, of basing your decisions on concrete facts, whereas in every phase of what Geni and I do, the vast majority of our battle is sifting through prevarication, perjury, and distortion in order to find the truth. Imagine the difficulty of a writer who wants to be honest when, as you describe, everyone is spinning their own tale. Taking away my verbs and the letter T is the least of my concerns. Do you see what I mean?"

I had no more argument left, was not even sure how Tod managed to turn my statement around as easily as he did, and flummoxed, I could only lift my whiskey and swirl around the remains of my near empty glass.

We finished our meal and began clearing away the plates. I watched Tod move about our kitchen in tandem with Gee, setting his own dishes in the sink, retrieving the electric coffee grinder at her request and then the bag of coffee beans from the fridge. The fluidness of their cooperation—following on the heels of their united front at dinner—unsettled me that much more. Such shared domesticity seemed part of a greater conspiracy I'd no idea how to thwart. Together they carried the coffee and cake, the tray of dessert dishes, saucers and spoons and forks out to the back porch, while I pulled the small glass table around and set the two green patio chairs side by side. The night had turned dark, the threat of rain mixed with a sort of measured stillness that warned of distant storms.

I flipped on the floodlight that shined out from below the awning into the yard. The buzz of insects and the song of evening birds filtered in from just beyond the screen, while shadows fell across the porch and slid serpentine between the chairs. Tod sat next to Gee, in the seat I planned to take for myself. I stared at my wife, and disappointed, refilled my glass with whiskey before dropping onto the end of the grey and blue chaise lounge.

Rea was upstairs with Sheri, changing for bed, and soon came down to say goodnight. I embraced my daughter in front of our guest. (Earlier, Tod mentioned how much of me he saw in Rea and I replied, "She is my girl.") Gee went upstairs with Rea and when she came back I signalled for her to join me on the chaise lounge. She ignored my invitation however and settled back beside Tod. (Shoulder to shoulder, their shadows overlapped.) We spent the next half hour talking in turn about the weather, the Renton Monarchs, and the latest book by Richard Feynman. We ventured briefly onto politics and twice Gee reached and set her hand on Tod's arm to emphasize a particular view. All my comments, in turn, were taken to task. (I'd only to say, "Umm," for my wife and Tod to cry, "Baaah!") At one point, halfway drunk and fully convinced that all measures of restraint had failed, I threw up my hands and spoke of love.

"Has Gee ever told you how we met?" I put the question to Tod, surprising Gee, upsetting the momentum they'd acquired during the course of the evening, their interaction transcending mere flirtation while conveying a sense of comfort and synchronicity I found all but obscene. I wanted to discuss my marriage for no other reason than to draw attention to its existence, to reestablish my place in the immediacy of Gee's life; wherever that might be. "It's quite a remarkable story," I went on.

"Really, Walter," Gee set her coffee on the glass table. "I don't think Tod wants to hear."

"No? Do you want to hear, Tod? But of course he does. Everyone wants to hear a good love story," I moved to the edge of the chaise lounge and set my glass between my feet. I looked again at Gee and, suddenly nostalgic, remembered a time early in our marriage when we spent a weekend at the Day Clove Inn, watching old Bogart movies on a black-and-white TV, ordering burgers and wine from the restaurant downstairs without ever once leaving the room. (How magnificently inglorious our sex was then, how many dents and stains we put on that old bed.) I recalled the birth of our daughter, and the summers we used to walk along the narrow path at Welbrooke Park, holding hands on our way to and from the lake. I thought of the winter a storm blew a branch through our front window and we covered the damage with cardboard taped over the open hole, lighting the fireplace and kneeling with Rea between us as we tended the flames. Here was what possessed the core of my love, the essence of memory that could not be swept away.

I recounted for Tod the story of the museum and if not for the ticket I received from a client, Gee and I would never have met. "Looking back, who can deny we were destined?" I stretched out my legs in the direction of my wife, and in the process nearly toppled my drink.

Twice Gee tried to stop me, and twice more I went on. I was boastful and gushing in detailing the triumphs and commitment of our relationship and, hoping to remind my wife of all we had, I made every effort to contrast my life with Tod's. "Have you ever been married?" I put the question to him, and when he answered, "No, I haven't," I gave a telling nod, and said, "No, of course not. And why should you? What a wild time you must have with all the liberal young ladies who volunteer at your review, the writers and coeds. All free spirits. What fun it must be. The lifestyle appeals to you, I'm sure."

Tod sipped at his coffee. He did not glance over at Gee. I felt certain I'd embarrassed him—at last—and when he said, "You've a colorful idea of my life, I'm afraid, Walter," I laughed as if he was attempting a bit of modesty, and answered with another half-drunk, "Do I?"

"My attitude toward women is not as opportunistic as you might think."

"And still, you make time for the ladies, I'm sure? As a liberal man with modern ideals."

"Being liberal does not mean I conduct my personal affairs like a dog in heat."

"Yes, yes. But you do get around?"

Again, Tod said, "It isn't as you imagine. The assumption people are always so quick to make about anyone possessing the least liberal leanings in their political views also being nonconforming in their personal life is a bit of a stretch."

"And yet, perhaps people believe as much because it's true," I continued to press the issue, feeling my advantage and refusing to let the matter drop.

"From a purely logical perspective," Tod responded, "there's simply no relationship between left-wing ideologies and libertine attitudes. The notion that anyone who challenges the powers that be must accept universally all iconoclastic conduct is a misconception left over from the '60s when the modern triumvirate of free sex, drugs, and rock and roll became synonymous with the progressive movements first introduced on college campuses. It's the sort of nonsense right-wing fundamentalists advance in their criticism of liberalism, but the hypocrisy among conservatives is severe. Hoover was a homosexual after all, Eisenhower slept around on Mamie, Whitaker Chambers was a pathological liar, McCarthy a suicidal alcoholic. Even today, Jesse Helms is a corrupt egoist, John Ashcroft a racist, George W. Bush a drunkard, and Chief Justice Rehnquist addicted to drugs. If the outward perception of these individuals can differ dramatically from their private lives, why shouldn't liberals be afforded the same luxury?"

I felt myself once again losing ground, and in an effort to hold on to whatever leverage I had, I quickly asserted, "But what of those liberals who espouse free love as part of their political views? What of the left-wingers who champion the impermanence of relationships and refer to monogamy as counterintuitive, insisting single-minded affairs inhibit the organic course of intimacy by ignoring the natural flow of human desire and affection?"

"Is that what you think, Walter?"

"Me? No. Of course not."

"Because you make a good argument." At this Tod looked toward my wife. "My problem is not one of sexual freedom," he said then. "I support unconditionally the right of all adults to behave as they choose in private. The necessity to force the issue however, to be liberal as you say in everything we do, seems to me a bit contrived. From my perspective, freedom is itself a discipline and truth is rarely found in the extremes. Consequence is the more revealing force. The result of what we do. Commitment presents the real truth of who we are, don't you think?" Tod finished and looked again at Gee who smiled while I bristled under the weight of a position I could not possibly support. How did I constantly wind up so manipulated, I wondered? Not ten minutes earlier I championed the heart and soul of my marriage, spoke passionately about monogamy and love, only to have Gee ignore me as if I was babbling in tongues, and here Tod spewed a bit of abstruse nonsense and my wife's ready to—what?—canonize his sanctimonious ass!

I slid forward on my seat in order to pour an additional shot of whiskey into my glass, and straining still to win Gee's favor said, "Your attitude mirrors my own then, Tod. We both value a good romance."

"It would seem so, Walter, yes," he smiled and turned further toward my wife. Gee poured him a fresh cup of coffee and cut him a second piece of dessert. (No such offering was made to me, and hurt, I sipped off the top third of my drink.) A cat cried in the neighbor's yard, startling me. (The sound was fierce and filled with fear.) I set my whiskey back down on the floor and, sullen, shifted to the far end of my seat.

Gee then spoke of love.

Crossing her legs so that her right foot, now bare, came conspicuously close to resting against Tod's thigh, she repeated what I said at dinner, giving me an odd look as she remarked, "It's like spinning plates on broomsticks, isn't it? Seeing what stays up and what crashes down." I resisted making any comment of my own, and concentrated instead on willing my wife to abandon her seat beside Tod and come join me, to slide between my legs, muss my hair with both her hands, and kiss me with reassurance. I needed this more than ever and hoped she might yet take up for me and say something favorable about a love which had learned to adapt and endure despite all obstacles and deterrents these last ten years. Instead, she stared into the yard where the light from just below the awning fell and cut a pale path through the dark. "I'm going to have a cigarette," she said then and getting up, she disappeared around to the front of the house, ignoring my appeal for her to stay.

Left alone with Tod, I made up my mind to address once and for all his conduct toward my wife. ("Now see here," I thought to tell him.) Although confrontation was something I evaded whenever possible, arguments, and altercations better left to men like Ed Porter and Jack Gorne who drew energy from the fight, I was determined to rise to the occasion, only before I could speak, Tod moved his chair closer to me and said, "I was hoping I might ask a favor."

Surprised, I could only stare back.

"A bit of business," he explained. "I was thinking about our conversation at the Dunlaps a few weeks ago, and your offer to help me if I ever seriously considered making an investment. If we could arrange a time for me to come by your office, there's a deal I'd like to get your opinion on."

"An investment, Tod?" the irony was too much, and insisting my office hours were booked for weeks, suggested he "Go ahead and tell me what's on your mind."

Tod sat with his legs crossed and ran his right hand back through his hair. "All differences aside, your knowledge on such matters far exceeds mine. I've examined my financial situation and have to admit I've fallen into a rather risky habit of funnelling all my available resources into current projects. Money comes and money goes, and after putting out nearly one hundred issues of the *Review*, I still have to worry about financing each edition. I've no investments to fall back on, nothing but the equity in my house and the Appetency Café." Along with the property Tod inherited from his late uncle—a three-bedroom brick colonial built in the 1920s that earned him a few extra dollars as he rented out one of the bedrooms to undergrad and graduate students who came and went in their turn—he also inherited Eddie's Bar and Grill, which he converted, with the help of two friends, into the Appetency Café. Large cushioned chairs, lowboys, and steamer trunks were brought in to replace the linoleum tables, the walls lined with shelves and books, the menu offering espresso, organic chicken sandwiches, tofu and bagels, pasta and green sprout salads appealed to his select clientele of local artists and writers, students and professors and the like, all readers and supporters of the *Review* whose patronage helped give the café a reputation as a New Age bohemian mecca, though very little in the way of a profit was ever earned.

"Despite what you may think," Tod went on, "I don't con-sider free enterprise a dirty business. It was free enterprise, after all, which allowed me to start the *Kerrytown Review*. My objec-tion has always been in the way an open market economy gives people the idea they can empower themselves through acquisi-tiveness, how corporations without the slightest hint of social conscience can alter our entire landscape." He came forward in his seat and looked straight at me. "That said," he smiled, "I'm convinced if I truly want to establish a successful power base for the good of the community, I need to put my capital to better use. I thought if I ran my idea past you, Walter, and you liked it," he let his voice trail off, allowing me the chance to respond. I brought my hands up to my chin, touched my lower lip with two fingers and gazed across the porch. "Go on then, Tod."

He spent the next several minutes describing in great detail the investment he envisioned. He identified a large plot of land on the far south end of Renton and said his idea was to build af-fordable housing for working-class families. "The land's available and priced to sell." He spoke eagerly of how the construction market was ready to boom and Renton was aching to grow, and, "I've heard from someone I know, a writer friend of mine doing a piece on an otherwise unrelated topic, that the city council's prepared to move on a proposal to expand the metro rail south. If that's the case, the value for all the land we're talking about, and the houses we'd build, would triple overnight. We can help young families get started while assuring ourselves of a sound profit."

I waited until Tod finished before rejecting his plan in total. "In the first place, there's nothing more speculative than the deal you just described. Until it's certain the metro rail's going up, you'd be sitting on worthless plots. In the interim, you'd have property taxes, insurance, and escalating building costs. You want a steady return on your investment in order to help support your review, and yet what you're talking about would suck up all your resources in two months. Even if things went perfectly, you're looking at six years before you made a dime on your original investment. Building the underground metro itself will take three years. Add to this the fact that, if as you say, the city's already decided to run a new metro rail south, there must be a dozen other developers already in the process of putting together such a deal.

"Furthermore," I could have stopped at any time, but enjoyed pressing the point, "have you any idea the sort of money required to put this kind of deal together? You want to buy land and build a subdivision for the working class, and yet what is it you have to invest? A few thousand dollars? If I was to get involved in what you've just described, I'd only be speaking to people who had a million dollars minimum they could afford to tie up. With no connections or money of your own, I don't see what your role in this project would be. It would cost Porter and Evans somewhere between thirty and forty thousand dollars of our own capital just to conduct the requisite research and put together the proper report before we could even go to would-be clients. Unless you're looking to hire us on and cover our costs, there's nothing I can do for you. I'm sorry."

Tod listened closely, disappointed by what I had to say. "I suppose I was hoping you might pull some people together for me."

"And if I did, where would you fit it?"

"As it's my idea, I'd receive a minority share."

"It doesn't work that way, Tod. In the first place, ideas are a dime a dozen. Why should you get anything when, at best, what you have to offer is information already in the public domain? Ed Porter would have my ass if I offered you as much as a finder's fee. Secondly, and as I've told you, even if it is your idea, no one investing a million dollars is going to let you in when all you're risking is pocket change. To make a go in business, you need to have the resources to pull the trigger. I suggest you focus on something smaller. Something that fits your immediate cash flow," I said as much in earnest, feeling quite generous in that moment and magnanimous enough to extend this bit of free advice. "If you'd like," I added, thinking nothing of it at the time, gloating still at my ability to make Tod grovel before I dismissed him absolutely, "if you want a safe return on the few thousand dollars you have to invest, I'm sure I can do that for you."

Tod came all the way forward in his chair and touched my shoulder. His disappointment was less severe and he seemed to understand and appreciate my advice. I could tell he was genuinely pleased by my new offer, his voice warm as he replied, "That would be excellent, Walter. It would be a start. I guess I am a bit out of my league on this one."

"Stick with what you can afford," I repeated. "I'm sure we can come up with something that will earn you a few dollars."

"I'll leave it to you then."

"That's a good idea, yes."

An hour later Tod left for the night and I immediately told Gee what he asked of me while she was out having a smoke. I recounted the way he begged for my assistance, how he pleaded with me and conceded his need for my expertise. "What do you think of that?" I pitched my voice and laughed on the way upstairs. "All his liberal mumbo jumbo and who needs who now?" I wanted her to admit the irony and see what a fraud he was, that people like Tod Marcum were no better than children set loose in the woods, incapable of surviving without the aid of more sophisticated and worldly men like me! I grinned with self-assumption, anticipating Gee's concession, anxious for her to acknowledge the superiority of my station, but all she said was, "I know," and shushed me in the bedroom, whispering, "Rea's asleep."

Gee refused to engage me further on the subject, expressing instead her annoyance at how I behaved that evening, accusing me of being a poor host, of drawing Tod into needless debate and confronting him every time he tried to talk. Her charge was sudden and startling, the suggestion that I had done anything wrong so preposterous that I could only stammer, "You have to be kidding. And what do you mean you know?"

"About Tod asking you to look at an investment? Because I encouraged him to do so. Why shouldn't he ask? And why shouldn't you want to help?" She disappeared into the bathroom, leaving me to react alone.

I stood in the center of the floor, astounded by this latest twist, frustrated and resenting again the way Gee always came so quick to Tod's defense. The alarm clock beside our bed was digital, the numbers red and lighted, and in the silence of our room I could hear the faint electric buzz that gave the air a fitful charge. I stripped off my clothes and sat on the end of the bed where, ignoring all impulses to the contrary, imagined my wife and Tod having sex. I worried about the physical advantages he might have, the size of his cock—no doubt larger than mine—his muscles supple and stamina superior, his ability to deliver Gee to wave after wave of orgasmic revelry, applying a sort of liberal— ha!—technique in order to fully satisfy her needs. My anguished mind worked overtime, the measure of fear and vanity, and I was staring blindly at a blank space on the wall when Gee returned and slipped into bed.

I crawled in beside her and resumed an enfeebled state of grousing. "All night long he's arguing with me, and then he has the gall to ask for a favor. In the grand scheme of things," I shook my head, and said louder, "do you realize I charge clients a thousand dollars for the consultation I gave Tod tonight for free? On top of that, his idea was insane, and still I volunteered to help invest what minor amount of cash he has. You should appreciate this and yet you're pissed at me."

"I do appreciate your taking the time to talk with him," she granted me this much. "And I appreciate your offering to help."

"But?"

"You should want to work with someone like Tod for a change, someone whose objective is not limited to increasing their own wealth."

"Believe me, Gee, my clients give more money to charity than Tod has ever raised in his life."

"I doubt that," she stared at me until I looked away. "Why can't you see Tod's idea to put whatever profit he earns back into the community is a wonderful gesture? You should be flattered he came to you."

"There's no reason for me to be flattered by a man I've only met twice. His asking me for anything is presumptuous."

Gee glowered. "If you're determined to go on this way, Walter Brimm, I suggest you let the subject drop."

Words of wisdom. A practical truth. I should have taken Gee's advice and said no more. Discretion would have gone a long way toward earning my wife's favor, but how was I to stop when I remained so otherwise anxious and unsettled after such a miserable night? I wanted more than a cold, convenient truce, required not compromise but something intimate and indivisible, a sense of assurance I could sink my teeth into. I wished again my wife would hold me in sweet prelude to the moment we put all this nonsense behind us, and desperate to feel her, to possess and be possessed, to have her on top of me so I could rise beneath her and be devoured inside, I slipped under the sheet and reached in her direction. Gee quickly turned away, and when I said, "What?

I thought you were appreciative?" she all but groaned and slapped at my hand. "Go to sleep," she said and rolling further from me, she switched off the light.

In darkness then. In the blink of an eye—one blink, yes—I was rendered helpless, cast out and transformed.

CHAPTER 5

Sunday morning, a few short hours removed from our dinner with Tod, I got up early and retrieved the *Renton Bugle* from the front porch. My head ached, and sitting inside my den, I read an article about three former executives of the Bankers Trust Corporation—Bruce Kingdon, Kenneth Goglia, and Harvey Plante—who were each indicted for diverting $15.5 million of customer money into the bank's own accounts as a means of covering shortfalls in their division's projected revenue and profits. I made a note to mention the piece to Jack Gorne who was friends with both Kingdon and Plante, and flipping ahead, scanned the pages until another article caught my eye.

There in the extreme, I read an account of love's labors lost: Yesterday the body of one Franco DeLima, age twenty-seven, was found in a field in Long Island by a woman out walking her dog. Pathologists determined from the injuries that Mr. DeLima had fallen from a passing plane, the speculation being that he was a stowaway and took his fatal tumble when the landing gear was lowered during the flight's final approach. Police said foreign coins and stamps were found among his possessions, along with a postcard from a woman named Maria who wrote, "Yo te amo," a dozen times, surrounding the one line printed in English: "Hurry to me, please, my love." Poor sap. Such a sad story. What a precarious entanglement. How often the most ill-fated acts were performed in the name of Love; the pairing of Eros and Amor producing the ultimate paradox. "Love, love, love," as the Beatles sang. ("All you need is...") But who can ever understand the risk one takes and the lure of such immoderation?

I put the section down and picked up another, finding by chance an article that quoted my wife. The piece addressed the suicide rate among teens and the knee-jerk response of certain conservative groups to blame popular music. ("What sort of faulty reasoning is it that condemns musicians for our social ills?" Professor Sharre wrote. "If music is so potent, and not merely a manifestation of more pervasive cultural concerns, why not fill our schools with soothing choral arrangements and inculcate our youth with a palliative calm?") Under normal circumstances, I would have agreed with my wife and felt her logic well conceived, but this morning I was querulous, and put off still by the events of last night, couldn't bring myself to agree with Gee on anything.

I dropped the paper, and pushing the heel of my hands against the side of my head, got up and retrieved a pad and pen from my briefcase in order to jot down the information Tod provided regarding the land on the south side of Renton. I reviewed the details in black and white, assessed my findings objectively, and concluded once more that his idea was nothing but a wish list, speculative and contingent upon ifs and whens and events which may or may not happen. I scribbled out a few more notes and set the pad and pen back in my case.

The day passed languidly. I took Rea to the park while Gee went to the library and researched her newest article. (The piece was tentatively titled "The Misconception in Cultural Objectivism and the Ethic of Community" for whatever that meant.) By evening, Gee and I managed to avoid the topic of Tod Marcum altogether. Such evasion, administered with deft efficiency, allowed us to bypass any further quarrels, yet the cooperation we effected was itself strained and we monitored our dialogue as if one false word would forever shatter the watchful calm I at least was struggling to preserve.

I left for work the next morning and was inside my office no more than an hour when Gee phoned to let me know, "There's a mailing I promised to help with tonight."

"Tod?"

"Yes."

"Why didn't you tell me before? Why wait until now and over the phone?"

"We won't be late," she said without answering, informing me of her intent to take Rea and suggesting I treat myself to a night on the town. "You'll like that, I'm sure," her tone was bright in an effort to persuade me.

"Fine," I grumbled, and said no more than, "go on then. Yes. Goodbye."

I spent the rest of the morning consulting with clients eager to invest in the Pacific Rim, and returning to my office after lunch, initiated a preliminary investigation into the property on the south side of Renton. I treated the task no differently than any other business venture, was most diligent and professional in my study. I had a clerk do a title search, and making several queries on my own, found out about the status of the metro rail. Everything seemed as Tod said, right down to the last detail. Shortly before six, I got in touch with the owner of the land, a widower who'd held the acreage for years and was anxious now to sell in order to relocate out west. To my surprise, I discovered no one had entered a bid.

I ate by myself that night at Talster's Bar, had a porterhouse and three whiskeys on the rocks. I realized I was drinking too much of late, and driving home, assured myself I'd take control of the situation before it got out of hand. Once inside my den, I poured a fresh whiskey and sat down in my chair. Gee and Rea were already upstairs, though I didn't go to see them, and when I did at last crawl into bed just after midnight I lay at a distance from my wife. Restless, I rose before dawn, showered and shaved and drove to my office where I sat at my desk and reviewed once again the information compiled yesterday. I still had no clear idea of what I was doing, no sure way of saying what I would or would

not have done had Ed Porter not stopped by my office that afternoon and mentioned that he was looking to put an investment
together for a select group of clients. I wasted no time and suggested a purchase of real estate, specifically several acres of land
on the south side of the city that was undervalued and ready to
be developed.

Two months later the property was ours. I contacted archi-
tects, city planners, and building contractors in order to lay the
groundwork for erecting a subdivision we'd eventually name
Happy Meadows. In November, the mayor's office announced its
plan to construct a new southern line for the metro rail. The
value of our property tripled overnight. Ed Porter's group of
clients, including Jack Gorne, whom I brought in on my own,
could not have been more pleased. They applauded my resourcefulness and the brilliance of my vision. I was cheered in the most
affluent of circles. "Walter Brimm! Walter Brimm!" (Brimming,
indeed!) I accepted their accolades with a modest shrug, and
mentioning nothing of my success to Tod, informed everyone
that I was only too glad to help.

We broke ground on the first block of houses in Happy
Meadows the following spring. I drove over with Rea, and together we watched from a hillside as a large yellow bulldozer
moved heavy mounds of earth, while men wielding shovels and
long poles jumped into the hole, measuring its depth, smoothing
out the base and sides in preparation for pouring the foundation.
Tod had learned by then of the property's sale, and called to see
what I knew. "Nothing," I said. "Not one word."

I lost little sleep as a result of my deception, convinced I'd
committed no crime, that if Tod was fool enough to bring me information on deals he could not otherwise afford to enter into,
then certainly I was free to take them on. That my deed entailed
a certain amount of deceit, and in this way varied from the firm
ethic I tried to uphold ever since my parents' crimes, was true

enough. And yet I had excuse for my behavior, and had only to look at Gee as she continued to slip away from me to feel vindicated and deny the reality of what I'd done.

That winter, in the months before construction began at Happy Meadows and no one suspected a thing, Gee continued spending far too much time with Tod. They met and phoned and otherwise arranged their encounters two and three nights a week, serving together on committees, civic boards, and community councils, cochairing fund-raisers, petition drives, and benefits held at the Appetency Café. Additional social evenings were scheduled for the three of us, invitations extended and accepted against my complaint. More and more, I grew to detest the man's presence, the way he spoke and smiled and touched my wife with familiar fingers reaching, caresses cast as insignificant, yet soft and telling. It was not uncommon for me to come home and find him sitting in our kitchen, a series of crayon-colored pictures laid out in front of him drawn by Rea.

I suffered those months in a sort of disabling fog, without ever once knowing what I should do. As a consequence of our conversation that first evening on the porch, Tod was more judicious in pressing me about matters of business. He picked his spots and let me know from time to time how he still hoped to become part of a deal with profits reinvested back into the community. Once, at a reading by Lawrence Weschler, he cornered me during the reception and told me of a conversation he had with a man looking for investors to buy into the midwestern distributorship of Duroflex Watchbands. He described the profitability of Duroflex over the last few years, how it was an American-held corporation, with manufacturing on the east coast, a union shop that treated its workers fairly and ran its operations without a hint of scandal.

I shook my head, explaining again that such an investment required tens of thousands of dollars, which Tod didn't have to risk let alone lose. "Watchbands are one of those luxury items," I said, "with a finite market base. The biggest mistake small companies make is trying to expand. Duroflex does alright in minor regions, but if they try to cut into markets controlled by larger companies such as Timex, they'll get eaten alive. An investment isn't supposed to be a gamble, remember that, Tod."

The next morning, I drove down to my office where I started a thorough review of Duroflex. My research could not have gone better. Every aspect of the company proved sound. I was impressed by their past performance, their liquidity, and patient plan for growth. Within days, I began contacting potential investors. I spoke several times with Mark Hillard at Duroflex who forgot about Tod the minute I mentioned the availability of my cash and the firm I represented. The deal went through without a hitch. Ed Porter came into my office and chimed, "Good for you, Walter. Watchbands, indeed! It's the sort of business I cut my teeth on. You're becoming a very clever fellow."

In April I was at a fund-raiser for the re-election of Senator Nancy Shelton and somehow wound up standing alone with Tod. "I've been thinking," he said, and went on to pitch another proposal for purchasing unsold tennis, basketball, running shoes, and cleats from warehouses around the country. His plan was to establish a new middle market for footwear. He envisioned a chain of stores that sold old model shoes at a discount, all the usually expensive brands marked down, the high-tops and training shoes no longer as chic as the current year's styles but just as useful and priced to sell. "Manufacturers are always looking to clear out old lines in order for outlets to carry the company's most recent items. Major chains only want to push what's new, but people want good deals."

I listened as always and once Tod was through said, "Your idea, for what its worth, has several serious problems that I don't think you've considered. In the first place, the availability of your product will always be limited to last year's stock. You'll have no control over manufacturing, and therefore no say in what you might otherwise wish to order. This in itself is a negative. Then there's the cash you'll need to raise, which will again present you with problems. As for venturing into the retail trade, the risk is unacceptable as a rule. The odds against survival are just too great. Once more, I'm going to pass."

I was ready to walk away, only my attention was diverted then by a large mirror mounted to the wall behind Tod. (We were in the Fenbrooke Banquet Room of the Renton Skylark Hotel.) The position of the mirror captured Gee's image as she stood across the room conversing with two other women I didn't know. The distance between us elevated her figure inside the mirror so that she appeared painted in as part of some beautiful mural. I was struck at once by how handsome she looked, and wanted only to invite her to come and reserve a room with me upstairs so we could lay together and cling to one another tightly until all the harm that had otherwise accumulated and complicated the connection between us was drawn out and put to rest. No sooner did the thought reach me however, than Tod shifted and blocked my view.

I was certain his interference was committed on purpose, and vexed, resorted to asking, "While we're on the subject, Tod, are you still interested in having me help you invest what money you have in the market?"

"Walter, yes. I thought you'd forgotten."

"Not at all. I've been keeping an eye out for just the right stock. I know you're only interested in socially conscious firms and finding the right fit takes time. I think I have something, however. A new company on the verge of developing a state-of-the-art water purification system. Cutting edge. Their stock is holding steady now, but as soon as they get FDA approval, well you just watch."

"Water purification, you say?"

"All new, affordable, and efficient."

"That sounds excellent, Walter."

"The company's called Adam's Eau."

"They're French?"

"Some French money, but it's an American operation. If you're interested," I continued, "I can get you a block of shares first thing tomorrow." Tod had four thousand dollars to invest. I told him I'd front him the money, that he could send me a check in the mail. "You're a player now," I said. "How does it feel?"

"Outstanding. This is very generous of you, Walter."

Generous, indeed. I was clever this time and refrained from boasting of my gesture to Gee, waiting instead for Tod to tell her. Let her come to me, I thought, and thank me with the appropriate appreciation. Later, in the next month or so when Adam's Eau crashed—as I was sure it would, having already conducted my research and knowing the company's struggles to satisfy the FDA placed it on the brink of permanent disaster—I'd have my reward from Gee in hand and could blame Tod's troubles then on the market. I didn't have to wait long. The very next evening, as soon as I got home, Gee expressed her thanks for my helping Tod. "Why didn't you tell me?"

I shrugged as if informing her was not important.

"It was very kind of you." She said this with a curious look on her face, her eyes half squinting as if there was something she was trying to see in me, a glimpse of what she otherwise wasn't quite sure was there. That night in bed, I tried to take advantage of her gratitude and presented myself with a keener sense of humility, pleased by her receptiveness, yet rather than rejoice in the spectacle of her company—as I longed to do!—I found after but the briefest of embrace that I was struck—how shall I say?—unresponsive to further celebration. Two nights passed in which I could neither sleep nor rouse myself to the task I desired. Resentful of such an ignominious interruption, I struggled for answers and after several vain attempts to reconcile my conduct, I began questioning the wisdom of misappropriating Tod's cash.

Perhaps my actions were a bit extreme. Unlike Duroflex and Happy Meadows, where Tod suffered no real harm, my duplicity with Adam's Eau was intended to cause specific damage. Such concerns—manifest in my inability to sleep and the limpness of my member—seemed a sufficient warning sign and clear reminder that I was, above all else, a good and decent man who did not come naturally to such prevarication. By the third night then, I decided to sell Tod's stock in Adam's Eau, keeping him from ruin a week before the company went under.

As a further show of good faith, I included him in the purchase of Affymetrix Inc. stock, whose photolithography patent for making computer chips on silicon was currently being challenged by Incyte Pharmaceuticals. (Incyte used a similar process for gene chip technology and the placing of DNA microarrays onto glass.) I predicted the court would find in favor of Affymetrix, and shortly after purchasing a block of shares for Tod, six clients, and myself, a judgement was entered. The value of Affymetrix stock soared while Incyte plummeted. I celebrated my triumph with an uncertain sense of relief, boasted to Gee of my perspicacity and how beneficial my efforts had turned out for Tod.

I slept well for several nights, regarded all earlier schemes against Tod as minor missteps I was now completely done with, and having tested the bounds of my personal weakness was sure that I'd come through the challenge unscathed. Eager then to receive my reward, I presented myself again to Gee. Unfortunately now my timing was off, for she had papers to grade, final exams to prepare, a new article to research, a gymnastics class she promised to enroll Rea in, several community meetings to attend, and a benefit to organize at the Appetency Café. She came to me in bed at night exhausted, smiling, yet with fixed resistance, apology, and defense, as if I was some further obligation she had neither interest nor the energy to deal with. Disappointed, I watched in silence as twice the phone rang just as I thought I was making progress, and twice on the other end was Tod.

CHAPTER 6

ⱳ

Another article in the *Bugle*: Rudy Castillo, age twenty-nine, spurred by the sting of Venus's retreat, burst into his estranged wife's apartment, and in front of their four-year-old daughter, shot Sugerih Fernandez, age twenty-four, to death before turning the gun on himself. "Jesus!" I thought. But weren't things now getting extreme.

That May, Tod and Gee organized a rally for Myra Falster, a freelance journalist jailed on a charge of civil contempt. It seemed Ms. Falster refused to reveal her sources in an article she wrote on six state legislators subsequently indicted for selling their votes to lobbyists and the judge locked her away. "We need to expose the dangerous precedent the courts are setting by denying journalists the right to rely on secret informants," Tod said one night as he dropped by the house to meet with Gee. "The first thing a restrictive government does is bind the hands of its newspapers."

"It's true," Gee touched Tod's elbow.

"The media may as well limit itself to printing recipes and box scores if a journalist can't guard her sources."

"Exactly."

"Imagine all the important stories which would never see the light of day."

"All the violations of government and big business which would go unreported."

"Myra's a pawn."

"In a fixed game of chess."

"She's a victim of a system that empowers ill-qualified judges to run roughshod over the fundamental needs of an effective free press."

"It's completely criminal."

"It's fascist."

"It is!"

And on and on they went.

With time at a premium, Gee spent the next three days rushing directly from teaching at the university to the *Kerrytown Review* where plans for the demonstration were coordinated. Rea was brought along each afternoon and remained downtown with her mother until six o'clock, when Gee hurried home and fed her a quick meal, kissed her twice, and ran back out the door. Barely a word was exchanged between us, my every complaint met with a reminder that "It's a unique situation, Walter. There's no choice involved. You need to understand."

"I do understand," I answered. "Completely."

The night before the rally, I waited up for Gee, sitting in the living room and turning the pages of a book by Nabokov. Hours passed and still I remained in my chair, anxious to see my wife as soon as she stepped through the door, otherwise unable to crawl up to bed and slip between the sheets. In her absence these last few days—added to the long list of prior evenings she was gone— I again imagined her with Tod, kissing and pawing and fucking their way through the night. My fantasies had mutated into something more dissolute than ever, and while I conjured these images intentionally, they soon got the best of me and refused to leave my head.

What a botched bit of bumble it all was. How I hated my own vulnerability! In the weeks since Affymetrix, as I elected to take the high road with Tod, I waited expectantly for all forms of intercourse, both sexual and otherwise, to improve between myself and Gee. This was the way the world was supposed to operate in the grand scheme of things, with a person's generosity rewarded in kind. How else was human decency to be encouraged if not through equal gains? And yet, rather than Gee drawing near to me, she remained distant and distracted, her features fixed in a defensive sort of mask whenever I looked her way.

What was I to do then? Where was the potency of my commitment? Of my pure American soul? Why couldn't I rush downtown and pummel Tod with my fists instead of sitting in silence and pondering my jealousy, rolling it around on my tongue like some sour slice of fruit I could neither swallow nor spit away? Another hour went by and nothing but time escaped. I switched off the lamp and sat in the dark. Gee came home at a quarter to one. I heard the turning of the latch and, staring out from my chair, could see her in the hall, setting her leather satchel down, hesitating there in order to get her bearings. (Was it possible after all these years the house felt unfamiliar to her now?) I waited a moment then called her name.

"Walter?" she came forward and found the light. Her face looked puzzled, annoyed and surprised. "Is something wrong? Is Rea alright?"

"She's fine."

"What are you doing up?"

"Nothing. Reading. Waiting."

"It's late."

"I know."

Again, as if my presence disturbed her, "Why aren't you in bed?"

"I'm not sure."

"Aren't you tired?"

"Yes."

"Me, too. I'm going up," she turned and started back toward the stairs.

I did not so much think of what I would say but offered no resistance as the words came out, all of my avoidance in the many months before having run its course, leaving me to put the question to her then behind the disquietude of a half-whisper, "Are you in love with him?" My asking seemed to fall out of the air, startling Gee as she turned and moved at once toward the stairs. I imagined as she disappeared on the opposite side of the wall that she was weighing her escape, wondering what would happen if she continued on up to our room. Would I follow after her or let the subject drop? I, too, wondered what I would do. (Having posed my question, was it possible now to pretend I hadn't asked?) I was about to call out and say she didn't have to answer and that I wouldn't ask again, when she returned to the living room and stood directly in front of my chair.

Her sudden nearness confused me. Had she remained at a distance, I'd have assumed her intention was to talk around my claim, dismissing and denying everything until we both wearied of debate and agreed to say no more. In drawing close to me however, her objective was different. The glow from the hall light lit the front half of the room. Gee remained standing near enough that I could touch her hand if I dared. I stared at the red tint of her hair, her green eyes, and hyaline white of her cheeks, waiting for her to speak. But she didn't.

Silently then, she knelt down in front of me, embracing me, settling against me as one might lean with exhaustion upon the trunk of a tree. When she kissed me—in a way she hadn't for a very long time—I hoped to feel real affection but knew at once her offering was something else. Still, I didn't resist, eager to enjoy the moment regardless of why it was bestowed. Only after we went upstairs and consummated the awkwardness of our sex, performed with the sort of harsh determination of two people intent on proving a point, did I succumb to melancholy and the bleakest sort of portent. Gee got up and went into the bathroom. I heard the water for the shower run, listened as she brushed her teeth, as she sat and peed away my undead sperm.

The rally for Myra Falster drew a crowd of several hundred people to the campus of the University. Television reporters recorded the event, speeches were given, and pamphlets handed out. A series of articles appeared in local papers, across the wire services, the Internet, and a special edition of the *Kerrytown Review*. (Gee's piece, "Allowing the Press to Press: The Risk of Extinguishing a Reporter's Right to Protect Her Sources," was particularly well received.) Although the matter was relegated to yesterday's news within a day or two, Tod regarded the turnout as a decisive victory and celebrated with a spirited editorial championing the inalienable virtues of civil disobedience and the inherent wisdom derived from the will of the people.

Judge Felmore Carson, presiding jurist in the case against the six state legislators and singularly responsible for ordering Myra Falster to jail, was not persuaded by any sort of public protest however. A strict constitutional constructionist, Judge Carson interpreted his powers as absolute, and pointed to the language of the statute, which held that a court, upon believing a witness would at some point come forward with the information requested under oath, could jail that individual indefinitely through a charge of civil contempt. "Give the girl time," Carson said. "Women can't take the heat. It won't be long before she cracks."

Disappointed public outcry failed to spring Myra from jail, Tod and Gee met the following evening at the Appetency Café to discuss their next move. I kicked about the empty house, stormed angrily from room to room, insisted Gee tell me the moment she and Rea got home, "What's going on?"

"Walter, nothing," my wife shook her head. Her expression showed surprise, as if she assumed her gesture toward me the other night entitled her to a period of grace when I wouldn't complain about her work. I was offended by her attitude. To be the recipient of a pity fuck from my own wife was a humiliation I'd no idea how to bear, and my demoralization continued the following afternoon when, just after three o'clock, on the eleventh day of Myra Falster's incarceration, Gee phoned me at work. "I need you to pick up Rea," she said. "See if Sheri can watch her for an hour. I'm at the twelfth precinct."

"What?"

"Don't get all excited now."

"Why are you...? Gee?"

"They've set bail."

"You were arrested?"

"And Tod. He needs you to bail him out, too."

I had no luck arranging a sitter for Rea, and together we drove downtown. (I told my daughter that Mommy was interviewing some policemen for work and we needed to pick her up.) The station house occupied half a city block along Ninth Avenue, between Westchester and Jefferson. We parked at the curb and hurried inside. The desk sergeant was a beefy man with an off-grey flattop and vermicular veins fanned out across his thick ball of a nose. I was told, out of earshot from Rea, that Tod and Gee had gone to Judge Carter's house that morning and chained themselves to his front gate. Local media was alerted, while a small crowd, all orchestrated beforehand, stood around and chanted, "Free Myra F! Protect the freedoms of the press!" until neighbors called the police. The crowd disbanded and the chains were cut. "We get this kind of crap from kids, Mr. Sharre," the sergeant shuffled through a stack of papers.

"Brimm," I said.

"Yeah, well, whatever."

I was instructed where to go and post bail, was asked to fill out several forms, told to wait in the lobby, then left with Rea until Gee and Tod were released. We sat for twenty minutes before the door to our far right opened and Gee appeared. Despite my agitation, I was relieved to see her. Dressed in jeans, hiking boots, a pale T-shirt, and blue cotton jacket, she looked as vibrant as one of her students. (Gee!) I made up my mind to temper my indignation until she had a chance to apologize. Obviously, she must realize now how irresponsible Tod Marcum was, that he was nothing more than a vain and selfish man who put her reputation, her job, and her family at risk, seducing her—yes!—with all his ridiculous talk of civil disobedience and righteous protest. I found reason for hope along these lines when spotting me, Gee signaled from a distance of some thirty feet, smiled and waved warmly.

The pleasure I took from her face soothed me, my anticipation heightened by the joy in her eyes. She seemed appreciative of my presence, convinced that I was her rock, her supreme steady ground. I smiled back, happy for the first time in months, certain everything was right again and that my wife still loved me. But just as I stepped forward, eager to greet her and hold her in my arms, Tod came through the opposite door and Gee shifted her gaze. Her expression changed at once from gratitude into a show of true elation, her face filled with ecstasy and unconditional glee, exhilarated and euphoric, shimmering with a rapture that caused all of my initial cheer to collapse and shatter like glass at my feet.

Rea ran toward her mother while Tod—after saying something to my wife—followed after me as I hurried outside. "I want to thank you for coming down," he said, "and to apologize for Gee's arrest. I'm sorry," he said then, but there was a look of ultimate pleasure and satisfaction about him, a contentment derived from Gee's having joined him on the fence. I stopped at the curb, and furious, asked, "What exactly are you sorry for, Tod?"

"How's that?"

"You said you were sorry for your part in Gee's arrest, and what sort of bullshit is that when being arrested is exactly what you planned?"

"Walter, truly," Tod answered as if he might somehow still explain, but I moved on across the street.

Gee rode in the rear with Rea. (Before sliding into the car, she came around to the driver's side and squeezed my arm, without warmth and more to test my mood.) The ride home started out in silence, but after a short while neither Tod nor Gee could resist and began recounting the events outside Judge Carson's house. How pleased and praising they were of the other's effort. I found their banter unbearable, and refusing to let them carry on this way, interrupted with, "Has it occurred to you yet that all your nonsense has caused more harm than good?"

"Actually, no," Gee was emboldened with Tod nearby.

"In the real world, you piss off a judge, your friend rots in jail."

"And what would you have us do?"

"Hold another rally. Write more articles. Don't chain yourself to a fence," I shook my head, reminding Gee of her position in the community, of her role as a mother and teacher. "You can't go around as if you haven't any other responsibilities, for Christ's sake. All your actions have repercussions. There is consequence. What do you think the regents at the university are going to say? What of my clients and senior partners at Porter and Evans? How are you going to explain things to your daughter?"

"It's because of my position in the community," Gee countered, "because I am a mother and teacher that I conduct myself as I do. The last time I checked anyway, a person still had a right to demonstrate."

"A legal demonstration. What you did broke the law."

"Someone has to stand up to judges like Carter."

"Radical rhetoric," I snapped.

Rea began asking questions then, wanting to know what exactly we were arguing about. Gee explained the situation in earnest, but I interrupted again to say, "There are laws, Rea, put in place to protect us and sometimes people don't agree with the law, but that doesn't mean we can break them as we choose."

"This country was founded on rebellion," Tod saw fit to interject. I squeezed the wheel until the tips of my fingers turned a deep purplish-red, and coming off the expressway, no longer able to contain myself, shot the car over to the curb, shifted into park and shouted, "Don't you ever interrupt me when I'm talking to my daughter, do you understand?"

"Walter, I'm sorry."

"Walter!" Gee called out, but I paid no attention. "You and Gee," I barked. "You and Gee!"

"Walter, that's enough!" my wife tried once more to cut me off, but her challenge only caused me to roar, "You, too! You, too!" The late afternoon sun shined through the side window, surrounding Gee in a pale white light. Her eyes—Christ, her eyes!—captivated me without the slightest effort, so green and lovely that despite my rage I felt the whole of my body warm, taken in and melted down. No one spoke again the rest of the way home. I pulled into the drive, got quickly out of the car, and went at a full trot to unlock the front door. I was supposed to drop Tod at his house first, but this was of no importance to me, and standing on the front porch, I shouted at everyone, "Come on, come on! Out, out, out!"

One by one, they made their way up the walk, first Rea, followed by Gee and Tod. I stormed passed them as I hurried back to the car, my anger rooted in such a thorny patch of hurt and fear that I felt my chest go tight. Despite everything, I hoped Gee would stop me then and say that I was right and how sorry she was for not seeing things my way before, but I'd only to look back at the house where Tod stood beside my wife watching me from the porch to know my wish would not be forthcoming.

Gee's eyes cut against mine, condemning me for what she regarded as my reckless outburst, insisting that I was the one guilty of poor judgement. I set the picture in my head and called up to them in a voice suddenly feeble. "There you go then. As you like," and sliding in behind the wheel, backed out into the street and drove off.

CHAPTER 7

How hot the afternoon became, how blistering the weather.
Somehow in driving off I expected to feel a sense of release—
from what I wasn't sure—but in shooting down the hill from my
house and out of our subdivision, accelerating toward the avenues and over the highway, I remember feeling hopelessly sad
and altogether less free than ever before in my life.

I went back downtown and had a drink at Talster's Bar. Men
I knew arrived after work and spoke in loud, unrestrained voices,
smoked their cigarettes and downed their drinks indifferent to my
troubles. I sat and stared at my hands, toyed with my wedding
ring and the packets of sugar that I stacked and then scattered
like so many bricks in an unsteady wall. The aftereffect from the
day's disaster was dreadful, and as I continued to steam over what
just happened, Jack Gorne spotted me and slid into the chair opposite mine. "You look like shit," he set his whiskey down on the
table. I didn't want to talk, wished only to be left in peace, and
immediately regretted coming to Talster's and not some unfamiliar dive on the east side of Renton. "So," Jack tapped my drink
with his middle finger. "What is it?"

"What's what?"

"The reason you look like shit."

"It's nothing."

"Work?"

"No."

"Money?"

"Jack."

"Women?"

"I'm fine."

"Suit yourself."

"I came out for a drink, that's all. There's nothing more to it."

"You're right. Good for you," he pushed my glass in front of me. "Drink up then. When you finish that, I'll buy you another." He sat back in his chair and waited for my resistance to give way. I tried to ignore him, but after two more sips of whiskey I did as we both knew I would and told him everything. Jack's eyes went wide as I mentioned Tod Marcum and the *Kerrytown Review*, his interest piqued as I worked my way through all Gee's private meetings and nocturnal rendezvous with Tod, their phone calls and rallies and dinners. I described the incident with Myra Falster, how they chained themselves to Judge Carson's fence and the look my wife gave Tod in the police station lobby as I bailed them out of jail. I ran through our argument in the car and how I left them together on the front porch before driving downtown.

"So your wife's seeing Marcum," Jack took a long swig from his drink, shook his head, mumbled something under his breath, and spreading his hands out flat, offered to tell me how he'd handle the situation, "if I was you."

I refused to encourage him, and repeated then, "I'm just here having a drink."

"Sure you are, Brimm."

"Tod and Gee work together. They do community projects together, that's all."

"Of course."

"He owns the *Review*, she writes for the *Review*."

"Then you needn't worry."

"I just wanted a drink."

"A wise idea. No reason to think about your wife and Marcum chained together."

"Jesus, Jack."

"What did I say?"

"It was a protest."

"Sure, and what chance is there, do you suppose, that they rehearsed the cuffs and chains beforehand?"

"Damn it, Jack."

"Brimm, Brimm, Brimm!" he tossed his head back. "Come on now, you wouldn't be sitting here if you weren't already thinking the same thing. Listen to me. Don't believe because I'm not married I can't be right. I know exactly how these things go. Relationships are like business, either you're in the black or you're in the red."

"What's your point?"

"My point should be obvious, but since you're asking, let me spell it out for you," he moved my drink closer to me. "Suppose there was a deal you wanted to make, but you were having a hard time, do you honestly think you'd be here now, crying in your booze? Hell no. You'd be working your ass off figuring out a way to put the pieces together. And why? Because you're trained to focus on the bottom line. Black or red, high or dry, in or out, that's what you do. It doesn't matter if it's a project for me or Ed Porter or keeping Marcum from your wife, it's all the same. It all comes down to knowing what you want and how far you're willing to go to get it."

"I know what I want," I said on reflex, leaving Jack to reply, "Sure you do, Brimm. Of course. Which puts you exactly halfway there." He set his glass beside mine, leaned forward in his chair and asked, "So now what?"

"I don't know."

"Brimm," again Jack shook his head, then offered to tell me a story. "This happened last month. I was with a girl from the service I use. We just finished and I took a shower while she dressed and waited to be paid. I put on a robe and came out to the main room. You remember my apartment, don't you, Brimm?"

"Yes." Jack owned the entire top two floors of Fordum Towers, a total of 5,000 square feet, overlooking both Pendelton Field and the Mitlankee River. Renovated to his satisfaction, all the interior walls—excluding the bedroom and bath—were knocked out, the ceiling between the twentieth and twenty-first floors cut away and skylights put into the roof. The main room was vast, with barely any furniture, a bronze spiral staircase running up and down the east corner of the room, the reason for its existence unclear.

"So," Jack continued, "I came into the front room and there was the girl on the couch, her shoes off and her feet tucked beneath her, comfortable as can be. I called down for the doorman to get her a cab, then sat in my chair. The girl yawned and asked if I had the time. I have to tell you, Brimm, seeing her this way, all relaxed and familiar as if we were the best of friends, pissed me off. I pay good money for these girls and expect them to maintain a professional appearance and don't want them yawning or kicking off their shoes unless I say it's OK. I made a note to complain to the service and insist in the future I be sent only girls who knew how to behave, and just as I was about to let the girl go and think nothing more of it, she fucked up again by asking, 'What's with the room? Why so little furniture in such a large space?'

"I decided to teach her a lesson," Jack tapped the table, "and let her know such chitchat was not what I wanted, and so I answered her with a question of my own. 'Tell me, under what circumstance do you suppose you'd give up being a whore?' My question caught her by surprise, and when I repeated myself, and said that I was curious, given the extreme of her profession, and was there a limit she imposed on her practice as a whore, she insisted I not call her that again, but I just laughed and said, 'You can't be serious. There's no reason for us to argue semantics. Call yourself whatever you like, it's all the same to me.' She started to get up, but I told her to sit back down. I didn't apologize for offending her, and wanted to know, 'Given the demands of your career, is there any place you draw the line? Can you imagine some particular thing you wouldn't do? An incident which might cause you to quit your job? What if you fell in love? Or were raped? What if you found Jesus, or were sent to a hotel room one night and your father opened the door?'

"The buzzer sounded and I went to answer it. I told the doorman to let the cab's meter run and I'd pay the fare. As I sat down again, I allowed the sides of my robe to slip off my legs and asked the girl what she would do if I offered her ten dollars to suck my cock right now? She was outraged, of course, and I said that I agreed. 'Ten dollars insults you doesn't it? Even a whore has her pride. But what if I offered you a thousand? One thousand dollars to blow me right now?' I went to my bookshelf and removed a small metal box, unlocked the top, opened it, withdrew ten one-hundred-dollar bills and brought them back with me to the chair.

"Now then, I said, and parted my robe even further, exposing myself so there was no misunderstanding of what I wanted. Let's see who you are. I told her not to look so glum, that she should feel lucky, that I was giving her a chance few people ever had, an opportunity to gain a clear perspective of herself. The girl studied the cash in my hand, wanting to refuse I'm sure, but what point would there be in turning me down? If she said no and still went out tomorrow and slept with another man for money, what would she be but a thousand dollars poorer? The bills I held were crisp and green. I had to wait only a minute before a great sense of relief came over her face. She told me to get a rubber, but I said no. 'For a thousand dollars, you taste flesh.'

"She got down on her knees. 'Tell me then,' I said.

'I'm a whore.'

"There now. There, there. You do what you have to. It's never about pride, is it? It's about survival. It's about knowing who we are, about what we need and finding a way to get it." Jack stopped and drank from his glass. Someone at the bar finished a story of their own and a group of men sent up a loud cheer. I pushed my back flat against the wood of the chair, and said in response to Jack's tale, "It's all fine, but you can't compare my situation to that of your whore."

"Really, Brimm? Why not?"

"Because my problems are different."

"Are they?"

"Yes."

"Tell me."

"I'm not trying to put her down, but people like your girl-friend have it easy when it comes to determining the value of their wants and needs. They can treat the world as black and white as you say, because the stakes for them are never too high. That girl sucks your cock and who cares? The repercussions are negligible while the decisions I make are more significant."

"But that's where you're wrong," Jack leaned into the table, the center of his red tie creased. "The fact the girl decided to take the money and suck my cock reconfirmed her understanding of the universe and what could be more significant than that? Listen to me," he jabbed a finger into the space between us and turned suddenly serious, "everything in life is based on dis-covering simple truths. Nature itself is designed this way. After all the external crap is wiped clean, moral mumbo jumbo and pseudo-sensibilities, self-interest is the driving influence in all our decisions."

"I don't think so, Jack. You can't just wipe out morality then claim because you deign it doesn't exist that everyone is driven by self-interest."

"Sure you can. What about you and Marcum? Tell me your concerns aren't selfish."

"Of course they aren't."

"Because?"

"I happen to love my wife."

"Ah yes, love. Nothing selfish there," Jack laughed and pushed his hand through the scattered packets of sugar. I noticed a scratch which ran around his wrist and settled into the center of his palm, and clicking his tongue in a tisk-tisk-tisk sort of sound, as if admonishing a stupid child, he said, "Only an idiot follows a strict moral code limiting what they can and can't do to get what they want. Listen to me, Brimm. Life is about the bottom line. That's all there is and ever will be. Forget morality. Forget right and wrong and a proper code of ethics. Those terms are fodder for poets and fools. We're talking about your very ex-istence here. You need to stay focused. The decisions of my little whore are exactly the same as yours. You both have to figure out what it is you want and what price you're willing to pay to get it. The only question there is for you, my friend, is what you intend to do about Marcum. Are you going to let this bullshit with your wife continue? How many inches are you willing to take, Brimm, before you stop Marcum from fucking you up the ass?"

I left the bar shortly after seven, refusing Jack's offer to take me out on the town and, as he said, release a little tension, and driving east on First Avenue, tried to rid my head of all his chatter. ("Listen, Brimm. Listen. Listen. What are you going to do now? How are you going to get what you want if you can't decide?" over and over and over again.) I pressed my hand hard against the horn, cursed twice, and hit the gas. The car lunged forward and I shot through a red light.

I drove past Milhaunder Mall and the Museum of Modern Art, out beyond the older side of town with its antiquated buildings and factories, toward City Airport and the distant landing strips where smaller planes came and went. Just before Interstate 7, I changed lanes, turned left, and wound up in an altogether unfamiliar neighborhood. The houses near the airport were small A-frames with sloped, black-shingled roofs, bricked fronts, and aluminum sides. I crept along slowly, turning at the second corner, and then the next, past a series of houses where the flickering glow of television sets shined through half-draped windows. After a time I took my foot off the gas, closed my eyes, and allowed the car to glide against the curb. The impact was minor, and still I shouted as if involved in a horrible wreck. ("Gee!") My voice echoed inside the car, fell away, and haunted the silence which returned.

The image of Gee on the porch came back to me, and unable to cope, I tried to distract myself by switching on the radio. A newscast reported on William V. Aramony, former president of United Way, convicted last year of defrauding the company out of several million dollars who, from his jail cell, filed suit and won a judgement holding United Way liable for $4 million in deferred compensation. "Mr. Aramony's contract did not include a clause forfeiting the money if he was convicted of a felony," his attorney was quoted as saying. "The law is the law. We expect United Way to stand by the terms of its agreement."

What a world, what a world! (The Wicked Witch again in my head.) Music followed the news, a song by Boz Scaggs, "What Do You Want The Girl To Do?", which I had to turn off, and shifting into gear, I drove out the far side of the neighborhood, down Hutzel Boulevard, which ran parallel to First Avenue some three miles south of the airport, past a series of Mini-Marts, a small Mexican restaurant, a check-cashing outlet, several gas stations, and a hardware store with a hand-printed sign: Keys Made While U Wait. I pulled into the parking lot of a Revco Drugstore where I bought a small bottle of aspirin, the day's edition of the *Renton Bugle*, and a fifth of Seagram's Crown 7.

Outside, a group of teenage boys in identical neon-glow orange coats tested the doors of cars parked at the far end of the lot. I sat in the front seat of my car and swallowed three aspirin with whiskey, then looking for further diversion, opened my newspaper where I found on the third page an article captioned "Man Drowns Inside Woodberry Aquarium." As reported, a watchman discovered the body of one Michael Nersonne, a journeyman welder, floating near the surface of the large fish exhibit, having plunged to his death sometime during the night and with two large muskellunge swimming beneath. According to the piece, dozens of other fish rushed the surface in an attempt to get at the body but the muskellunge remained resolute and forced the intruders away. "The body would have been devoured for sure," the watchman said, "if not for them big musk."

I read further, curious to know what the muskellunge were doing, disbelieving the watchman's account and surprised when an ichthyologist at the university was quoted as saying, "Fish are no different from other intelligent creatures. They share varying and often sophisticated degrees of conscience. They have distinct and otherwise inherent social inclinations, feelings of sympathy, loss and woe. It's no surprise to me what the muskellunge did. It's quite apparent they were trying to save the man."

I set the paper down, stared out across the parking lot, and taking in the whole of the ichthyologist's claim, pictured myself as the man in the tank falling into deep waters. How would Gee react if she was there and saw me slip from view? Would she shout out in panic, attempt to save me in the same way the muskellunge tried to protect the welder, or would visions of Tod fill her with an altogether different sort of anticipation? The question was one I didn't care to answer and drinking again from my bottle, I checked the time—8:10—turned the key in the ignition and headed north.

Traffic going into the city was heavier than coming out. My mood was high strung and feeling slightly drunk, I watched the road for surprises. A man in a dark Ford pickup stared through my window at a red light and I hid the bottle of whiskey from view; knocking down another shot only after he was gone. For some reason, I thought then of my parents. Despite the many years, I still felt their presence acutely, and often wondered at what point in the course of their crimes their love for me became so insignificant that they lost all sense of grace and grew indifferent to the perceptions I now carry as a permanent reminder.

The first time I visited my father in jail, just after his arrest, he was brought to me dressed in a stiff orange jumpsuit, his thin black hair brushed in clumps by way of his fingers instead of a comb, exposing the reddish-white of his scalp. His glasses were missing, his naked eyes cast downward. (He appeared smaller than I otherwise remembered.) We were inside a small room with a square metal table and two grey chairs. A policeman was posted outside the door, the tiny window set high up in the left wall allowing a single ray of light to pass through. I stared at my father, afraid for him and anxious to hear his explanation regarding the ridiculousness of his arrest and how each charge was a terrible mistake. I placed my faith in him as always, yet seeing him enter the room, his shoes missing their laces, his cheeks unshaved, walking in a tired shuffle as if shackled, I was struck at once by the reality of the situation and understood how completely things had changed.

As he approached the table and sat down, I stood back in what minor distance the room allowed, not quite sure what to say before I managed to ask, "Are you all right? Are they treating you OK?"

Something in my question caught him by surprise. He seemed prepared for a different conversation, a more direct interrogation, and startled by my concern, looked once around the room, back down at his hands, and then up again at the thin ray of light spilling in from outside. I inquired about bail, but he pretended not to hear, and only later did I learn that all his assets were frozen and no one came forward to help. When I asked again if he was OK, his expression changed, the show of weakness first evident when he entered the room replaced by something more baffled and severe. He shook his head, smirked, stared down at his fingers, then up at the silver light, muttering, "Shit." (I could not recall him ever once cursing before.) Only as the guard came in and said it was time to go, did my father speak to me. "You shouldn't blame your mother," he rose as he said this, the guard holding onto his arm.

I was confused, and told him, "I don't understand. What does Mother have to do with anything?" He seemed about to answer, then set his jaw and changed his mind. "I don't understand," I said again. "What do you mean?" but the guard already had him out in the hall and was leading him back to his cell. I called out once more in vain, for by then my father was gone.

I turned off Hutzel Boulevard and drove back along the numbered avenues until I reached the Woodberry Aquarium, parked, and went up to the door. The sign stencilled in small black letters on the front window reported the hours of public admission as 10 a.m. to 9 p.m. I stepped inside with fifteen minutes to spare and purchased a five-dollar general ticket. The

woman who took my money was heavyset, grey haired with
sallow skin, a thin mustache, and dark eyes, dressed in a multi-
colored smock with the word Woodberry sewn in gold thread
above her left breast. She squinted harshly when I asked for
directions back to the muskellunge, reproaching my curiosity to
visit the tank where the journeyman welder drowned. I offered
neither comment nor defense, and walked off in the direction she
pointed with a quick wave of my hand.

I went down two corridors where the smaller tanks were set
into the walls and an assortment of colorful fish swam in specially
lighted pools of filtered water. The larger tanks were in the east
end of the building, the saltwater trophies, the puffers and angels,
sand sharks, discus, and eels in 150- and 300-gallon tanks, with a
special 5,000-gallon unit for the lemon sharks, groupers, and
other large catches. The main freshwater display was a 10,000-
gallon system built between the east and west wings, home to the
muskellunge and additional lake and river fish ranging from fifty
to two hundred pounds.

I made my way back to the tank and stood staring in through
the glass. The setting was natural, with plants and stones and a
silt-clay bottom lighted by lamps hidden along the inner columns
and down beside the larger rocks. I identified the muskellunge
from a chart on the side wall and waited for them to swim by. I
could find only one at first and followed her around the circum-
ference of the tank. She was without question an impressive creature. Even in the confines of the tank, the muskellunge, at over
eighty pounds and shaped like a steely torpedo, exuded a powerful presence. Intricate creases topped her brown-green skin, with
a series of black spots set along her rearmost fin and tail. Her face
was lined and handsomely wrinkled, her mouth long and centered back beneath a stout nose. She had intelligent grey eyes, at
once dark and soft, which lent themselves to a keen and obser-
vant expression.

I leaned against the tank and began at once to imagine the
sequence of events from the other night. I assumed the journeyman must have hidden somewhere until after closing, then found

a way into the water from the covering on top. I saw him diving straight down, setting his arms around one of the massive rocks at the bottom, remaining there until losing consciousness and bobbing back toward the surface. (Why he did all this, I could only speculate.) I pictured the muskellunge trying to protect him, could all but feel the cool dark water, and how slowly the minutes must have passed last night; the full black pitch of disaster and chaos within the tank as the muskellunge set themselves against the other fish circling and charging the dead.

A taped message played over the loudspeaker, informing those of us still wandering about that the aquarium was now closed and the doors would reopen at ten a.m. tomorrow morning. I didn't move from the tank, maintained a quiet vigil, watching and waiting for the second muskellunge to appear and the other to come back around again. An attendant approached after a minute and politely told me it was time to leave. I asked him then about the mate. "I can only find one musk," I said. "Is this the right tank?"

"Yeah, it's the one." The attendant was a boy of maybe twenty, pencil thin, with short cropped brown hair, three gold studs in his right ear, and a maroon Woodberry Aquarium vest over a short-sleeved Ski the Ute T-shirt.

"I thought there were two muskellunge?" I was now confused.

"There were," he said. "The other's dead."

"What?"

"A virus, they think. Something gotten from the dead guy."

"But it hasn't even been twenty-four hours."

"Yeah."

"A virus can kill a large fish that fast?"

"A human disease. A foreign strand. It can happen."

I didn't know what to make of this news. I found it hard to believe such a robust creature could die that fast, and walking back outside was genuinely disturbed by word of the other musk's death. What a horrible night! One thing after another. I imagined the dead fish drawn from the tank with a large net and chain and shaking my head, tried again to make sense of the muskellunge's decision to stay near the journeyman's body. I sat in my car and contemplated the question in full, thinking about the fish, and as all things now flowed back to Gee, once more about my marriage. I compared the decision of the musk with that of my father, how faced with the fear of his own marriage crumbling—as Mother's affair got the best of him and he scrambled for a way to salvage her love by acquiring a steady infusion of cash—he committed himself to a course of action; his effort purposeful, prodigious, and organic, his determination fully realized and not compromised by some insular claim of propriety—and fear—for which Jack had mocked me.

Of course, just as the muskellunge wound up dead as a result of acting with too much moral hubris, so too had my father's crime ended in disaster, and how could I say then that one choice was better than the other?

"You can't, Brimm." Jack Gorne was right. "There is no right or wrong, only consequence. Self-interest, Walter! Valuate your desires, ignore all extraneous influences, assess the situation, size up the competition, and do what has to be done!"

I sighed with a knowledge which seemed long avoided, and shifting back into gear set my jaw exactly as my father had years before and drove across the avenues to my office.

CHAPTER 8

ᘛ

Other than the cleaning crew and a few young associates hired to keep an eye on the overseas markets, all of Porter and Evans was quiet. I signed in with the night watchman and took the elevator up to the fourteenth floor of the Mortimer & Long Building where I went first into the washroom and rinsed my face and emptied my bladder of whiskey. The lighting inside was unnaturally bright, and as I glanced at myself in the mirror, the coloring of my cheeks and lips appeared a particularly bloodless shade of pale. I went down the hall to my office, shut the door, and sat behind my desk. In my bottom drawer—locked—I kept a small folder fastened with a broad elastic band containing some sixty sheets of paper; all the information pertaining to Tod's proposals for Happy Meadows and Duroflex Watchbands, along with my research and the purchase and sales transactions from Adam's Eau. (It was, I suppose, part of my fastidious nature to keep such a record of these deals and all related work product.) Hand printed on a few separate sheets of paper, less detailed than the other notes though sufficiently recorded, was the proposal Tod brought me for selling last year's athletic shoes in a new second-tier market. (Tod called the project Old Soles.) Although I rejected his pitch early on, I had done some initial investigating and placing the papers for Old Soles in front of me adjusted the glow of my desk lamp and began reexamining the proposal.

I spent a good hour pondering the possibilities and what it would take to get the project up and running, made a series of new notes on a fresh pad of paper, used the Internet, Standard and Poors, and the Corporate Digest to identify existing manufacturers and distributors, tracked down phone numbers and addresses of potential suppliers, and jotted out the names of people I should contact in the morning. After this, I outlined what I should say to my clients and to Tod and sometime after ten thirty, I returned the pad and notes to its folder and locked everything back in my drawer.

The whiskey I drank earlier had worn away, leaving me with a residue of weightiness in my arms and legs, though my head remained surprisingly clear, and shifting my attention from Old Soles to the complemental plan conjured while driving from the Woodberry Aquarium, I reached for my Rolodex and retrieved Jim Catrell's number. I'd known Jim ten years, had worked with him on several deals, and followed his career closely. (Jim made his fortune buying and selling companies, liquidating or improving their holdings, merging weak sisters into efficient operations, cutting and revamping as the situation required.) "Hey, Walt," he had an animated, high tenor tone of voice, forever pitched at a level of exhilaration.

"I hope it isn't too late to call, Jim."

"What? No. Nonsense. I'm glad you did. We were just watching your wife on the news."

"Were you now? How'd she look?"

Jim laughed. "How do you think? Like a goddess in chains!" I heard the creak of a leather chair as he sat down. (A stout man with short legs which seemed too thin to support his weight, his stride was top-heavy, like a wooden toy designed to rock back and forth at the slightest provocation.) "So it's civil disobedience now, is it? Excellent! I'll say this for Geni, she has spunk," Jim laughed again, then added, "For what it's worth, I think this whole thing about that girl reporter is bullshit. Civil contempt my Aunt Fanny. They let thieves and addicts post bail, don't they? The next time your wife wants to chain herself to a fence, you let me know."

"I'll be right there beside you, Jim."

"And you should be!" Ruthless in business, Jim's politics leaned nonetheless left of center. ("Hell," he crowed, "I'm rich enough to afford it.") He enjoyed attending parties accompanied by the Greenpeace candidate for city council, and often appeared in restaurants and at the theater with union organizers and the local director of the ACLU. Whenever Gee wrote a controversial article, Jim phoned to mock my more conservative ethic. "So then, Walt," I pictured him settling back in his chair, "What's on your mind?"

I answered his question directly with "Tod Marcum."

"Ahh. Geni's pal."

"That's right."

"Quite a character, I've heard. Likes to stir things up with his *Review*."

"I thought you might want to meet him."

"Really? Why?"

"I don't know, Jim. For whatever reason people like Marcum amuse you. Besides, he could use your advice. He has peculiar views about business. I've helped him out a few times on some stocks and ideas he's run by me, but I'm no longer comfortable operating in that capacity."

"His getting arrested with Geni has soured your good nature?"

"We've had our differences," I went so far as to admit.

"So why not hook him up with someone else at P and E?"

"If it's all the same, I'd rather not. Anyway, you're better suited for dealing with his eccentricities."

"I see. And it was important for you to set this up tonight?"

"It was on my mind. There's a few details I'd like to finish off business-wise with Tod, and it occurred to me to give you a call."

"Well, alright then. Yes, I'd love to talk with him."

"Excellent."

"I can take him to the club, shake the boys up a bit. Let me check my calendar and I'll call you tomorrow."

I hung up the phone and made a quick notation beside Jim's name, imagined Tod joining him for dinner, how they'd hit it off and the conversation they'd fall into. In my capacity at Porter and Evans, I saw Jim socially at a number of functions throughout the year and we sometimes met at Talster's for a bit of friendly imbibing. I knew from experience Jim's fondness for brandy and blood-rare steaks, that he liked to talk sports and particularly the Renton Monarchs, and after a few rounds of drink he couldn't resist boasting of some secret bit of information: future mergers and business deals, impending stock offerings and bank trans-actions, trades involving corporations and financial institutions he had a fiduciary interest in. Material meant to be held in the strictest of confidence under the letter of the law was all suddenly submitted for discussion. I could remember a half dozen times or more when I found myself saying with a mix of good humor and alarm, "Jim, Jim! Shut up! Don't tell me anything. I can't trade on this now with you talking so much. Hell, Jim, you're costing me a fortune! Stop! Are you trying to get us both arrested?"

Shortly after eleven, I phoned Gee. I was nervous and took a moment beforehand to consider exactly what I would say, asking first, "Did I wake you?" and hearing Gee's voice tired on the other end of the line, wondered about Tod. "Is he still there?"

"No, Walter. Rea and I took him home."

"Listen," I began softly enough, offering then the speech I prepared, affecting an earnest tone, convincing in my delivery, eager to let Gee believe I was sorry for what happened. "I apolo-gize for flying off the handle and not managing the situation better. Your arrest caught me by surprise, that's all. Still, I should have focused more on what you'd been through and not on how the circumstance affected me, and for that I'm sorry." I hoped this was enough to regain Gee's trust, thankful to be speaking by phone, knowing if she had a chance to look at me she'd see at once that I was lying. "I'm sorry," I said again, and was relieved when Gee answered, "It wasn't all your fault, Walter."

Her concession pleased me. That she sounded, if not absolving, receptive to explanation was good enough for now, though just as I wondered if my apology might actually possess a grain of truth, and if perhaps this was all we needed, a recognition of our errors to put us back on track, Gee found reason to mention Tod. "I'm sure he'll also forgive you, Walter," she said.

Shocked, I could do no more than clench my teeth. "When the time comes, I'll have to ask him." I replied, and telling Gee not to wait up for me, that I wanted to finish something I'd started at the office, I promised to be home soon—for she insisted, "There are things we still need to talk about."—and hanging up, I came from behind my desk, turned off the light and went back down the elevator in a smooth and silent descent.

The air outside seemed somehow hotter by the time I reached my car, and driving across the numbered avenues, toward Marshall Boulevard and in the direction of campus, I thought about continuing onto Fetzer Street, but decided surprising Tod was not the best-laid plan. I needed him unruffled, not set back on his heels suspicious of me, and parking in front of Greely Hall I walked a block until I found a pay phone. Liddi Faine—Tod's tenant the last year, halfway through her dissertation on French Female Writers of the Renaissance, and part-time waitress at the Appetency Café—answered on the second ring. It was nearly midnight, and after identifying myself and apologizing for calling so late, I asked if Tod was still up.

We were casual acquaintances, Liddi and I, having been introduced at a reception Gee brought me to, and at subsequent events, and while our conversations were mostly cordial, I sensed she didn't like me very much. (She enjoyed teasing me with reference to the amount of time Gee and Tod spent together and no doubt had heard about the day's debacle and was wondering why I'd called.) "I'd like to stop by if it isn't too late," I said.

"Sure. Wait. Let me check. Tod's finishing up some work," she informed me, then left the phone for a moment. The next voice I heard was Tod's who sounded a bit startled yet invited me over, "Of course, Walter. Yes, come on by.", without asking what was on my mind.

I bought a bottle of wine at an all-night drugstore—the gesture seemed a good idea—and returning to the street, walked past Charlie's Coffeehouse and the Blind Pig. I didn't plan on leaving my car behind—the distance from campus to Tod's house was approximately a mile—but turned left off of Marshall and kept on going. The heat in the air plastered my shirt against my chest and caused my pants to chafe my inner leg; the night somehow growing hotter by the minute. Fetzer Street was part of an older neighborhood where more than half the homes were subdivided into three and four apartments rented out to students. I quickened my pace against the arching heat and arrived at Tod's front door a short while later.

Liddi let me in. She was one of those oddly attractive women, around twenty-five, her slender form a handsome mix of angles and curves. Slightly tall with a dark complexion and light brown hair cut short and brushed to remove the slightest trace of curl, she wore jeans and a blue T-shirt imprinted with a picture of Che Guevara, a weaved rope bracelet encircling her left wrist, her feet bare and toenails painted a bright shade of orange. "Walter Brimm," she smiled as if happy to see me.

The light from inside spilled onto the porch. I stepped into the hall, glad to be out of the heat. The house was small, with narrow halls, a rectangular front room and dining area to the right of the kitchen. Stacks of books, magazines, and newspapers were interspersed around a collection of old furniture, while a print by Milton Avery hung on the wall alongside framed photographs of writers, radicals, and politicians Tod had gotten to know over the years. "Walter," he approached me from the stairs and clasped my hand.

I passed him the bottle of wine and asked then for a glass of water. "It's hot as hell out tonight."

"Is it? I hadn't noticed," he returned in a moment with ice water for me, a corkscrew, and three glasses. I hoped we might speak alone, but as he motioned me toward the front room, Liddi followed after us and settled into one of the chairs. I sat on the couch across from Tod. "I'm glad you stopped by," he said. "I phoned your house a while ago, but Geni told me you were still out. I want to apologize for this afternoon. You'd every right to be mad."

"All the same," I waved him off, "I overreacted."

"I shouldn't have butted into your conversation with Rea, and I should have made sure you knew what was going on from the start."

"You don't owe me an explanation, Tod."

"I have a check for the bail."

"Don't worry. That isn't why I'm here," I hoped to sound as earnest as I had with Gee on the phone, and when Tod said, "Still, I should have discussed things with you first," I insisted, "What you and Gee do is your business. It wouldn't have mattered if you told me. Even if I objected, Gee hardly needs my permission for the things she does."

"As a courtesy."

"Would that have made you feel better?" a hint of anger found its way into my tone, and determined to compose myself, I leaned forward and said, "Let's change the subject, shall we?"

I felt Liddi's stare and wondered if she already suspected me of delivering up a Trojan horse, but refusing to be thrown off, I said to Tod, "I've been meaning to speak with you anyway, and as you were still up and I was anxious to put the events of today behind us, I thought I'd stop by and tell you that I've been reviewing your idea for Old Soles."

"Really?" again Tod sounded surprised.

"I've done some initial research and feel with one or two modifications the venture just might work."

"My idea?"

"Are you still interested?"

"But I thought you said there were too many risks?" he reached toward the bottle of wine. I declined what he poured for me, the aftereffect of the whiskey and the absence of food making my head and stomach unreliable. Liddi lit a clove cigarette and dropped the match into a red plastic bowl. "There are risks, of course, in any deal," I answered. "And I won't lie, in many ways the investment is too large for you, but there's promise."

"You think it's possible?"

"Yes."

"And I can afford it?"

"There are ways."

"Then I'm interested," he had on a pair of reading glasses, wire-rimmed with rounded lenses, which lent a certain counterbalance to his otherwise narrow face.

"Good," I shifted around on the couch, angled more toward Tod and away from Liddi. "Now then, I've already spoken with distributors and several shoe manufacturers. I've also checked out potential sites at local malls. If we can purchase a good block of shoes for say six dollars a pair which you, in turn, retail at between twenty-five and fifty dollars, even with your overhead and interest on your loans, you stand to make a nice profit."

"My loans?" the first hesitation—predictable—entered Tod's voice. I ignored as much for the moment and went on. "I'm afraid Porter and Evans isn't prepared to represent you officially as a client, which means I won't be partnering you with any of the other accounts I manage, but I can put you in touch with some friends of mine at institutions I believe you'll approve of and I'll help you get the loans you need. Unofficially, I'll assist you any way I can."

"I don't know what to say," he took another moment to consider what I just told him, weighing the reality of my proposal, and staring at me, I could see in his eyes further signs of doubt. (More proof of Tod's pretention, I thought, for how quick he was to discuss business in the abstract and how fast he fell into a panic when the time came to risk his own cash.) "Of course," I said, prodding him on, asserting my position of command over the figures and facts, "if you don't want to pull the trigger."

"It isn't that."

"I understand. You're worried about the money. How are you to cover the expense, and wasn't I the one who preached to you about not getting in over your head?"

"It does seem a bit much for me to take on."

"Then don't. Do the deal or not, any way you like, that's your choice. If you're unsure, we can always keep reinvesting your stocks. In a few years, you'll probably have earned ten, maybe twelve thousand dollars, but that really isn't what you're looking for, now is it? In terms of investing your profits back into the community, you need more."

"I would like more, yes."

"The thing of it is, making real money requires risk. I've encouraged you to play it safe until now because the deals you've presented me with were too speculative. As your friend," I said, "I discouraged you. But you remained persistent, and now I agree, if you want to make some serious cash, you have to consider taking the plunge."

Tod ran a hand back through his hair. He adjusted his glasses and stared over at me, ponderous and still unsure yet otherwise unsuspecting. "It's true. It is what I want," he said. "And I've been thinking lately about a project I'd like to fund. Do you remember the first night we met?"

"At the Dunlaps' party."

"We debated Jack Gorne's purchasing Wintmore Towers and the closing of Melstar Clinic."

"I remember."

"I'd like very much to purchase a building on the east side of town and lease the property back to the city in order to see Melstar reopened."

"Well," I let my voice go high as if I was entirely supportive of this most ludicrous new idea and, tipping my head back, said, "There are certainly plenty of vacant buildings on the east side. All the more reason to try and earn some money through Old

Soles. In fact, if you're serious about Melstar, there's a friend of mine I think you should meet. Jim Catrell. You may have heard of him. Jim knows all the ins and outs of doing deals with the city and I'm sure he'd love to take you to dinner and answer every one of your questions about getting a property for Melstar. I'll give him a call and let you know tomorrow. I wouldn't mention Old Soles just yet. Jim's a businessman, after all, and a bit ruthless. He might steal the whole project from us. Concentrate on the clinic and how to get things started. Now then, about Old Soles."

Liddi stood up unexpectedly. The space between her chair and the lowboy was less than eighteen inches, and she could have easily reached over and placed her wine glass down without leaving her seat. Instead she rose with her glass in hand, and after bending forward, turned and positioned herself in front of me, close enough so that our knees almost touched, angled so that I, but not Tod, could see her face. All of this lasted a matter of seconds and yet I took from her stare a measure of caution. "And what do you get out of all this, Walter?" she asked while sitting down again. "What is it you want?"

"I want to see Tod do well," I answered at once. "I want my wife to be happy. I want her pleased with me for helping out. That's it. That's all I'm after." I set my gaze against my accuser with particular firmness and continued. "As for money, if you're wondering about that as well, the answer is I won't make a dime off Old Soles."

"And you won't lose a dime either if the store fails," Liddi continued letting me know with just her eyes that she regarded my words as meaningless, that everything we had to say to one another was already exposed. I looked back at Tod. "Nothing is for certain in business, it's true. All the best projects are easily shattered with the slightest error, but that's why I'm here, to help make sure nothing goes wrong."

"Que nous sommes tous dans un etat d'equilibre affreusement instable, qu'un rien pourrait rompre," Liddi spoke at me, quoting no doubt from one of the obscure female writers she was studying in her graduate program. "And if you're not careful, Walter?"

"But I am by nature. You can count on it. Now then," I directed my comment again to Tod, pulling at the front of my shirt as the room we were in seemed unbearably hot, "I can help you with the banks. I can put all the initial pieces together. In terms of what I've already done, the research and lining up of loans, the contacting of the mall and shoe manufacturers, the bargains I've hammered out and the assistance I'll provide in the future, I've already saved you thousands of dollars before you invest a dime. The decision's yours, Tod."

"I'm quite grateful."

"I understand."

"And appreciative."

"Yes."

"And I am interested, Walter."

"Excellent," I let him know I took this as a commitment.

"I'm a bit overwhelmed is all," Tod qualified his response. "There's still a lot we have to discuss."

"Certainly there is. Of course," I got up then, my back to Liddi and facing Tod's chair. "It's late. Why don't you sleep on it. We can talk tomorrow. If you don't feel comfortable, that's fine. That'll be the end of it." I forgot about leaving my car on campus, and should have agreed when Tod offered me a ride, but I turned him down. For the first half mile, walking up Fetzer and out toward the main road, the torridness I experienced earlier was offset by the afterglow still pumping through me. I was relieved to have gotten things rolling, pleased with myself for not giving ground, accepting the Gospel according to Gorne in order to do what had to be done. After ten minutes however, the strength in my stride began to fail, the sweat across my neck producing an ache while a stiffness entered my knees and a heaviness filled my head and chest. I brought my hands up to my face in order to wipe at my eyes, while on Marshall Boulevard a hot wind swirled and pushed at me from behind, sending me awkwardly forward. I stumbled once and almost fell, my legs threatening to abandon me as I wound up exhausted and drenched by the time I reached my car.

CHAPTER 9

Love is a fever, who can deny?

I crawled into bed sometime after three and spent several minutes lying there staring at my wife. Gee tended to sleep curled away from me, but tonight in my absence she had turned toward my side. I saw her face clearly, my eyes having adjusted well to the dark, and unable to resist, leaned over and kissed her. I had no expectation but was disheartened nonetheless when, in her sleep, she brushed at her cheek and rolled off.

The ache in my bones still lingered from my walk and as a consequence, when I finally slept, I wound up having strange dreams. I saw the two large muskellunge strolling, not swimming, down a crowded avenue, one in a bright red dress and the other sporting a bowler. I saw my father decked out in an old-fashioned bank teller's uniform with a visor and elastic bands pushing up his sleeves, handing money to people from between the bars of his jail cell. I pictured my mother floating past the musk, saw Tod and Gee rowing a boat on waters so calm the surface seemed a sheet of glass, and Jack Gorne in a coal-grey suit and tie, a flower in his lapel that looked like a lily, toasting me as I sat in my underwear at a rear table in Talster's Bar.

Jack's image stayed with me and I soon had a dream about a man I thought was he—though I couldn't quite make out his face—driving his car outside the city, parking far up a dirt road, and marching into the woods late in the night. The moon and stars did not quite reach the path where he was walking, their glow suspended in the branches of the trees like strips of torn silver tinsel. A light rain was falling, and instead of comfortable boots, Gore-tex pants, and a hooded windbreaker, the man in my dream had on thin leather shoes, a nicely tailored pair of slacks, silk tie and white dress shirt, all very expensive and utterly out of place in the woods.

A large black dog trotted beside the man, a thick rope drawn around its neck, a makeshift muzzle strapped over its nose and jaw. The path through the trees was narrow, unused for some time, disappearing altogether a half mile into the woods where a railroad car sat inside a partial clearing. (Years ago, Anthracite Corporation transported coal through the woods outside of Renton, but the building of the highway made the route obsolete, and in the process of dismantling the tracks, I suppose—for purposes of my dream—it was possible for an old boxcar to have been left behind.) The man and dog strode on together in a curious sort of syncopation. Soon other dogs could be heard barking, weak, imploring howls that echoed and cut through the dark.

In the clearing, the man let out the rope, released the muzzle, and gave the black dog more of a lead. He retrieved a ladder from behind a tree and propped it up to the front of the boxcar. The walls of the container were a good twelve feet high, the top opened and exposed to the rain. The man removed the rope from around the dog's neck, replaced his hold by wrapping a harness underneath the animal's belly. A series of pulleys with additional ropes rigged and set were attached to the top of the railroad car, allowing the man to hoist the dog with little trouble. Once he had the dog lifted, he ascended the ladder, raised her over the wall, and lowered her inside.

The rope was pulled back out and the man shined his flashlight down into the box. The remains of two dead dogs, scattered and torn apart by the others, lay within, while the surviving members—four in total including the newest dog—shied from the light. The man observed his handiwork before climbing back down the ladder and listening for any sort of commotion. Although the newest animal was stronger than the others, the events of the evening were still too confusing for her and only later, as days passed and the last remaining scrap of bone was gone, would the stronger dog realize the full extent of her predicament and by instinct turn and attack.

The man walked from the woods under branches slightly bowed by the rain. He laughed to himself, understanding the function of his deed and how in a world as perfectly formed as ours—where half our days were spent in darkness and half in light—a person had to train himself to manage all forms of being. The rain fell harder by the time he reached his car and wiping his palms, he turned and shouted back toward the box, "Eat the bones, you mutts!" He drove home then, entered his apartment by way of the service elevator, changed his clothes, dried his hair, had a meal, and went to sleep.

I woke in the morning to the sound of our alarm clock radio and a voice I didn't recognize singing moodily of days gone by.

CHAPTER 10

i\J>

I spent the next two weeks discussing Old Soles in great detail with Tod. I worked diligently to bring the deal together, made dozens of calls, contacted manufacturers and independent distributors anxious to move their old stock and permit resale if we agreed to purchase a set number of shoes up front. I arranged loans through three of our city's more progressive institutions at rates Tod could not have gotten without me, inquired at shopping malls about available space, reviewed all incoming and outgoing documents, filed the requisite papers, and advanced the initial costs of registering with the state under the name Old Soles, Inc. Tod convinced two friends to back him in the venture. (Their investment was negligible however, and hardly worth the effort.) As a further show of good faith, I loaned Tod the money necessary to pay off the remaining $30,000 on his mortgage, enabling him to acquire a new loan against the current value of his house and put the cash into Old Soles. I assumed the debt without complaint and accepted it as a cost of doing business.

Gee learned of my plan to help Tod and very nearly kissed me, settling instead for a touch of my arm which felt light and cool against the ache in my muscles that had not yet left me. We agreed—tacitly—to skip for now the serious conversation she alluded to before on the phone, and in the days that followed conducted ourselves at a cooperative distance.

Early in June, Tod had dinner with Jim Catrell. "Your friend was very helpful," he called to inform me the next day. I listened to all the more meaningless details of their evening, impatient to hear some significant bit of information, and was rewarded after several minutes. "Have you heard of Sun Lytes?" Tod asked.

"They're an L.E.D. developer," I said. "They went public last year but their first offering didn't do much as I recall."

"Jim said they're underfunded but ready to take off."

"Are you saying you want me to sell your stock in Affymetrix and buy Sun Lytes?" (We agreed earlier, for purposes of financing Old Soles, not to cash in Tod's Affymetrix stock unless there was good reason.) "If you want me to buy Sun Lytes, I will," I tried to move him along.

"What do you think I should do?"

"You're the client, Tod," I was careful to avoid asking specifically what Jim had said, was ready to interrupt should Tod provide too much information. "I can look into the company and arrange the trade if it appears sound, as long as you give me the green light. Is that what you want?"

"If it seems good to you, Walter."

"You're telling me to buy the stock Jim recommended?"

"Yes."

"Alright then," I did as told that same afternoon, selling off Tod's shares of Affymetrix and purchasing Sun Lytes. I bought no shares for any of my other clients and certainly none for myself.

Old Soles opened just in time to catch the late summer and back to school rush. In order to stock Tod's shelves, having contacted all the manufacturers, I approached the same clients I brought together for Happy Meadows and Duroflex Watchbands and convinced them to invest in the purchase of 8,000 pairs of shoes for just under $60,000. "Trust me," I said. "You'll turn a tidy profit in less than a month, I guarantee." I next spoke with Tod and explained how I'd contacted a broker who was in a position to sell us 8,000 pairs of shoes for $90,000. "He won't sell you any less than that. Still, it's a fair price. I've done business with these people before. Dealing with a broker rather than the companies directly is the way to go. It's best you let me handle the exchange. If they sense you're a novice, they may try to jack up the price. Don't worry, I'll take care of everything."

Initial sales at Tod's store were brisk. The idea of creating a retail market for last year's high-tops, cleats, and running shoes proved visionary and went off without a hitch. By mid-August however, a competing store opened in a crosstown mall and sold its shoes for several dollars less. Tod was nonplused. Business fell off at Old Soles almost at once. "I can't believe it. What's happening, Walter? How did this store get open so fast?"

"Don't worry," I said. "Competition is a natural consequence of success. You'll weather this storm just fine."

By earning my clients a quick $30,000 profit from the sale of their shoes to Tod, I had their backing to enter into further negotiations with the shoe companies in order to convince them that the sale of last year's shoes was an untapped market. I laid out a plan for partnering my clients with the manufacturers directly, and after several meetings, the manufacturers agreed to supply us with an unlimited amount of their old stock for a minor charge. The companies, in turn, would maintain a twenty-percent proprietary share in the sale of each shoe, while my clients would cover the day-to-day expense and management of each store, the leasing of the facilities, employees, and so forth. "It's a perfect arrangement for both sides," I told the partners. "And best of all, by doing business this way, we don't have to worry about competition. Technically we're entering into a franchise agreement with each manufacturer and as such, they can deal with us exclusively under the letter of the law."

What a clever man I'd become. How resourceful and innovative. ("Walter Brimm!" the partners cheered.) So pleased was I by the course of my deception that I barely noticed the fever that returned and lingered in my head. I assumed the trouble I had sleeping was nothing more than my mind's inability to wind down, that I was excited by the promise of things to come, of Tod being cast into financial ruin, all his free time given over to keeping creditors from seizing his home, his restaurant, and the *Kerrytown Review* until he was forced to confront his note holders in shame and driven from Renton absolutely.

A week into September, Tod received word—as delivered on false letterhead from the "broker" I told him of before—explaining that the manufacturers currently supplying Old Soles with shoes had decided to go into the business of selling their back stock for themselves and as a consequence, Old Soles would receive no further shoes in the future. Tod phoned in a panic. "How can they? What are we going to do?"

"Unfortunately, Tod, there's little we can do. Our contract was only for last year's shoes. Remember, I warned you going in, this is the problem when you don't control production."

"But the deal was sound."

"I said your plan had excellent potential. I also said there were risks. I'm afraid this sort of thing happens all the time in business. As soon as someone hits upon a good idea, the big guns take aim and try to blow them out of the water."

"But my debt."

"It's a tough break, I admit."

"And you were so encouraging."

"Are you blaming me, Tod?"

"Walter, no. Of course not."

"I don't understand what else you expected from me."

"I didn't mean to imply."

"I cautioned you."

"I realize that."

"I'm not prescient. I told you all along, if you're reluctant to pull the trigger, don't. I said the deal had potential, but there were no guaranties. I helped you get started. I did everything I could to minimize your risk. Nothing I did was for any reason but that you asked."

"I understand."

"I should have been more insistent. I should have made sure you understood the risks. I tried to dissuade you initially, remember? I warned you what can happen. I'm very sorry."

"It isn't your fault, Walter."

"Let me make a few calls. I'll try to bail you out the best I can."

I hung up the phone and turned my attention at once to Tod's file. Under the language of his lease at the mall, his loans through the banks, his new mortgage, and the money put toward purchasing the shoes, I estimated his outstanding debt, not counting interest and liability to his limited partners, would top $250,000 by the time Old Soles was forced to close. What a victory this was! (Welcome to the real world, Mr. Marcum!) Here was what came of men who tilted at windmills, who filled their heads with foolish visions, and assumed the purity of their intentions protected them from defeat. Here—indeed!—was what came of false prophets who dared to strut and crow and hide behind a facade of moral impunity as they attempted to seduce the wives of friends and neighbors.

I phoned Tod back that evening and feigning a sympathetic tone said, "The ship is definitely sunk. It's a matter now of salvaging what you can. There's no sense throwing good money after bad. My concern is keeping you from absolute bankruptcy, which is why I've cut a deal I think you'd be wise to accept." Having decided I could do away with a portion of Tod's debt and still accomplish my goal, I assumed the role of savior and said, "All things considered, you're in a bit of luck. Most times, when a business goes under, the carcass is left for the buzzards to pick apart. I don't normally do as much, but for you, I've exchanged a few favors and persuaded the companies to buy back whatever stock you have remaining at two dollars a pair."

"Two dollars?"

"That's right. And they've also agreed to assume your lease the day after Thanksgiving."

"But I paid eight."

"Paid, yes. One deal has nothing to do with the other. I'm telling you, it's generous, Tod. The companies could easily let your stock rot, but they want the shoes now and don't mind doing you a favor."

"And the lease?"

"They're looking to capitalize on the start of Christmas sales."

"What if I held out through the holidays?"

"You're not listening. You won't have any shoes. They want your stock now."

Tod sighed hard into the receiver, paused several seconds, and then sighed again. "Alright. If you think it's best. I appreciate your helping me like this, Walter. Truly, I do."

"Not at all, Tod. Don't mention it. What are friends for?"

To the victor then, yes? The effect of my effort deserved celebration and I waited for my reward, convinced it was only a matter of time before Tod disappeared altogether, his days occupied by financial matters and keeping the wolves from his door.

How happy I was—how ecstatic!—and yet immediately following the closing of Old Soles, the intensity of my sleeplessness increased three-fold. I lay in bed and listened to the wind move the branches of the trees, and some nights, unable to keep still, I pushed back the sheet and drifted down to the den where I sat until dawn. My restiveness acquired mass, while such brutal fits of fever turned my dark eyes red and swollen, brought an unhealthy pallor to my cheeks, caused my mouth to dry, and produced a shudder in my shoulders, hands, and hips. Time and again an ache seized my muscles, arrested my joints, robbed me of appetite, and increased the heat on my brow. What nonsense it was, how utterly unjust!

Gee was sympathetic at first. She felt my head, commented on how haggard I looked, diagnosed my affliction as a stubborn strand of flu, and made an appointment with our doctor. (He prescribed Zithromax, suggested a daily dose of vitamins, gave me a B12 shot, none of which helped.) At night, with the rest of the house so utterly quiet, my insomnia became part of a cruel and dark exclusion. One evening, after pitching about too long, I got up and went downstairs where I stood in the darkened bathroom and washed my face in cool water. My hands trembled and a weary ache passed through my bones as I stared at the mirror, somehow afraid to turn on the light, searching and failing and searching again in an effort to locate my face. I brought my head closer until the tip of my nose was pressed flat against the glass and there I could see an outline, the contours and outer edge of what seemed vaguely familiar. Beyond the shape of my brow and thin puff of cheek however, I found nothing that appeared remotely as I remembered.

By October, the resale of Tod's remaining shoes was complete and Old Soles was officially shut down. (Tod paid rent on the empty space for another six weeks, the cash drawn from his reserves at the Appetency Café.) On the day the papers were signed, I sat quietly in my office, the symptoms of my flu attacking me in endless waves. I rested my head against the cool surface of my desk, stirring only when Ed Porter came in and asked what I knew of Dewiche Corporation. "You don't look so hot, Brimm," he said this with a disapproving click of his tongue. "Some of us have noticed. If you're ill, you need to keep it to yourself. Clients take it as a sign of weakness." I told him I was fine, though the moment he left, I turned my office light off and put my head back down on my desk.

I remained that way until shortly before noon, when a search I was running came up. (I had programmed my computer to conduct hourly checks on Sun Lytes stock as well as any new articles referencing Jim Catrell and here suddenly eight separate sources flashed on the screen.) Each report confirmed Sun Lytes's merger with Kolor Beeme, Inc., and Panunscia Sciences, the three companies restructured under the name Kolor Lyte Sciences, Inc. Word of the merger—as handled by the investment bank of Dorfetcher & Kline—came on the heels of Kolor Lyte obtaining $14 million in R and D capital from the Swedish Deuhaman Bank to help advance a patent on a unique L.E.D. design. Overnight the value of Kolor Lyte stock soared from $12 to $32 a share.

I printed out the articles, circled the names of Dorfetcher & Kline and Jim Catrell, who was not only a board member of D&K but chief negotiator in the deal. I documented Tod's purchase of Sun Lytes and the profit he earned as a direct result of his dinner with Jim—all original shareholders received a split of their stock which was then transferred into Kolor Lyte securities—and after typing out a draft of the anonymous letter I planned to send the SEC, locked Tod's folder back in my desk.

The events of the last few hours invigorated me, the final piece of the puzzle. The money Tod made was not nearly enough to affect his outstanding debt but was certainly sufficient to land him in serious legal trouble. I thought of driving to Talster's and drinking a toast, perhaps even inviting Jack Gorne so I could brag of my decisiveness and have him exclaim, "Goddamn, Brimm, but that's the way!" Instead, the pleasure of the moment proved fleeting and I wound up pitching forward, leaning to my right, and throwing up into the plastic liner of my wastebasket. I spent the next twenty minutes trembling and feverish, and struggling to recover, finally went to the washroom where I rinsed my face, brushed my teeth, and straightened my tie. I insisted again, "It's only a bug," and promised to go home and sleep as soon as I felt well enough to drive, but even the effort of waiting weakened me, and frustrated I tested my fever with the palm of my hand against my head, felt the heat within me burn and burn some more.

I left my office at a quarter to seven and drove straight home. Rea greeted me with an embrace about my legs, her grip stagger-

ing me with its sweet intensity. As I bent down to reciprocate and
lift her toward my face however, I nearly blacked out. Rea
squealed and raced away, altogether playful and imitating of her
mother who had her own deftness now for avoiding my touch.

Gee settled Rea in the front room with a large pad of paper,
markers, and scissors. "Daddy's a bit under the weather," she explained. "We don't want you to catch what he has." I sat in the
kitchen, sipping at a warm cup of green tea. Gee was at the far
end of the table, a stack of student essays in front of her. I appreciated her company, how she made an effort of late to look
after me, compassionate in her concern even as the atmosphere
surrounding us remained tenuous; a broad barrier of secrets and
confusions I could not wish away. "So?" she asked without looking up.

"So what?"

"Anything new with Tod?"

"You're asking me?"

"You're helping him, aren't you?"

"I have helped him."

"Better than before, I hope."

"Gee, please. I feel like shit." When Old Soles first began to
falter, Gee assumed an attitude of confidence, convinced of my
ability to help Tod weather the storm and make everything all
right. After weeks of praising my efforts however, she grew uncertain, and fearful of Tod's financial reversals—the current obligation on his debt was extreme, his credit in shambles, the
interest on his loans compounding his liabilities by the minute,
the profit he made on Sun Lytes stock a drop in the bucket, his
Review, his home, and the Appetency Café one late payment
away from being seized—she took to challenging me. I was disappointed that she still refused to see the incident with Old Soles
as further proof of just how bumbling and incompetent Tod was,
how in the grand scheme of things men were measured by the
consequence of what they created and not the superciliousness of
their ideals, and to that end Tod was worthlessly inept. "One does
what one is; one becomes what one does." I took to quoting

Robert Musil, a claim Gee threw back in my face, questioning my responsibility, approaching me with imputation. "What happened, Walter?"

"Everything. Nothing. Who knows? Bad luck."

"You were supposed to help him."

"I did everything I could and then some."

"He came to you for advice. You suggested he go forward with the deal."

"I wouldn't have touched the deal but for his insistence."

"What does Tod know about business?"

"My point exactly. He should never have pitched his ideas to me."

"But you encouraged him. You went to his house and suggested the deal."

"As a way of doing him a favor," I rubbed hard at a pain in the side of my chest. "I also loaned him $30,000, remember?"

Gee interrupted. "That wasn't a loan. We invested right along with him."

"Wait now."

"The deal went bad for everyone."

"Are you telling me it's alright for Tod to take our money, but I'm a bastard if I want to be repaid?"

She didn't answer, forcing me to go on. "What about the thousands of dollars I saved him by calling in favors to lessen his debt? Don't I get credit for that? If not for me, he'd already be ruined."

"That's all fine, Walter, but what are you doing for him now?"

"What more can I do?"

"A lot, I think."

"You're wrong."

"Am I?"

"Gee."

Our talks went around this way, circular and unresolved. I grew nervous, embittered, and afraid of what was happening. I had hoped—naively perhaps, desperately I admit, and still with anticipation—that Tod's need to confront his financial troubles would leave him no time for my wife. Instead, she rallied to his side, applauded his brave front, encouraged his fortitude while insisting—together!—they'd find a way to stem the tide.

I looked across the table at my wife, my hands wrapped meekly around my tea, the pain in my back, in my head, and chest and neck unremitting. I was worried about my health, about what was afflicting me and why, and eager then to extend a gesture suggestive of future promises and commitment, said, "Perhaps when I'm better we can get away for a weekend. Your mother could watch Rea."

Gee looked at me then, cautiously yet clear in her response. "I'm not sure now's the right time," she replied, and before I could ask why not ("Why, Gee? Why?") she added, "I've been thinking."

"About?"

"Tod."

"Gee."

"I have an idea," she said. "I want to give him a dinner, as a way to raise money for Melstar and help pay off some of his debts."

I sat without moving, my shoulders stiff and knotted. The discomfort in my body crushed me with disappointment and alarm as Gee continued to explain, "We can rent a hall at one of the nice hotels and have people pay a few hundred dollars each to celebrate the work Tod has done in the community. The money can go into a trust for Tod to reopen Melstar and satisfy his loans."

"You're kidding, right?" I groaned, whatever wind remained in my sails was now completely gone and at best I managed to stammer, "You want private citizens to pay off Tod's personal debts?"

"People will be happy to give."

"But Old Soles was a private investment."

"Made to earn money for the community."

"Everyone has a reason for why they go into business. Not everyone has the luxury of a dinner to help cover their losses." I slid forward in the chair, leaned over and settled my arms on the table. Rea had gone upstairs to her room where I could hear her bouncing about on the bed while singing the theme song from some early morning television show. The sound of her voice, both fragile and sweet, produced an odd sort of accompaniment to the argument taking place below. I cleared my throat and tried a different tact. "Have you spoken to Tod about this?"

"Not yet, no."

"Well, you can't expect him to agree. A dinner like this is not his style. He won't appreciate being singled out for special treatment." I struggled to remain firm, but was feeling ill again, the ache in my head heated and pounding. Gee's face, otherwise lovely, was absent of compromise. She took offense to my objection, and determined to brook no complaint, insisted a bit cruelly, "I know what I'm doing. I know what Tod needs."

And there it was. What a farce the world! What an ever churning bit of folly. I felt the support of my body give way and bracing myself, by sheer will, before my chin crashed down on the table top, I cried, "A dinner? For God's sake, Gee! (For my sake, please!) Why can't you leave the man be!" I got up then and went into my den where I paced about until my illness got the best of me—it didn't take long—and I collapsed in a chair. My heart beat wildly. I lost track of time, did not know whether I remained seated a few minutes or half the night.

When I at last made my way upstairs and changed out of my clothes, the house was already dark. Quietly then, I slipped into bed beside Gee who, not yet asleep, reached over and touched my hip with her fingers.

All of life is ground in such moments of brief encounter, either accepted or denied. (Love is a moment not stolen but dared.) Fool that I was, angry and weak, I lay silent and still, waiting for her to extend me more, but she didn't, and when I reached for her finally, my effort was eclipsed by the cool blanket pulled over her vanished form.

CHAPTER 11

ۣۮ

Mid-November. A cool, dry patch of days filled the city with a crisp, frozen charge. The windows of our house were long locked against the breeze, and we flooded each room with a steady stream of preternatural heat.

Despite my objection, Gee went ahead and organized Tod's dinner. She rented a banquet hall, put together a menu with caterers, ordered flowers and linen, tables and chairs, contacted fellow writers, teachers and scholars, and social activists who made their own calls for support. In the end, more than 300 people put up $250 a plate. Two members of the city council agreed to sit at the head table along with Tod and Gee, the writer Wendy Doniger, civil reformer William Sloane Coffin, and Dr. Janus Kelly of the free medical clinic.

On the off chance I might yet come around and agree to help, Gee asked if I'd assert what influence I had and persuade a few of my clients to attend Tod's dinner. How perfect her request. ("My clients, did you say?") Here was the ultimate irony, for what could possibly be more absurd than turning to Ed Porter and Jack Gorne and anyone else who'd ever made a dime from one of Tod's ideas—from Happy Meadows, Duroflex, or the collapse of Old Soles—and encourage them to support a dinner meant to bail Tod out of debt? I refused as a matter of principle, but then in a moment of weakness—and in an effort to please my wife—I went ahead and called a few clients, soliciting minor donations to the cause. I expected little to come of this, and was surprised when Nancy McClarin, retired chairman of McClarin Paints, longtime Democratic stalwart and original patron at Porter and Evans, took it upon herself to contact and ultimately persuade eight local companies to underwrite the cost of the entire dinner. (Placecards were printed with the names of each business and left in front of every plate.) I could not believe the amount of cash brought in, and with no way to refuse the donations, went ahead and took full credit, boasting to Gee, "There? You see? Who doesn't come through in the end?"

I received for my effort a warm embrace, hastily tendered, my wife stepping in and out of my arms so fast it was hard to be sure she was ever really there.

The dinner was scheduled for December 15. A Friday night, a week after the latest edition of the *Kerrytown Review* was put to bed. On the calendar in our kitchen, hung on the wall beside the phone, Gee marked the day inside a neatly drawn blue square. I, too, had referenced the date in my personal organizer, circling 12/15 in red.

Thanksgiving came and went with little notice while Gee busied herself with all the endless details of Tod's dinner. I, in turn, found myself alone again each night. (The aches and pains that destroyed my sleep and weakened my already shaky constitution were no longer of interest to my wife, whose application was demanded elsewhere.) I weathered this latest indignity poorly, and sitting with a cold compress posted against my rising fever, cursed my empty house—"Goddamn you, Tod!"—over and over, until my head filled with such a resounding sting I could but barely take the sound of my own breathing.

The Tuesday before Tod's dinner, I was in my office when a Mr. Thomas Mumphore called and identified himself as a field agent for the Securities and Exchange Commission, "Enforcement Division." He was most formal and without once mentioning the anonymous letter the Commission received explained that he was interested in a purchase I made for a Mr. Tod Marcum involving Sun Lytes stock. He said his questions were all routine. "We often conduct random audits of trades made on the eve of large mergers and sales."

The record of Tod's selling Affymetrix stock and acquiring Sun Lytes was registered by law through Porter and Evans and easily traced back to me. I was most cooperative in my responses, and took advantage of certain opportunities to paint the picture of Tod as a man desperate for cash. "Mr. Marcum has a history of approaching me with various proposals," I said. "I dissuaded him several times from getting in over his head, but finally agreed to help him open a shoe store. It was just after the store closed and left him nearly a quarter million dollars in debt that he called and told me to sell off his only stock, Affymetrix, and buy Sun Lytes. I was surprised, but he insisted I do as he wanted. Why, is something wrong?"

I was asked a few more questions, queried and quizzed, and eventually let go with no hint from Mumphore that he was in any way suspicious of me. The thermostat on my office wall was set at seventy degrees, but for days now felt considerably hotter. I sat back in my chair and tried to gauge my reaction to Mumphore's call, wondering if now was the time to play my final card and phone Gee with the news. I hoped such a revelation might at last raise doubts in her mind about her inviolable Mr. Marcum, but the prospect of her providing a less favored response gave me pause. What if I informed her of the SEC's investigation and suggested—as a consequence of Tod's debt—he knew exactly what he was doing when he accepted the illegal tip from Jim Catrell and forced me to purchase Sun Lytes stock, and instead of misgivings, Gee came quickly to his defense? ("Don't be ridiculous, Walter!") What if I found the nerve to ask, "Yes, but what if he did deceive us? Desperate people, Gee. (And don't I know!) What if he proved himself less than you think?" and to this my wife answered, "If anyone ever deceived me that way, Walter, I would never forgive him. (There!) Is that what you want to hear?"

I was still digesting the whole of such possibilities when my secretary buzzed through and announced that a Mr. Marcum was here to see me. "I won't keep you," Tod apologized as he entered my office, saying that he was across the street at the bank— "Giving blood," he quipped—and thought he'd stop by.

I'd not seen Tod for several weeks, and hearing from Gee how he continued to cling vigilantly to the sideboards of his sinking ship even as his financial situation went under, I was nonetheless disappointed to find him looking so well. Where I hoped he might appear haggard, his usually hale frame worn about the edges, his shoulders slumped, and a dark cast encircling his eyes, he seemed, if not unfazed, otherwise unchanged. Still, his voice was somehow off, the inflection behind his words oddly weighted, and while it was the dead of winter, he wore no more than a tweed sportcoat with a thin grey sweater beneath. His hair was moistened by a few flakes of snow, his jeans wrapped stiff around his legs from the cold wind outside. "How are you feeling, Walter?" he extended his hand.

"Fine, fine," I had him sit in the chair in front of my desk.

"Geni tells me you're still under the weather."

"It's nothing. A bug I can't shake."

Tod nodded. "There's something going around," he brushed his hair back with his right hand. "I won't keep you," he repeated, then reached inside the pocket of his sport coat and produced an envelope that he placed atop my desk. I noticed the printed return address, Enforcement Division of the SEC, and picking up the letter read the contents. "Apparently, my quick profit has them curious," Tod forced a smile, his expression unsettled, absent its usual confidence and verve.

I slipped the letter back inside the envelope and answered Tod with the same lines Mumphore said to me. "It's nothing. It's all routine. Happens all the time. Someone must have traded heavily before the merger and now the SEC's beating the bushes, looking at anyone who bought in close to the time of the deal. Don't worry," I made myself go on, rubbing at the side of my head while I spoke, quelling as best I could the ache of my fever. "The letter means nothing. I get these notices about clients all the time. It's an inconvenience at worst. Let me make a call and see if I can't get you out of it."

Tod took Mumphore's letter and folded it back inside his pocket. He thanked me, and for a moment I thought he might leave, but then he sighed and said, "I'm broke now, you know."

I made no reply.

"Oh, I'm sure the banks will let me scramble about for awhile, but eventually I'm going to lose everything. Whatever money's raised at this dinner Geni has planned won't help. Those funds can go toward Melstar or some other charity, but not for me."

"You know about the dinner?" I wasn't expecting this, the last I was told Gee hoped to keep things a secret from Tod until the fifteenth.

"It's hard to plan a surprise when so many people are involved," he gave me a strange look, turned away, paused a moment then glanced back. "Sorry. I feel rather foolish under the circumstances." Tod set his hands flat against his legs. "Just a little more cash, a little more, a little more, and I could save the world, but it seems the emperor has no clothes." He shook his head, his expression suddenly failing until he was all but unrecognizable to me. "I'm sorry," he said again, and standing, "I don't want to disrupt your work. I know you're busy. This letter from the SEC was just a shock, that's all. I'll be fine. A year from now we'll look back on this and laugh."

I remained sitting behind my desk long after Tod had gone. The pounding in my head returned in full force and I grew fearful, waiting nonetheless for a sense of satisfaction to greet me, the knowledge that all my handiwork had hit its mark, but what I felt instead was a raw rasp of error. I grew angry at what seemed a show of weakness, such questioning in the face of Tod's defeat an unacceptable defect, and grabbing at the sides of my head, I chanted, "Be glad! Be glad! Be glad!"

Ten minutes later, my secretary informed me that Jim Catrell was on the line, but I was feeling much too ill and in no mood to talk. My response was the same an hour later when I received a second call from Jim. "He says it's urgent," though sick as I was, I insisted, "I can't talk now. Tell him that. Tell him I can't, I can't, I can't!"

The night of Tod's dinner the sky was clear. Gee had reserved the Fenimore Banquet Room at the Imperial Hotel on Waverly Boulevard, not four blocks from my office. The plan was for Gee to pick up Tod at the *Kerrytown Review* sometime after six and drive across town where—as pretext—I was supposed to meet them for a drink at the Imperial Bar. The dinner was scheduled for seven p.m. with people instructed to arrive no later than six forty-five. At ten minutes to six, I was still at my desk at Porter and Evans, the aching in my joints and raw stinging in my head unabated. I shut off my computer, loosened my tie, and fishing out my keys, removed Tod's file from my locked bottom drawer.

I'd no idea what I was looking for, but spread the papers across my desk just the same and studied the accounting for Happy Meadows, the profits made on Duroflex, the purchase and sale of Adam's Eau, Affymetrix, and Sun Lytes, along with each transaction involving Old Soles. Eventually I went and stood at my office window where I could see from the fourteenth floor nearly all of west Renton and a section of the Mitlankee River. (How cold the water must be this evening, I imagined.) I brought my hands up to the window, set my fingers flat against the chill of the glass, and thought of Gee. Last night, as she prepared to dash off on some last minute errand for Tod's dinner, a sense of urgency and sorrow swept over me and I grabbed for her in the hall, catching hold of her arm and drawing her close, surprised as she permitted me this, allowed me this, allowed me—yes—one brief embrace which caused me to suffer the unfamiliarity of her touch and unmistakable depth of our estrangement. A second later, she and Rea were running out to the car. I stood on the porch and watched them depart, then returned inside alone.

I went down to the washroom and readied myself for the night. Few people were in the office at six thirty on a Friday evening and I left my door open, surprised to find Ed Porter waiting for me as I came back. He was standing behind my desk, several sheets of paper from Tod's file in his hand, a grim look on his face. "Close the door, Brimm," he said.

Confused by his presence, unsure how to react, I took two strides then stopped and composed myself as best I could in the center of the room. The snow outside fell in flakes of fractured white. Ed Porter maintained his position behind my desk, having pushed aside my chair. "I received a call," he said. "Two calls, in fact. Do you know a Liddi Faine?"

"We're casually acquainted."

"And Thomas Mumphore?"

"From the SEC."

"Enforcement," Ed passed his hand through the remaining papers on my desk. "I don't like getting calls from Enforcement, Brimm. And I particularly don't like hearing that one of my senior associates has placed a suspect trade. What's going on here? What is all this?" I took another half step forward, terrified and dizzy, and struggling not to panic while straining hard to think. "It's just old records, Ed."

He bent over my desk, picked up a sheet of paper with Tod's name on it. "Is this Marcum a client?"

"No. That is, not technically."

"What the hell does that mean?" the old man's face was red, the corpuscles in his cheeks rushing to the surface. "If there's something going on here, Brimm, if you're screwing with the reputation of Porter and Evans…"

"It's nothing like that, Ed," I did my best to answer.

"No? This Liddi person seems to think you've committed a series of frauds. She paints a rather detailed picture, in fact, and all these documents appear to back her up. How is it you were involved with Marcum to begin with? What's Marcum have to do with Duroflex and Happy Meadows? What the hell is his relationship to Old Soles, and why is Jim Catrell phoning me and screaming in my goddamn ear?"

I muttered, "I've no idea what you're talking about," but this simply caused Ed Porter to throw the papers back down on my desk and shout, "Quit bullshitting, Brimm!"

I was by this point pleading, warning him off with a bleak, "Stop, please. You don't understand," my voice anxious and suddenly loud, "Stop!" as I lunged forward and grabbed up the papers, holding them against my chest as I fell back, groaning, my hands flailing, the papers scattering in the air, my head dizzy as a violent heat cut through me and I stumbled again, balling my fists that I waved high in the air, the angle of my arms unmistakable even to someone as otherwise impervious as Ed Porter.

I don't remember how I got from my office out into the street, coatless and cold, running as best I could through the wetted chill. Despite the evening's wind and the blowing snow—clinging to me as if I was a heated coil trying to pass through an icy obstruction—my fever remained. I tripped twice and fell to my knees, panting and feeble as I climbed back to my feet and made my way the four blocks to Waverly Boulevard and the Imperial Hotel.

The carpeting inside the lobby was a dark orange cut across blue mosaic tiles. A chandelier hung in the middle of the ceiling like a giant crystal squid, with dozens of tentacles surrounding a blazing white light. The banquet hall was to the left, a large antique clock set between two oil paintings of ducks and dogs swimming in a marshy pond read seven thirty-five. I ran as best I could, the soles of my shoes soaked through and caked with ice, the front-desk clerk, two bellhops, and the concierge giving chase as I stormed past them, my shirt untucked and plastered white against my chest. I smelled freshly baked chicken, the perfume of cut flowers, and the smoke of a nearby cigar as I shot through the doors, charging in with such force that everyone jumped and several people close by fell out of their chairs, bone-white plates and finely polished silverware spilling. Gee and Tod were at the main table, though as I tried calling out, my voice became caught in my throat, knotted and useless against all I wished to say. Panic appeared in a series of colors—gold and violet, blue and orange and green—as I staggered on, sending even more chairs and one entire table crashing.

People remained far back long after I collapsed, the room reduced to a narrow strip of light, the periphery of all I could see a thick, woolen grey with Gee and Tod now kneeling beside me, their voices mixed and muffled inside my head. ("Walter? Walter?") I tried once more to speak, still gasping, begging them with my eyes to understand—"Please!" and "Sorry. Sorry."—though in the end my every effort failed. (Of course.) At some point someone slipped their hands beneath my arms and I was loaded into the back of a car, driven soiled and sweating, stretched out like a bony fish broiling in its own juices to the emergency room at Renton General.

PART II

"When a lot of remedies are suggested for a disease, that means it can't be cured."

ANTON CHEKHOV

The Cherry Orchard

CHAPTER 12

I woke the following afternoon hooked to an IV, my mouth dry and head aching, the inside of my throat so unforgivably raw that when I tried to speak, I produced only a soft, hoary "Gaahhrr." I looked about for Gee but there was no one else inside my room. A nurse informed one of the doctors that I was awake, and after an hour he came to see me. I had my reflexes checked, a light shined into my eyes, my back and stomach pressed. ("Tender? Tender?") "We're waiting on your lab work," the doctor said, convinced that I was incubating a serious sort of virus that infected my kidneys. (My coloring was jaundiced and I'd passed a bit of blood.) "Another week and you'd have done yourself permanent damage," he gave me a judging look, then left without saying another word.

I spent the rest of the day alternating between the coldest chills and convulsing with fever. I felt the effect all over, on my lips, in my joints, between my legs, and even in my hair. I shut my eyes for a time and when I opened them again the room was dark.

Eight days into my stay at Renton General and my muscles have turned into a sort of lumpy pudding, sloshing beneath my flesh as if I was nothing but six feet of waning bone and tissue. A

121

weakness ruins my grip and when I pee, sometimes in the plastic bowl and other times stumbling to the john, my stream comes out dripping and truncated like an old man. I fault the drugs and am quick to admonish my doctors, insisting their treatment is only making me worse, that my decline is rooted in external factors and I can't be cured with traditional medicines. Each time my nurses come with pills I weep and shout, "What is this? What? What? What? Why can't you understand what I need?"

Gee doesn't visit, has sent word instead that she wants a divorce. (She insists she knows everything and slams down the phone when I call.) Yesterday, I received a stack of papers from her lawyer setting out the terms and conditions of our separation. I won't be permitted visits with Rea until the doctors are satisfied with both my physical and mental health. The monetary figures are of no interest to me—she can have it all, it doesn't matter—and after being asked several times by her attorney to sign the papers, I have an orderly buy me a blank mailing folder and send Gee's requests on to my own lawyer with the briefest of instructions.

I lay awake, hour after hour, my head flat against the pillows, a mass of boneless rubber, a sack of boiled spaghetti spilled out on my bed. I regret what has become of me, loathe both the justice and injustice of it all, and wish I had but one more chance to handle things better. The sheets on my bed are starched and sterile, chafing against my flesh. Twice a day, one of the nurses appears in my room in order to make sure I've altered my position. They warn me against the sores that will otherwise gather on my shoulders and elbows, my ass and heels and hips. I shift as they tell me, though as soon as they leave, I sink back into the same immobile pose.

The weakness in my arms and legs is constant. No matter which pills I take, I remain feeble and pale. My doctors are more baffled than ever as to the actual root of my illness—my lab work reveals nothing—and frustrated by their inability to diagnose my collapse, they become divided in their thinking and subject me to a dozen new tests. One ambitious physician suspects I may have a brain tumor and sends me off for a CAT scan. The results are negative. My doctors are disappointed. Physical therapy does nothing to rid me of my languor. I'm put through my paces by a cruel son of a bitch named Griswald who tugs at my enervated frame and demands I go "Faster!" as I shuffle and groan on his creaky machines. I'm losing weight, and after two ridiculous sessions, refuse to submit to the torture of this insane man's devices.

Another one of my doctors suggests I start keeping a journal, in order to chart my state of mind and perhaps reveal what otherwise lies at the root of my trouble. After a period of hesitation, I purchase a notebook, red and spiralled with 300 sheets of paper, and record my thoughts in a shaky hand:

> Gee.
> GeeGeeGeeGeeGeeGeeGeeGeeGeeGee
> GeeGeeGeeGeeGeeGeeGeeGeeGeeGee
> GeeGeeGeeGeeGeeGeeGeeGeeGeeGee
> GeeGeeGeeGeeGeeGeeGeeGeeGeeGee
> GeeGeeGeeGeeGeeGeeGeeGeeGeeGee
> GeeGeeGeeGeeGeeGeeGeeGeeGeeGee.
> And again, Gee.

And the next day:

> Aaaaahhhhhhhhhhhhhhhhhhhhhhhhhhh!
> Aaaaahhhhhhhhhhhhhhhhhhhhhhhhh!!!
> Aaaaahhhhh! Aaaaahhhhh! Aaaaahhhhh!
> Aaaaaahhhhhhhhhhhhhhhhhhhhhhhhh!!!!!
> Aaaaaahhhhhhhhhhhhhhhhhhhhhhhhh!!!!!
> Aaaaaahhhhhhhhhhhhhhhhhhhhhhhhh!!!!!
> Aaaaaahhhhhhhhhhhhhhhhhhhhhhhhh!!!!!
> Aaaaaahhhhhhhhhhhhhhhhhhhhhhhhh!!!!!
> Aahh! Aahh! Aahh! Aahh! Aahh!!!!!

Ah, Walter. How eloquent! There you go now. At least you have it all figured out. After such an effort, why don't you just lie still for a while and be quiet? Why can't you be a good boy now, and "Shut up! Shut up! Shut up!"

Fine. Yes. OK.

I toss the book aside and give in.

Jell-O and tuna are all I eat. I favored neither food before, and while there's nothing so especially irresistible now about either—the Jell-O is often hard, the tuna dry and difficult to mash with the minor amount of mayonnaise I'm given—I've no taste for anything else and consume only this for my day's refection.

I've begun asking the orderlies to bring me the morning and afternoon papers, and on successive afternoons I read about eight fashion models who plan to auction their eggs over the Internet to would-be parents who desire a beautiful baby—with bids beginning at $50,000—and of Alistair Duncan, world-renowned expert on Tiffany stained glass, who was recently indicted for arranging the theft of a nine-foot Tiffany window from a Brooklyn cemetery which he planned to sell to a Japanese collector for $250,000.

Insane? (But true.) I read as well of Love and Madness:

Carlos Angel Diaz Santiago, twenty-two, in the midst of an unfortunate fit of passion, rammed his former lover's car into the path of an oncoming train, killing her instantly. Upon his arrest, a contrite Mr. Santiago insisted through heavy tears, "I... I... only wanted to talk to her."

Fate and Folly:

Rex Allen, age seventy-seven, the former country singer and western movie star, known—along with Koko the Wonder Horse—for such films as *The Arizona Cowboy* and *The Hills of Oklahoma* was accidently run over and killed in his own driveway by a friend who failed to see him bent over behind the car. "One minute he was there and then he wasn't," the good friend noted.

Vanity and Ego:

A cosmetic procedure known as Botox allows for a small amount of botulinum bacteria to be injected into the muscles of the forehead and around the eyes, erasing all preexisting wrinkles—the effect paralyzing the muscles, leaving the patient with eyebrows and parts of their cheeks that will not move. So popular is the procedure in Beverly Hills, people actually line up outside select clinics for a $99 Wednesday Botox special.

Tragedy:

In Warrenton, Virginia, Scott Zeigler, forty-one, hoping to free his six-year-old son's toy rocket from a power line, used a fishing pole to knock the gadget down. Assuming the rod was plastic, Mr. Zeigler erred in not realizing the shaft was graphite and was electrocuted upon contact.

And back again—of course—to Love:

On the front of both the *Renton Bugle* and *New York Times*, an article on James J. McDermott, forty-eight, former chief of the investment firm Keefe, Bruyette & Woods, accused of leaking information about potential billion-dollar bank deals, mergers, and public offerings, to Kathryn B. Gannon, thirty, an X-rated movie actress, known in the trade as Marylin Star, whom Mr. McDermott was dating. As a consequence of their relationship— referred to in writing as "Mr. McDermott's ill-advised affair"— Ms. Star profited in excess of $90,000, disappearing after cashing in her stocks to parts unknown, while Mr. McDermott, surprisingly earnest in his lament, confessed, "But I've lost everything!" An attorney for Mr. McDermott, hoping to plant a seed of doubt, said, "Things are not always as they seem. When all the facts come out, we expect the court to be sympathetic."

Certainly, yes. All the facts, indeed. (Why shouldn't we be sympathetic?) There always seems to be two sides to every story.

My night nurse is a small woman, the size of a child, who sneaks into my room at least once an hour to check up on me. I've no idea why it matters to her if I'm asleep or not. On nights she's off or assigned elsewhere, none of the other nurses peek in or care in the least about my condition. Only this tiny creature comes and creeps inside while I lay in the dark. She seems intrigued by me, puzzled or perhaps perturbed by my presence. "What are you doing here?" I expect her to ask. "What's wrong with you?" but she doesn't say a word. Not once does she speak to me though I'm usually awake, frustrated by my inability to drift off when everything around me is silent and I'm so awfully, awfully tired.

Tonight she lingers longer than usual, stands nearer my bed, her face in the shadows neither young nor old, innocent nor corrupt. I remain with my head atop the pillows, my eyes staring at the ceiling, and still I can see her, perched and quiet, as inert as a bird removed from flight. Finally, after what seems an inordinate amount of time, I can take no more, and ask, "What is it you want?"

The room resonates with the sound of my voice, and when I look again she's gone.

I feel my fever pitch as I roll on my side and glance out my window while listening to the emerging sounds of the city: car horns and distant whistles, the cry of voices, metal doors on creaky hinges opening and slamming shut. The ease with which the world outside continues on indifferent to my absence causes me to grow despondent, and pulling the sheet up over my head, I shout, "Fuck!" and "Fuck!" again and again, in desperate bursts. "Fuck. Fuck. Fuck. Fuck. Fuck! Fuck! FUCK!" until the word becomes my holy mantra. I cry so loud, in fact, that the day nurse eventually enters my room, and snaps, "Mr. Brimm?" (You there, beneath the sheet!) "What is the matter?"

Precisely, what? "I'm not sure," my voice gives way to a flag-ellant dissolve. "I can't seem to decide one way or the other," and curse again the constancy of my irresolution.

After three weeks my doctors can find nothing wrong with me, and convinced I'm incubating no infectious disease, that my heart is undamaged and my organs are absent cancer, having billed all they can for my care and seeing no reason to keep me, they arrange for my discharge. I don't protest though I'm only the least bit better and suffer still from a fever that shreds my bowels, blurs my vision, and dissolves my remaining muscle.

A few days before my release, flipping through the paper, I spot my own name in the "Coming and Going" column in the Business Section of the *Renton Bugle*. The reference is complete with photograph, my head and neck inside a pale grey square, and a brief note about my leaving Porter and Evans. "After fifteen years," the single line states, no fond farewells, good wishes, nor explanations mentioned, the terms of my dismissal already pro-vided in a letter from Ed Porter.

I drop the paper and reach for my notebook, determined not to think about all that's happened, and concentrating on the future, write: "What to do?" The response comes as part of a per-verse denial: "How should I know? I've no idea. I'm in limbo. I'm in agony. I'm in hell. Consider who you're asking."

I turn the page and try again, and in a more deliberate tone, wonder: "Is it ever possible for events which have gone awry to, at some future point, be repaired?"

My answer this time is just as swift and instinctively I print:

> Afraid not. Fait accompli. What's done is done. All of life is aftereffect, the sting of the bee, the prick of the nail, mud slides and moun-tains collapsing into the sea. Our days are a

process of crossing slippery slopes where each successful stride is all well and fine but it's the one false step which forever fucks us.

The assessment is sound, though a bit one-sided, and as part of my hope for healing, I sneak into the margin: "Of course, at times, there are moments of brief redemption."

As I can't go home just yet, I begin reading the classifieds in anticipation of my discharge. I want to move somewhere that suits my condition, and ignoring all ads to buy or lease a handsome high-rise on the north end of town, houses to the west, and quaint getaway properties to the south, I focus instead on finding a place more unassuming; a small refuge where I can serve a period of reparation and recovery without being disturbed. I spend the morning scanning the pages until I find an ad for a one-bedroom walk-up and that afternoon place calls to the landlord and building manager. Once a deposit is wired and my attorney takes care of the papers, I'm able to obtain, sight unseen, the perfect hideaway on the lower east side of Renton. No one comes to assist with my release, and a week after the New Year I move downtown without fanfare or assistance.

CHAPTER 13

Dr. Janus Kelly lies naked on his lover's bed, his long frame stretched out raw and spent, razed and gnawed about the edges. Despite a certain boyish glint in the flash of blue in his one good eye, his body at forty-seven appears betrayed by the consequence of several queer disasters; his left hand and right foot gnarled by separate acts of physical dissent, his otherwise handsome face conveying a slight miscarriage in its smile, his black-grey hair, narrow nose, and unshaved jaw giving him the gentle look of a man whose conflict with the world is nonetheless fierce and vulgar.

Myrian moves about the bedroom of her flat with three paint brushes of varying width and fiber held between the fingers of her left hand. A fourth brush in her right is used to shape the center of a large and lushly variegated mural with influences of Gorky and Nicolas De Stael evident throughout. "The trouble is you think too much," she says. "Your mind's like one of those pill crushers."

"A mortar and pestle."

"That's right. You mull and mash everything down to paste." Part of her hair is dyed orange, the center streaked blond, while an inch above the root is her natural shade of red. Her eyes are green, the surface of her skin snowy pale. Also naked, there is a pleasantry to her form, a fluidness in both her figure and motion as she wields her brushes with her back to Janus. "You can worry yourself crazy, if you want," she says, and replaces one brush with another, drops of blue and green falling onto her feet; cool colors passing down between her toes. The paints—all water soluble— produce a harmless trace of smell, easily washed off and rolled clean with a can of Sears white when a wall is finished and the surface made ready to start over.

Janus considers and eventually concedes her point. "Maybe so," he says. "I do think too much at times," he has two pillows behind his head, his good eye turned and following Myrian as she moves across the floor, his legs laid out atop the blankets despite the cool air in the apartment, and taking in the whole of the scene with a mix of amusement and confusion, he thinks, "Here I am and how is that I wonder?"

Myrian shrugs her shoulders. She has long fingers and lithe arms. Her cheekbones are sharp, as is the shape of her nose, her wrists and elbows and chin. At twenty-eight, she waits tables at the Appetency Café when not freelancing for local decorators who hire her to create murals for private clients. Janus enjoys watching her work, imagines her movements as possessing the appeal of a beautiful bird in an erotic cubist painting. "I just think."

"There you go again. Read into it whatever you like."

"Some things should not be decided because of money."

"In a perfect world, maybe," she doesn't turn to look at him, annoyed with herself for having brought the subject up. Her flat is too small after all, and how could she possibly accommodate Janus and his possessions, few that they were? What of her schedule and the way she kept odd hours working and painting? How would Janus handle those nights she didn't come home until three or four o'clock, staying out to drink with friends, maybe dancing at the Blue Dolphin or one of the after-hour clubs where she liked to feel her body pressed against by strangers while the noise and music from some new band beat loud and louder still inside her head? What, too, of the late hours Janus put in at his clinic, the danger of addicts wandering in off the street and de-manding drugs? How wouldn't she worry about him then if they were living together when she already did so now?

Janus shifts his body back on the bed. "It isn't that I don't appreciate," he says, then stops and self-consciously brings the sheet up over his waist. His penis has gone soft, collapsed down on the inner seam of his leg like a sleepy snake. Although he's tired—it's past midnight, six hours removed from when he'll wake and walk the two blocks to open the doors of his clinic—he fights the urge to rest, and watching Myrian in motion, shields the sensitive half of his bad eye from the light.

Since the start of their affair, almost two years ago now, as they first encountered one another in the lobby of their building and a few neighborly conversations led to something more, Janus remains surprised by Myrian's attraction to him. That he's in love with her now—captivated by her intelligence and energy and the knack she has for providing him with such sweet pleasure—only makes him more attuned to the reality of their situation and the inevitability of their ultimate parting. He predicted going in she'd tire of him, put off by his half-crippled frame and the difference in their ages, and determined to keep perspective, he focuses on the end of their affair and how eventually a younger man will come and spread himself naked and wanting on this very bed. That such has yet to happen, and seems more and more unlikely, is but another thing Janus can't quite understand and complicates all his recent decisions.

Myrian steps from the wall and turns to face her lover. A few small streaks of violet and blue appear on her bare stomach as she brings the tips of her brushes up and places them across her nipples. "What else do you appreciate, doctor?" she tries to make light of the situation, standing at the foot of the bed, her attempt to remove the tension from their exchange causing Janus to smile. He teases her then in turn, replying with a sentiment he knows reflects her own convictions. "I appreciate all of this, the absolute perfection of the moment and the whole of everything now."

"And well you should," she moves the ends of the brushes down, then spins away and returns to painting the wall. Several astral-like shapes are set onto a bluish-grey backdrop, the circles and lines, squares and half-moons, cylinders and indented spheres appearing to float across the surface. Myrian drops to her knees and begins working on one of the moon figures. After a while, she bounces to her feet again and steps away in order to gain a fresh perspective, her concentration unaffected by the lateness of the hour and the sex she and Janus had not thirty minutes before. (Inexhaustible, she's able to transform herself completely from one event to the next.) Once last winter, warmed by the heat of the old radiator and bathed in the light of a single lamp, she mounted Janus with brush in hand and paints beside her, leaning forward in order to work the wall behind the bed while Janus moved slowly beneath; undulating in a steady rhythm, his body liquid and floating along in short, hypnotic waves, like water coursing through an ancient stream, reproduced by Myrian's hand in a series of prismatic strokes of light green, beige, and crimson.

Still in bed, Janus continues to watch her work, taking in the movement of her arms and legs which are mercurial, not nimble like a dancer but somehow more natural, her gestures unrehearsed, genuine and unpredictable, perfect in their collective display. The glow of the lamp casts Janus's shadow up along the left side of the wall where Myrian notices him there, goes and traces his silhouette in blue with the thinnest tip of her finest brush. Janus considers the placement of his body inside the mix of Myrian's other anomalous shapes most apt. "See how she treats me as one of her discrepant forms," he smiles, and thinks about her invitation to move upstairs from his flat below. Tempted, he allows himself a moment when his weariness gives way to wanting. "Why not?" he wonders, but then a sudden throbbing enters his foot, cuts across his arch and down into his poorly healed bones, distracting him from imagining further. He tries to ignore the pain by focusing on the curve of Myrian's hips and the sweet shape of her breasts, only the contrast between her beauty and his own mangled landscape frustrates him, and reaching down he bends his toes hard, working his splintered remains until the existing ache subsides briefly.

The electric heater Myrian uses to warm her bedroom clicks on and the lamplight dims, regathers itself beneath the shade, and glows then as equally bright as before. Outside, blind gusts beat against the window. (Winter seems to take a perverse delight in bullying the east side of Renton.) Janus stares out at the cold, knows all too well from his work at the free clinic how inclement weather effects his neighbors: the falls that shatter elbows and hips, the bouts of croup, pneumonia and influenza, laryngitis and high fevers, frostbite, hypothermia and hyperventilation, the burns suffered by those who try warming themselves with cheap kerosine lamps and the skin that cracks and splits raw from the chill. He prescribes antibiotics for every sort of illness the winter months bring on, treats as best he can the people who come see him: the indigent and uninsured, mothers struggling on ADC, children neglected and run off, addicts and derelicts, victims of alcoholism, those with syphilis, blastomycosis, botulism, diph-theria, pertussis, hepatitis, trichomoniasis, typhus, and AIDS, young and old, black and white, Asian and Muslim and Latino, all pass through Janus's clinic at one time or another, in seasons warm and cold.

"Come to bed," he whispers as Myrian stands before her wall.

"Let me shower first," she answers, and goes to rinse away the smearing of paint and sex. When she returns, she slips in beneath the blankets and sets herself against Janus's hip. "Garvey Interiors called this morning. They want me to paint a mural of dinosaurs and cavemen for the lobby of Peterson's Pancake House. The Fred and Dino look."

"You'll have fun with it, I'm sure."

"Maybe so," she gives a soft laugh, and letting the subject drop, describes her idea for a new canvas. "I've made a few sketches and want to start soon, but nothing I've drawn feels right," Myrian switches off the light and runs her hand down the length of Janus's leg. In the dark, the heat of his body flows through her. She stretches her toes along his damaged foot, strokes gently at his dented flesh. "Tell me," he says in reference to her canvas, wanting to know what she has in mind, interested as always, hoping it will help her to describe the piece. Rather than say more however, Myrian asks if he's heard anything new about the man who collapsed at the Imperial Hotel.

"Nothing really."

"Tod's been in a strange mood ever since it happened."

"He's not thrilled by what he found out."

Myrian sighs. "It's crazy, isn't it? The things people do, I mean."

Janus squeezes her fingers inside his good hand, enjoys the feel of her this way, how his palm is able to enclose a part of her so completely. He measures the narrowness of her bones against his own and staring off recalls the events of Tod's dinner, how he was delayed at the clinic and arrived late, greeted by commotion as he and Myrian entered the hall where a man had fainted. The room was in ruins, tables and chairs overturned, and people scattered left and right. Janus examined the man's eyes, took his pulse, and checked his arms for marks as a woman rushed out for her car and Tod phoned ahead to Renton General, alerting emergency of what to expect. In the days that followed, Janus heard the whole story as Tod came to see him at the clinic. "The things people do, yes," he repeats what Myrian said.

"It's a mystery."

"Who can ever know?" and squeezing her fingers tighter, feels them wiggle warm inside his grasp.

He remains awake for a time, listening to the sound of Myrian's breathing, her foot still pressed close to his own, and reaching then with his injured hand, runs it gently down her cheek. He thinks about Tod, whom he's known for years, and how curious the events which pass in a lifetime. Back when he was a young doctor completing his residency at Renton General, Janus earned a fellowship in thoracic studies. The grant was a great honor and he was initially excited, though by fall he began having doubts. Disillusioned by the administrative constraints of practicing medicine in a large hospital, he wondered if there wasn't something more he could do with his medical training and mentioned the possibility of opening a free clinic to his wife.

Sarah Fenriche was a fellow resident finishing her rotation in reconstructive surgeries. Possessed of a firm, inflexible mind—her father was a scientist, her mother an engineer—Sarah was raised with empirical restraints, her imagination subjugated to the intransigence of sound judgement; she laughed when Janus first mentioned leaving the hospital. "All this talk. You're just over-anxious. Wait until you finish your residency and you'll see what you're feeling now is nonsense," she sat with her elbows propped and her nose pushed inside the *Merck Manual*, refusing to entertain any more of Janus's ridiculous suggestions.

Eventually he stopped discussing the clinic with her, and when she learned from others that he'd contacted state agencies and applied for grants, had scoped out potential sites while abandoning all thoughts of becoming a thoracic surgeon, she accused him of betrayal. "You're romanticizing everything. You're neglecting your responsibilities. You're out of your goddamn mind!"

"I don't see it that way."

"But this is absurd! You're supposed to be a doctor. How are the patients living on the north side any less deserving of your skills than those people in east Renton?"

"I never suggested anyone was less deserving. The point is people on the east side have limited access to suitable medical attention."

"So? Can't they drive? Can't they take a bus? You can't save everyone, Janus," she shook her head, her limbs pendulous, her trunk weighted through the hips in such a way that her every step seemed to celebrate the existence of gravity. Resentful of his position, bristling against his pious views, she shouted at him whenever he tried to explain. "How are we to live?" she proceeded then to the root of her complaint. "How much does charity pay? You're not thinking clearly." She rejected his answers, demanded he reconsider, accused him of misleading her from the start. ("If I had known!" she cried.) Despite all this,

Janus went ahead and opened his clinic. Sarah distanced herself at once from the process, and during the next sixteen months, as the grant money trickled in and Janus labored to keep his clinic afloat, she remained busy with her own work. Week to week, their marriage lost momentum, veered off the road, and eventually crashed. They divorced in the winter and Sarah moved to Brentwood where she became a successful plastic surgeon, shaving wrinkles from the cheeks of wealthy patients, tucking double chins, and carving crow's feet from the corners of otherwise senescent eyes.

Janus also moved. He found a one-bedroom flat two blocks from his clinic on the lower east side, worked long hours, and was twice awarded a plaque for his commitment to the community. Still the city saw fit to routinely cut his funding, claiming it couldn't manage the money under each new year's budget. Confronted by mounting costs, limited federal aid, and inconsistent private donations, he worried about being forced to close his doors, drained off what remained of his savings, sold his furniture, his framed lithograph, a gold pocket-watch, two lamps, four pairs of pants, and three wool sweaters. His effort was but a finger in the dike however, the fiscal demands of operating a free clinic ominous and unrelenting, and strapped for cash, he stayed up late, night after night, wondering, "What to do?"

At last, fate intervened. (If necessity is the mother of invention, desperation remains her bastard child.) In the course of an otherwise slightly drunk meditation, exhausted and fearful and with no other immediate way to keep his clinic open, Janus suffered an act of providential good fortune, resulting in his right foot being crushed beneath the weight of a 300-pound metal chest. ("How could such a thing have happened?" sympathetic neighbors were curious to know.) Rendered permanently disabled, Janus collected $40,000 from the Great Mercantile Insurance Company, which he coolly sank at once into the coffers of his clinic.

CHAPTER 14

The afternoon of my release from Renton General, some fifteen pounds lighter and with the emaciated look of a shipwreck survivor, I took a cab across town to my new apartment. The solitude of my liberation provided another cruel dose of reality as I bore the process of reentering the land of the living with just my cab driver as guide. A dark-skinned Malaysian man with a large purple birthmark on the left side of his neck and a wiry crop of hair, he cursed in his native tongue when I gave him the address of my new flat. "What you want to go there for? You pay me first if that's where you want to go."

I sat with my forehead resting against the side window as the car moved along, pale inside my old winter coat—sent over by Gee at the request of one of my nurses—a white shirt and thin pair of pants that hung on my hips with the constant threat of slipping lower. Earlier that morning, I entrusted one of my orderlies to cash a thousand-dollar check for me and I paid the cabby for his troubles. Despite my dismissal from Porter and Evans, money was not an immediate problem. I arranged through my attorney to put nearly all of my holdings in Gee's name—she made no such demands though I was eager to do so—and also deposited cash and stocks in a special account to pay off Tod's debt. I received a fair—if not generous—severance package from P and E, and of the assets I held onto—a few securities, one cash account, and interest in three minor businesses—my liquidity was sufficient to support me for the immediate future.

The streets along the east side were filled with tumbledown buildings and cheap motels, newspapers and the plastic lids to Styrofoam cups blowing in the breeze as if part of some tremendous shaking. I arrived at my new lodgings at a quarter to one and went inside to find the building manager. (Alphonzo Pearl was an old man in brown baggy pants, a frayed yellow shirt, and weathered black Eagle shoes, grizzled and dignified in speech and manner.) "I've been the super here going on twenty-nine years," he announced proudly, and set the pages of the lease out in triplicate atop his stained linoleum breakfast table. My apartment was on the third floor, the building five stories in total, fifty-two units in all, responsible management having kept the property in good repair. The lobby was freshly mopped and smelled of ammonia and pine, the tiles inexpensive sheets of a beige and blue mosaic cut into the corners and around the radiator, the red carpeting on the stairs worn flat in the center, transformed over the years into a shade of light clay. I pulled off my jacket and rolled back my sleeves, the muscles in my legs weak; when I walked there was a weariness in my stride that let me get only as far as the first floor landing—there was no elevator—before the exertion proved too much and I had to stop and rest.

When I at last opened the door to my new apartment, I was greeted by a musty smell. The walls were a pale yellow-white, cracked and replastered and cracked again. A small kitchen was set to the right, the bedroom and toilet a few paces back, the distance from the hall to the rear window less than fifteen feet. I went to the window and opened it, then stared down at the alley below. The knots in my legs made it hard to stand for long and I soon drifted back and collapsed on the couch. My furniture—two chairs, a brown sofa, a bed, and desk—were each delivered along with three suitcases of clothes, a few assorted pots and plates, and four crates of books, shortly before I left the hospital; the entire enterprise entrusted to Alphonzo Pearl's supervision as Gee refused to help. (I phoned to ask, hoping my decision to move downtown would alarm her and that she'd realize how far I was willing to go to make amends, but she said only, "Whatever you want packed, you contact the movers and they can call me for a convenient time to come by," and once more hung up the phone.) I sighed deeply and sank further into the couch, the chill from outside reaching me, and after a period of some delay I managed to get up and close the window tight.

Now what? I gazed at the far wall and the few boxes containing my collective possessions, my sense of isolation and exile heightened by the sight of these items so far removed from where they belonged. Slowly, I approached the first box filled with books and undoing the tape picked out *Doctor Faustus* and found underlined inside: "Adrian had not asked for a physician, because he wanted to interpret his sufferings as familiar and hereditary, as merely an acute intensification of his father's migraine," and then, in a paperback copy of *God Bless You, Mr. Rosewater*: "Eliot took a drink of Southern Comfort, was uncomforted. He coughed, and his father coughed, too. This coincidence, where father and son matched each other unknowingly, inconsolable hack for hack, was..." What, I wondered? I didn't remember underlining these passages, and thinking of my father then, miles away in his own single flat, I pushed the box of books back and shifted my position against the wall.

I closed my eyes and thought of Gee, who appeared at once, lovely as always, her green eyes large and bright, her red lips full, her nose thin and angled out between high, round cheeks. Her figure was fine, not overly curved yet sensually set as if drawn by a confident hand. I let my imagination wander up and down the length of her and bastard that I am, unable to resist, I slipped off her clothes, desperate to enjoy having her with me once more. No sooner did I do so however, then I realized the mistake I made, how receiving her image in the form of a ghost only drew attention to her absence, and the moment I opened my eyes she was gone.

Alone, I told myself not to panic—"Settle down, Walter. Settle down."—and gripping the side of my legs, repeated, "Here is where you are. Here is where you've come and here is where you need to be." Eager then to demonstrate my resolve, I leaped to my feet with the intention of unpacking my books and clothes, only my light-headedness got the best of me and I wound up dropping to my knees, the abrupt fall jarring loose the last of my resistance, and before I realized what was happening, I began to weep. ("What's this?" my mind was slow to catch up.) The sound I emitted was loud and gasping, not cathartic but bleak, confused and dire, and hunched over, I rubbed at my eyes with the heel of my hands, the warm tears rolling down as I cried out, each wail torn between my teeth.

I held my breath in order to swallow back my sobs, but the result was an even more pathetic whimper, and as I tried to stand I stumbled and fell toward the door. The desire to leave—on hands and knees if need be!—struck me worse than ever, but I was much too weak, and howling then, helpless and writhing, I lifted my head as best I could and stared across the room at the shape of something moving. Baffled, I squinted through my tears, blinking hard several times in an effort to be sure, and called out tentatively, then delirious, "Gee? Gee!" The very sound of her name lifted my spirits (Rejoice! For she is here!) and scrambling to my feet, I wiped my face, staggering forward until I could see clearly enough, devastated and giving way again, falling burdened and grievous back to the floor.

Myrian worked the lunch hour at the Appetency Café and had added extra shifts to her schedule in order to purchase supplies for her new canvas, but the crowd that afternoon was less than average—a handful of regulars and a few other people straggling in off the street—and the minor amount she made in tips was disappointing. Walking home, she ignored the chill and occupied herself with thoughts of her newest painting. She had in mind a woman set opposite a man, the female form a more outwardly physical force, while the male figure possessed the same dashed and damaged beauty as Janus. She wanted to convey somehow a sense of harm and strength, of injury and endurance, yet none of her sketches came close to achieving her vision.

She climbed the stairs to her apartment, still lost in thought, and only as she reached the third floor landing was she alerted to the sounds coming from the flat next door. She stopped and assessed the wails, unsure what to do, and finding the door ajar, called out, "Hello?" and took two tentative steps inside. "You there. Are you all right?" She walked around the boxes, coming within a few feet of the man who suddenly jumped up, sobbing and calling out what sounded like a woman's name—Jean or Jane—before collapsing a second time, dropping to his knees and groaning in great gusts of torment and surrender.

Myrian got him to the couch where she checked his forehead and found him hot with fever. As a means of testing his coherence, she questioned him further, asking, "Are you the man who's moving in? Who exactly are you? What's wrong? Are you sick? Do you need a doctor?" She decided to call Janus, and with the phone in the man's apartment not yet turned on, transported him next door. Walter felt himself being lifted, guided into the hall, and settled once again into a chair before Myrian disappeared into the kitchen and phoned the clinic. She returned a minute later with a dishtowel soaked in warm water. "For your face," she said. Walter took the cloth. "Thank you," his voice was tremulous, low and weak.

Myrian removed her jacket, kicked her wet shoes across the room, and sat on the couch as Walter sank further down inside the chair. He was dizzy, and looking about the apartment with its painted walls covered in so many colors and shapes and arresting configurations, his head continued to whirl and he felt for a moment as if he was inside the body of an enormous canvas. He thought once more of Gee and the art she admired, of Miró and "The Beautiful Bird Revealing the Unknown to a Couple in Love," and before he could catch himself and keep from dissolving again in front of his new neighbor, his lower lip began to tremble, his eyes filling with tears, his hands shaking as he hurried to bring the wet cloth over his face.

Janus entered the apartment to the same sobs Myrian first heard a half hour before. He stood for a moment, then approached the chair, studying the man quivering in expensive shoes and slacks, with hair once nicely cut now grown out, his face hidden, though even before he lowered the cloth and stared up, Janus somehow recognized him and mouthed the words to Myrian, "How in the world did he get here?"

CHAPTER 15

I've been in my apartment a week now and mark my time by the familiarity of sounds: the footsteps of the fat man overhead as he shuffles across his floor; water running through the pipes whenever a toilet's flushed; the comings and goings of other tenants; my radiator in a full convulsive hiss; the creaks and clangs and mélange of voices through the walls. Even the silence in between is recognizable, and when I wake now in the night— lonely and thinking of Gee—I no longer fumble about and wonder where I am, but sense instantly my emplacement.

Myrian comes each morning and evening to check on me. I appreciate her kindness and how generous she is even after Janus informed her of who I am. She brings me groceries, fruits and chips, assorted juice and soft drinks, lunch meats in white butcher shop paper, whiskey and ketchup, mayonnaise and fresh wheat bread for which I pay her, and insist, "Please, take some for yourself." Already she's helped unpack my books, my clothes and dishes, and arranged for a friend to sell me a second table on which I now have my phone, my notes, and pens. Despite her friendship with Tod, she remains sensitive to my needs, knows that I'm helpless and requiring of her care. (That I set aside money to pay off Tod's debt makes her clemency easier, I'm sure, though I wasn't the one to inform her of my gesture and we've yet to talk of it in detail.) In our conversations, Myrian is patient while I try to explain what brought me here. My account proves a poor narrative however, with no smooth transition from middle to end, and often I do nothing but show her the snapshot in my wallet of Gee and Rea. She stands beside me then for as long as I require, until I sigh and put the picture back.

Janus's friendship with Tod complicates our involvement a bit more, though he, too, is generous by nature and makes every effort to be kind. That first afternoon as I broke down and was rescued by Myrian, Janus checked my heart, my eyes, and throat and pulse. He asked questions about my history, inquired as to the drugs I was given and continued to take, discussed my current discomforts and the symptoms of my attack, and after arranging to have my records forwarded to his clinic, retrieved a B12 supplement from his bag and gave me a shot. He then grabbed my coat, and pulling Myrian's red knit cap down over my head, dragged me out into the street where he paced me twice around the block, his own fractured shuffle countered by my weight against his hip.

I find myself quieted in his presence, and appreciate how he continues to monitor my condition though he otherwise keeps a cordial distance. I wish we might sit and talk of something other than my health and while I don't force this on him, I remain hopeful. There's something in his stoic poise which intrigues me, the way his injured body seems to add rather than diminish from his grace and strength, how his eyes are set deep and dark like warm stones cast into a gentle pool. One morning, I asked Myrian about the accident that caused the damage to Janus's leg, eye, and hand, and rather than answer, she replied, "That was before we met," and said nothing else.

Yesterday, as Myrian worked the evening shift at the Appetency Café, Janus knocked on my door just after nine p.m. and inquired how I was getting on. I invited him in, offered him some tea, and assuming he'd come straight from the clinic, a sandwich with the meats and bread Myrian brought. "I want to thank you for checking in on me this way," I said.

"You've only been out of the hospital a short while."

"Still, my own doctors aren't as conscientious. They haven't once called. Plus, I know your friendship with Tod makes this awkward."

"My relationship with Tod has nothing to do with whether or not I look in on you."

"All the same."

"If you're doing all right then," he stood a few feet inside the door, watching me in the kitchen. "No dizzy spells? No odd pains?"

"None at all."

"And you're getting outside?"

"I go for short walks."

"Good. If there's nothing else you need then."

"What about your sandwich?" I held the plate in Janus's direction, and after a moment he accepted. We went into the front room where he sat in the near chair, his head turning slowly as he surveyed the scene in front of him as if my presence remained a riddle. Seeing him this way, I decided to confess my own confusion, and said, "To tell the truth, I'm not quite sure what I'm doing here either."

Janus stopped eating and glanced at me. "Aren't you?"

"Well, yes, of course," I cleared my throat, went back to the kitchen where I added a splash of whiskey to my tea. Janus eyed me from his chair and, holding out his cup, requested a bit of the same. I returned and sat on the couch where I asked about Tod and whatever he might have said about the situation. "I'm afraid we spoke in confidence," Janus answered.

"Sure. I understand. I realize you're friends. But Gee," I said. "Did he say anything about my wife?"

Janus drank from his cup, his left hand with smashed fingers bent inward balancing his drink in the permanent curl of his fore-finger and thumb. His reluctance to answer was frustrating and yet his air remained charitable, his eyes—as always—carried a note of sympathy. I stared at the floor, then up again, and with a further note of confession, said, "The thing of it is, I never expected any of this. And I sure as hell don't know what to do now."

Janus set his tea and whiskey down and for the first time I could remember asked me a question that did not concern my health. "What do you want to happen?"

I slid forward on the cushions of the couch, my shoulders curved and the arch of my back bowed, and answered in terms of recovery—both physical and otherwise; about perspective, yes; and the possibility of redemption, why not?—until all my words ran together and I tossed up my hands and admitted, "I don't know. It's one big blur. I thought I'd have it figured out by now, but I've been here a week and barely left my room and look at me. My first day and I collapsed and what does that tell you? Look how I rushed down here, all spastic and stumbling. Look how unfit and pathetic I showed up."

Janus smiled and leaning toward me, close enough that I could see the measure of consolation in his eyes, said, "How one arrives is never so important." The largess of his statement wasn't lost on me, the kindness and willingness to encourage me greatly appreciated, and comforted, I nodded and answered then, "Yes, of course."

Myrian sits on the couch inside Janus's apartment, fresh from her shift at the Appetency Café and with Janus beside her, the book he's reading, *The Deltoid Pumpkin Seed* by John McPhee, now closed. His apartment is smaller, a studio with only two rooms plus the bath. The main room is arranged neatly with newspapers stacked in wooden crates to the left of the door, books and journals, articles clipped or copied from select publications placed inside three separate sets of shelves. "A Painting of Pears"—in homage to Josef Albers—by Myrian Cale, hangs on the front wall. The couch is an ancient piece of furniture purchased thirdhand years ago—flat brown cushions, tortoise-shell tacks, and thick wooden legs—with a metal standing lamp and dark steamer trunk stationed nearby. "So? Myrian asks. "He seems OK?"

"He's fine."

"I'm glad you kept him company."

"I stuck my head in, he made me a sandwich."

"I think it's sweet," she leans against his shoulder, touches the curl of hair dangling behind his ear. "I wouldn't have expected, but I like him."

"He's likeable enough in his neutered state."

"Janus," she slaps at the side of his head. "He's been in the hospital, not to the vet's."

"Renton General," he winks, and barks, "Aarf, aarf, aarf!"

"You're incorrigible," she slides away, laughs, and adds, "I think he's truly sorry about what happened."

"Perhaps."

"Everyone makes mistakes. Not everyone's remorseful."

Janus sets his book down on the floor, brings his bad leg up onto the couch, and massages the ache in his calf. He considers Myrian's comment, wonders if it's worth remarking further, then says, "He wants his wife back. This is what feeds his contrition."

"That's alright. At least he's not defending what he did."

"It's true."

"And don't you think his being here proves something?"

Again, "Perhaps."

Myrian frowns. "You'd be more sympathetic if Tod wasn't involved."

"My sympathy isn't the point."

"I think he regrets more than losing his wife."

"I do, too."

"Then why are you being so hard on him?"

"I'm not," Janus rubs further down his leg, toward his ankle and foot. The light from the lamp falls over his right shoulder, finds its way to Myrian who sits with her hands in her lap. Janus studies her profile, speaks softly while explaining his opinion of Walter. "He's obviously come here looking for a way to unburden himself. That's fine. I don't see anything wrong with it, but when he starts asking questions."

"You don't think he has a right to ask?"

"Sure I do. That doesn't mean it's my place to answer."

"But don't you think it makes a difference whether or not they're sleeping together?"

"In terms of what Walter did? As for what's justified and what isn't? I don't know. I can't answer that."

"Oh really?" Myrian reaches for Janus's bent hand, kisses the crushed knuckles while staring over the top, and says, "Since when?"

CHAPTER 16

Next door to Myrian's apartment, Martin Kulpepper stands with his ear pressed and head turned like a dog to a whistle, listening as best he can. In the early evening, in the morning, and again late at night, he hopes to catch her laughing—how he loves the sound!—and otherwise settles for the sweet inflection of her voice as it echoes nearby. His devotion to the auditory tapestry, the notes and chords that compose her sonance, her phone calls and visits from friends, how she sings to the radio, and speaks with old Janus Kelly is constant and Martin never tires of listening to Myrian's voice transmitted through the wall.

Several crates of photographs and a sampling of glossy picture magazines are placed about the room. At twenty-seven, Martin is a thin vole-like creature with a long nose, dark grey eyes, small pointed ears, and a patchy moustache. (Last year, before moving into Myrian's building, he rented a room at the Red Sky Motel where the sounds through the walls were more feral and kept him up late at night.) He came from Boston to take a new position as a claims adjuster at Great Mercantile Insurance, certain untoward events leading him to Renton, where he looked forward to getting a fresh start. Working the files for GMI paid the bills, but Martin's real ambition was photography and he spent all his free time trolling the streets with his old Mamiya, snapping pictures and sending his best shots to newspapers and magazines, which rejected his efforts as a matter of course.

While still living in Boston, on his way to work each morning, Martin ate breakfast at Abelman's Diner where Donna Neilbrite waited tables on the early shift. A pretty girl, slightly shy with narrow shoulders and smooth, pale arms so thin they seemed without bones, Martin was amazed by Donna's ability to manage the heavy trays; her movements more natural somehow when set beneath the weight, for she looked otherwise confused—like a quill tossed about in a high wind—when nothing of substance was there to hold her down. Martin hesitated several weeks, then finally invited her to dinner. They began dating and he took her with him as he shot photographs of the city at night. He brought her to his apartment where she looked through his pictures and listened to him talk about such things as color fidelity, ISO ratings, focal lengths, apertures and shutter speeds, exposure and parallax compensating projected framelines. They made love with the lights on; Martin said he liked to look at her, to keep her there in front of his eyes like a photograph by Kith Tsang. Eager to please, attracted to the sweet insistence of his passion, Donna was comforted by his attentiveness, secure within his single-mindedness—for she believed serious men were less inclined to deviate in their commitment than those otherwise undevoted boys—which in turn inspired her sense of trust.

When he asked her to pose for him then, she agreed. He shot her first while she worked at the diner, and later in more intimate detail; partial and complete nudes as Martin was eager to try. That fall, he approached her with the suggestion that she assist him in taking his vision to a higher plane, and pose for him alongside two male graduate students who'd already agreed to the shoot. Donna hesitated, until the weight of Martin's persuasion settled over her and she felt safe again in his assurance that, "There's nothing wrong, really. It's all for art."

That night, the apartment was lit by lamps stocked with bright white bulbs. A blanket was laid out in the center of the floor, the old beige couch pushed to the side. Martin posed his models in studied frames, managed and monitored shadow and light, and only as the first roll of film was shot did he loosen the reins. Stationed behind his camera, eager to observe where things went on their own, he no longer orchestrated the scene, and setting the shudder speed accordingly, encouraged Donna to "Go with it," while pouring whiskey for her and the boys who exposed and opened and guided her down.

Afterward, with the two students gone and Martin disappearing into his darkroom—a closet with one narrow table, two pans of chemicals and water, a clothesline and clips—Donna sat in the front room, still slightly drunk and wearing Martin's brown terry-cloth robe. She finished her cigarette, then went off to shower, rubbing her body where the boys' hands had been, rinsing her mouth, and cleaning herself between her legs. Warm water disappeared down the drain. She shut off the shower, and wrapped once more inside the brown robe, returned to the front room. The light from beneath the door of Martin's closet let her know he'd finished developing what shots he wished to review that night, and refolding the blanket while pulling the furniture back around, she felt desperately in need of reassurance. She was not so naive as to think life was ever simple enough to be explained one way and not another, and still she hoped—just this once—what happened would remain consistent with her faith.

Anxious then, her arms threatening to float up above her head if she didn't find something else to weigh them down, she reached for the handle on Martin's darkroom door. Involved as he was however, still standing before the pictures he'd developed, his right hand gliding while his eyes devoured the images of the three bodies entangled, he didn't hear her and only as Donna called out, the fragile wires holding her together becoming dissevered as she stumbled back into the hall, did Martin spin around in full exposure to the glory of his art.

A whiskey glass broke on the hardwood as Donna rushed through the front room, sharp slivers slicing her bare feet as Martin bent quickly to pull up his jeans and run after her. He caught hold of her sleeve, but the robe parted easily and she slid free, naked again and gliding on an invisible tide toward the window. Untethered, stumbling still as her hands came up and appeared for all the world to be preparing her for flight, she crashed against the pane of glass, shattering it as the shards cut deep into her flesh, her wrists and belly stained at once with a mix of tissue and a dark outpouring of blood.

Angry, Martin wrapped Donna's arms tight in towels, then called for an ambulance which came ten minutes later; her coloring so pale by then she looked for all the world like a porcelain doll. How they managed to save her, to sew her veins and fill her once again with blood, then dope her so she couldn't decide their effort was futile and slip away for good, was a sign—Martin believed—of better things to come. He hid the photographs before the ambulance arrived, and to those who required an explanation, said that Donna tripped on her way from bed to retrieve a drink in the kitchen. Her nakedness resolved, he repeated for everyone who chose to listen, "It was an accident, that's all."

Donna left town and went to stay in Scarsdale with her mother. Restless, convinced the photographs were his finest work yet and determined to place them with a gallery outside the city, Martin blamed Donna for retarding his career and being a much too sensitive and narrow-minded girl. The bloodstain on the floor of his apartment made him uncomfortable nonetheless, and thinking perhaps it might be time for a change of scene, he made a number of calls. When an opening in Adjustment and Fraud at GMI came up and his supervisor at Boston Peneltone Insurance provided a strong recommendation, he eagerly drove the 400 miles to Renton, where he arrived on a crisp winter day.

His room at the Red Sky Motel was small and poorly insulated and he planned to hunt for a cheap apartment as soon as he had enough cash. He did not think of Donna much anymore, did not call or write, and felt it best to leave the past dead. The couple next door were a loud and libidinous pair, full of pranks and uproar, and intrigued by the short, murine-faced man with the fancy old camera, they invited him in for a drink and to regale them with his art.

Two days after my conversation with Janus, Myrian invited me to keep her company as she painted the front wall at Peterson's Pancake House. I was feeling slightly better, my fever more sporadic and my aches less severe, though I was still weak and times I thought of Gee and Rea brought me as close as ever to despair.

We left early in the morning, all of Myrian's supplies—her paints and pastels and dozens of old brushes, the drop cloth and tin of turpentine, sketch pad, charcoal, and several buckets and pans—already stowed away in Janus's old car. I dressed in warm slacks, a flannel shirt and sweater, a blue down jacket, brown gloves, and black buckle boots that Janus loaned me. Myrian monitored my exertion as we arrived at Peterson's and began to unpack. I was given the empty buckets and brushes to carry first, and once the drop cloth, awkward and surprisingly heavy, and the remaining paints and pans were unloaded, I rested from my effort in one of the wooden chairs.

Myrian arranged her brushes, unrolled the cloth, and laid out her flat silver pans. She walked up and down the length of the wall measuring the space, and after this retrieved a large white pad and sat next to me. I watched the motion of her hand as she began sketching the figures she envisioned on the wall. The ease and innocence of her creation appeared as if by magic, reminding me of pictures drawn by Rea. I missed my daughter terribly—the psychological evaluations I was ordered to take before being granted a visit were scheduled for next week—and imagined her then on the kitchen floor, drawing with crayons and markers, producing her own series of works: trees and flowers, people with enormous smiling heads, circles and squares shaded with every available color. Myrian looked my way, and seeing that I was lost in thought, asked if I was all right.

"I'm fine."

"You're sure?"

"Yes."

She finished her sketch and returned to the wall, prepping the surface before stirring azure blue paint inside a clean silver pan, then mounting her step stool with broad brush raised, she applied the first coat of sky above the space where the dinosaurs would eventually appear. I was no longer used to rising early, my habit since moving downtown to stay up late, afraid to cede the day and crawl off to bed where Gee's absence was even more acute, and in my effort to shake off the last vestiges of fatigue, I focused on Myrian and the wobble in her stool as she moved back and forth. "Be careful," I couldn't help but warn, however adept she seemed while scooting about.

"Careful who?" she mocked me with a quick little two-step.

"Who's going to catch you if you fall?" I also tried to sound in good humor, though my voice lacked energy and trailed off.

By morning's end, Myrian had finished a portion of the sky— the first coat without clouds—and moving to the left side of the wall, she dipped a fresh brush into a newly stirred pan of brown paint and began outlining a large brontosaurus. We ate a lunch of pancakes and eggs and then Myrian returned to work as I settled back in my chair where I continued watching her. She chatted easily with me, impervious to disruption, never once losing focus on her painting as we conversed about some of the other tenants in the building, the predicted snow for this evening, and bits and pieces from our personal histories we were inclined then to share. (Myrian, I learned, was born in New Baltimore, her mother a bookkeeper for a small chain of grocery stores, her father—"a professional shit"—gone before she turned six.) I moved my chair from the flow of traffic, sat just beside the coatrack while Myrian worked left to right, the crease in her canvas tennis shoes bending straight across the top of her feet as she stood high up on her toes and reached for an upper section of sky.

Toward mid-afternoon, the image of a tyrannosaurus and a velociraptor appeared. (Later in the week would come a stegosaurus, a diplodocus, and a triceratops, three cavemen with stone-age spears, two pterodactyls, and a wooly mammoth.) People walking by the front window stopped to take a peek, while customers seated at tables stared over their sausages and steaks and flapjacks, entertained by Myrian's work. One woman passing outside caught my eye, her red hair and long legs looking very much like Gee. I rose part way out of my chair and stared after her, only to realize my mistake. Myrian turned and noticed my change of expression, the way I gaped then pouted and audibly sighed. She stopped painting and set her feet flat on the stool, once again asking, "Are you all right?"

I wanted to let go altogether then and talk to her of love, to ramble on about Gee and Rea—as I so often did—but Myrian kept me from trouble once more, and coming from the wall she approached my chair, her face filled with pathos and eager to soothe me, she gently rubbed the side of my cheek with her warm hand, and whispered, "It really is a sorry bit of nonsense."

Around four o'clock, she went to the bathroom to rinse her brushes. I helped seal the cans of paint and placed them beneath the drop cloth that, along with the other supplies, was stored against the wall. Myrian laid her brushes out on a soft orange cloth. "How are you holding up?" she asked.

"Well," I replied, though I was, in fact, quite tired. "We should stop at the market. You'll eat dinner with us, alright?"

"Thank you, but I need to lie down first."

"Sure," she agreed. "I'll take you home."

"Home?" (Yes!) I thought again of Gee and slumped back in my chair, sinking through my shoulders and hips, my legs dangling in front of me as Janus's black rubber boots shifted unbuckled and loose at the end of my feet. The collar of my coat was disheveled and I tipped far to the left, barely braced against the fall as I continued to think of my wife. (For some reason, I conjured the image of her ankle and how she read at night in bed with her leg bent out from beneath the sheet, the light and shadow falling across her foot so that the curve in the space behind her bone and the smoothness of her skin in the shaded dent seemed uniquely sensual and warranted my slipping down and kissing her flesh.) In the process of picturing her this way, I froze and emitted a bleak, disconsolate groan.

Myrian stared back at me, then suddenly she was tossing off her coat and retrieving her sketch pad and stick of charcoal.

"Don't move," she said. "Can you hold it?" her request needless for I could not have stirred even if I tried. Half tumbled, the twist of my shoulders and tilt of my head, my arms tipped over and hanging in midair—reaching and rejecting—my booted feet like large black weights anchoring my narrow legs, I remained immobile while Myrian sketched my pining form. Unlike with the dinosaurs, these drawings demanded her full attention, and she worked in silence, explaining only as she finished about the canvas she hoped to paint and how her earlier attempts to conceptualize her ideas had failed. "I almost have the woman, but the man keeps giving me fits. I tried to use Janus as a model, but he never looks vulnerable enough to me. I see him in a certain way and wind up leaving out the cracks and dings. But you, Walter," she reached over and squeezed my arm. "With you, everything's right there," she smiled as if offering me a compliment, then stared back down at her work.

I lifted myself at last and rubbed the ache and numbness out of my arms, my neck, and thighs. The series of sketches Myrian drew embarrassed me—there I was, all contorted in my weakness and confusion—and yet I also noticed a hint of perseverance in my eyes, in the curl of my hand and the way my arm was bent in an effort to hold on. (I was pleased Myrian had what she wanted and said as much later.) The afternoon had a strange vermeil cast to the sky which I observed as we drove off, and soon I was standing in the dwindling light outside my apartment building, watching Myrian head toward the market as the first traces of snow began to fall. I waved, and bracing myself against the chill, turned and walked upstairs.

Coming inside, the jangle of Janus's black boots marked my steps as I reached the third floor landing and fished out my keys. I was tired and thinking still about Myrian's sketches, about Gee and Rea and all the rest, I was about to open my door when Martin Kulpepper appeared from inside his own apartment, shot a quick look toward the stairs, then called, "Hey, Walt," and quickly toward me. We'd spoken only once, a brief introduction in the lobby a few days ago, though occasionally in the morning and sometimes late at night I heard Martin in the hall as he surprised Myrian with conversation. Now here he was, using the same unctuous tone, for what reason I wasn't sure. "Damn cold day, isn't it, Walt? Why don't you come by my place? I'll get us a drink to warm us up."

"No, thank you. I'm going in to rest."

"Come on. There's something I want to show you," he slapped at my arm, stood waiting until I gave in, relocked my door, and followed him across the hall. "So how are you feeling, Walt?"

"I'm fine, thank you."

"That's good," he disappeared into the kitchen, returning with two beers. "I understand you've just come from the hospital."

"I'm sorry, but how do you know this?"

"Alphonzo Pearl."

"I see."

"Nothing serious I hope?"

"No."

"You look all right. What was it? I hear you had some kind of breakdown?"

"It wasn't, really."

"No? And your being here now is what?"

"A period of convalescence."

"Ahh."

I twisted the top off my beer while Martin sat in the opposite chair, his legs crossed, his black hair cut to fall just above his eyes, the gaps in his thin moustache further aggravating the runty features of his face. He pointed a hand in my direction, and said, "I heard about you at work. I'm in A and F at Great Mercantile. That's Adjustment and Fraud."

"I understand. But I don't have an account with Great Mercantile. Why should they have an interest in me?"

"Tod Marcum," he grinned and drank his beer. "Your friend has a policy with us, covering his home and business, and GMI's

legal department was looking into the effect of your fraud on in-
demnification," Martin clicked the heels of his shoes together.
"Legal wanted to see what civil actions were available in GMI's
role to protect Marcum against foreclosure. Lucky for you
Marcum doesn't plan to sue you, though I can't say why. Seems
his debt got covered, but GMI would have come after you for sure
if they had to pay anything out," he took another sip of beer.
"So," he raised an eyebrow, "why'd you do it?"

"Excuse me?"

"Marcum. Why'd you screw him?"

"I should be going," I got up from my chair and made my way
back across the room, with Martin following after me. "Wait,
Walt. Alright, we'll talk about something else," he caught hold of
my elbow. "Finish your beer. I still want to show you something.
Do you like art? I'm a photographer. I'm sure Myrian told you.
We're good friends, you know."

"I didn't realize."

"Oh, yeah. If it wasn't for old Doc Kelly. What do you make
of that anyway? My take is there's nothing really going on there.
The guy's a mess, all ancient and beat up. I give it another month
at most."

"I have to go," I repeated.

"The two of them together defies nature, don't you think?"

"Myrian and Janus are good people. They're happy together."

"I don't see it."

"Nevertheless," I reached for the doorknob.

"Alright, wait. Come on, I want to show you something," he
guided me back around to the far wall where he pointed to a
picture of Myrian in the moonlight. The photograph was encased
in a silver frame covered with a clear sheet of glass, the sky and
space around Myrian a velvet black, the trees and buildings
nearby faint in shadow just after dusk. She was walking with a
long scarf, white with flecks of sapphire, wrapped around her
neck, a grey coat with deep side pockets into which her hands
were sunk, and her shoulders slightly arched as if shielding herself from the wind. (Although I refused to say as much, the shot

was actually quite good.) The power of the camera's lens brought Myrian's face in close, revealing her lost in thought, her path lit by the moon, a single white ray falling over her. "What are you doing with this?" I asked, vexed by the image of Martin standing at his window spying down on the street below. "Does Myrian know?"

"Of course, of course," Martin waved me off. "Now look," he took the picture from the wall and handed it to me. "What do you see?"

"I see a woman at peace," I answered, and determined to dispute Martin's claim of Myrian only biding her time with Janus, went on to describe how tranquil she looked, how serene in her stroll. "I see how content she is. I see a woman unperturbed and completely at ease. She's happy."

"Of course," Martin took the picture and placed it back on the wall. For a moment I thought he was about to stroke Myrian's face with the side of his hand, but he stopped short of this, and without turning around said, "She's by herself, you see, without the good doctor weighing her down, with the moon I hung watching over her. She feels a change in the air and this appeals to her. She knows I'm watching her. She can sense me there. Hell, Walt, what else does she need?"

CHAPTER 17

Jack Gorne bought a bottle of Dewar's and left the west side of Renton shortly after five o'clock. The snow outside was heavy with larger flakes mixing together, producing a white counterpane against the dusk. At a stoplight on McLarren and First, at a crossroad near Holiday Market and the Warwick Congregational Church, a much smaller car than Jack's black Lexus lost traction and skidded into his bumper. The slight tap was insignificant, and still Jack sat through the green light, forcing the driver of the other car to come out into the cold and approach his window. "Did you dent me?" he asked.

"Sorry," she answered.

"Fuck that. Is there a dent?"

Myrian went back to look, and as she did, Jack accelerated through the intersection, sending up a spray of snow and ice in his wake.

Inside my apartment, I kicked off Janus's boots and hung my coat on the hook behind the door. I stood exhausted, the measure of silence sweeping over me in stark contrast to the rattle and buzz which had otherwise occupied much of my day. My mouth was dry, my head and limbs weighted as if with sand, and just as I settled down to rest after my outing with Myrian and encounter

160

with Martin, I was disturbed by a sudden knock at the door. The pounding was fisted, as if by someone trying to startle me or in a hurry to get inside. I called from the couch, "Who is it?" then got up and undid the lock.

Jack came in, pulled off his gloves, and unbuttoned his coat. "So this is where you've been hiding out. Jesus, Brimm. Your world and welcome to it, eh?"

I reclosed the door as Jack handed me two small bags. We hadn't spoken since before my collapse, though unlike other friends, colleagues, and clients and peers who found my circum-stance indecorous and avoided me with grave intent, Jack said, "I've been looking all over for you. I was out of town for awhile and phoned you a few weeks ago from L.A. to talk up a deal and that was the first I heard of what happened. By the time I got someone to tell me you were in the hospital they'd released you. I actually had to hire a man to track you down. Your wife wouldn't tell me a thing," Jack smiled. "I heard about Marcum. Goddamn, Brimm. Goddamn!"

Jack pointed to one of the bags he'd given me. "Dewar's," he said. "Let's have a drink. You look like hell," he tossed his coat and gloves on the couch while scrutinizing the apartment. "What are you doing in this shithole anyway?" he took the Dewar's from me and went into the kitchen where he poured us each a glass. The heat inside my apartment clicked off and the air was chilled. Jack put his glass down on my writing table, and placing a hand atop the radiator, gave a quick yank which produced an immedi-ate rattle and hiss. He turned and sat in the chair across from the couch just as the heavyset man in the apartment upstairs came home and stormed through his flat. "Christ, Brimm, the sky's falling," Jack laughed, and smoothing a crease from his slacks, asked, "So, what's the story? What are you doing here? What's this all about?"

I allowed myself a small sip of whiskey, and cupping the glass in both hands said, "Nothing. I caught a bug. I was laid up for a while and was looking for a quiet place to recover my health."

"Here?"

"It isn't so bad."

"And the wife?"

"Gee's not with me."

"I see that." Ever since our evening together at Talster's, I'd avoided discussing Gee with Jack. Even after Old Soles closed and rumors of Tod's financial reversals began circulating through the city, I said nothing, but there seemed little reason to avoid the subject now. Jack settled his legs out in front of him, and chimed, "I warned you, didn't I? I told you to figure things out first and not fuck around. You should have come to me for help before everything blew up in your face."

"Maybe so."

"Maybe nothing. What you need now is to get back on your feet. Let me get you out of here and put you up some place nice."

"Thanks, but no. I can't just yet."

"What do you mean? What are you waiting for?"

"I'm not sure."

"What do you think's going to happen hanging around here?"

"I told you, I don't know." The wind rattled my window, whistling along the brick. Jack sipped at his drink, slid his chair toward the couch, bent forward, and set his jaw. "Listen, Brimm. Forget whatever it is you think you're doing. What's done is done. You need to regroup."

"That is what I'm doing."

"Like hell. You're hiding out is all. You're punishing yourself for no reason. Give yourself some credit. There was absolutely nothing wrong with your plan."

"What are you talking about?"

"Jesus, you were this close to pulling everything off," he moved his thumb and forefinger a half inch apart. I stared at the distance, and after a brief calculation, said, "I was never as close as you think."

"Sure you were. You had your foot on Marcum's throat. All you had to do was push down."

"I couldn't. You don't understand."

"What don't I?" Jack leaned further forward and slapped at my knee. "Listen, Brimm, you were clever enough to get the ball rolling. You'd be home right now with your sweet wife and daughter if you hadn't crashed and burned."

"I got sick."

"You gave in."

"I made a mistake."

Jack rolled his eyes. "Fuck, Brimm, what mistake? We're talking about real life here, not some fairy-tale landscape. Right and wrong are just words. They're arbitrary abstractions at best. The only legitimate definition for what's fitting is that which gets us what we want."

"I don't believe that."

"Well, maybe you should," he pointed then at the second bag he brought which I'd set on the floor. "Take a look," he said. "A housewarming gift." Inside was a dark grey revolver. "If you're going to live in a sewer, you should at least arm yourself against swine."

I voiced my protest—to no avail—and finally went into my bedroom where I stashed the gun deep in my closet. Back in the front room, I sat again on the couch as Jack picked up where he left off. "If you think your breakdown establishes some sort of moral correctness, Brimm, you're wrong. Your collapse is just an excuse. There's nothing noble about your collapse. The only thing your illness proves is that you got weak and quit. Look where you are now and think how much better off you'd be if you hadn't stopped to question what you were doing."

Music came from Myrian's apartment, an old tune by Jackson Browne. ("The world keeps spinning round and round, into the deluge.") I sipped at my drink. The whiskey warmed me, then passed on and left me chilled. My head ached and my hands in my lap looked suddenly frail. I stared at the ceiling where the sounds from upstairs continued, more rhythmic in their cadence, as if the fat man was dancing. I let my shoulders fall and my head roll to one side as I considered what Jack said, the idea that my collapse amounted to nothing more than a fundamental weak-

ness. ("For Christ's sake, Brimm, what's the point if you can't finish what you start?") The question plagued me. For weeks I had
wondered the same, confused by the inconsistency of my conduct, the speed with which I abandoned my moral compass and
the paradox of orchestrating Tod's ruin only to break down over
the corruption of my deed. What good was there in maintaining
rigid canons if, as Jack said, everything was arbitrary and at the
most critical time morality could be suspended, beaten back by
circumstance, and dislodged with the ease of removing a pebble
from one's shoe?

I put what remained of my whiskey on the floor, suddenly
saddened and tempted to argue, though I said instead, "Yes, I
understand."

"Good. Excellent. Now then, we can get down to business. I
want you to forget about sitting around here crying in your beer
and come work for me."

"What? Jack, thanks, but no. Not now. I can't. I'm not up to
it."

"Sure you are."

"Besides, my license is suspended."

"I'm not looking for a broker. You won't need a license for
what I want you to do."

"I'm sorry."

"Go ahead and name your salary."

"Really, no."

"Brimm."

"I'm sorry."

Jack frowned. "What are you doing?"

"Nothing."

"Exactly."

"You know what I mean."

"No, I don't. Tell me."

"I'm waiting for things to sort themselves out. I'm trying to
decide what I should do next before I leap again."

"You're cowering is all."

"If I am, that's my business."

"But it's my business, too, Brimm. You're fucking with my operations, quitting on me like this. Don't forget, you're my goddamn talisman."

"Maybe in a few weeks," I put him off.

"Suit yourself," Jack reached out and grabbed up his gloves. "I'm late for a date as it is. I'll call you next week and we'll have dinner," he stood and slipped his coat back on. "In the meantime, think about my offer."

I promised I would, said that I appreciated his stopping by, then reclosed the door. The hiss from my radiator had stopped and when I went and tried to adjust the knob as Jack had done, I was greeted by a chilly reception. I stared out the window at the falling snow, and looking then around my flat, wondered if I hadn't made a mistake and whether I shouldn't hurry and call down to Jack and tell him I'd take whatever job he had to offer. ("We need to get you out of here, Brimm!") I went to the wall and listened once more to the music passing from Myrian's apartment; a new song, sweetly concordant, lyrical and harmonic, arranged with piano and guitar. I placed my hand on the surface and immediately felt the vibration enter me, imagining the notes filling my veins, the music's rhythm, all the elements of meter and harmony, euphony, and symphony evolved and flowing in infinite waves, one after the next, enduring despite occasional static, undeterred in its will to carry on.

I remained this way for some time, and afterward washed and dressed and went next door to join Myrian and Janus for dinner.

CHAPTER 18

ひひ

Mid-February. I fill my days sitting about reading or staring into space, occasionally writing in my notebook. I scan the newspapers Myrian brings me, stand at my window and observe the vacant alley below, sometimes drinking though mostly not. (Now and again I find the nerve to phone Gee, though my wife remains chilled and unreceptive, and only as I stop trying to engage her in conversation does she allow me to speak with Rea.) Yesterday, as I did each afternoon in an effort to jump start my rejuvenation, I bundled up in a jacket and cap, gloves, and scarf, and the black rubber boots borrowed from Janus and went for a walk.

My route took me across the Avenues, down Mission Street, past Chick's Bar & Grill, Reed's Market, and Lilli's Wigs and Rugs. After some fifteen minutes, I turned and headed back east where I spotted a car identical to Gee's. The leap of my poor heart—mistaken again—brought me from the curb where I stumbled awkwardly in my haste, twisting my ankle and falling into the road. ("Fuck!") Disappointed, I limped off in the direction of my apartment, and soon found myself in front of Janus's clinic where I stopped and went inside.

The waiting area was crowded, each of the several plastic chairs occupied. There was a hook for coats, a coffeemaker with powdered cream and Styrofoam cups on an old metal table, pamphlets discussing the necessity of infant immunization, the dangers of unprotected sex, HIV, herpes, and gonorrhea, how to guard against hypothermia and influenza, signs of sickle cell and diabetes, tests for breast and testicular cancer all set out on a smaller table near the front window. A severely gaunt young woman who may or may not have been asleep sat in one of the chairs, a large man in dark work boots and stiff blue jeans, his right hand wrapped in gauze and held up straight at the elbow two chairs down, while an older woman in a threadworn dress and brown pants beneath, her knuckles knotted against a grey metal cane, sat across the way. Three other men stood over by the coffee machine, conversing among themselves and trying to keep warm.

I pulled off my scarf and hat and gloves and when one of the chairs became free sat looking about the room. The floor was a faded blue tile, swept clean, the walls a rough white brick with cracks and fissures running from ceiling to floor, the patches of water stains behind the bricks impervious to a fresh coat of paint. Janus was in the examination room directly behind the waiting area. (A storage space for files and supplies was further back at the end of a narrow hall.) A retractable partition separated the two rooms, and opened, I could see Janus dressed in a green flannel shirt and faded jeans tending to the bare foot of a child. Inside his damaged left hand, Janus managed to hold a small light that he shined toward the boy's arch, and speaking soft words of encouragement to mother and child, he removed a large sliver of wood. The procedure lasted no more than a few seconds, though preparation—the swabbing and soaking of the foot—followed by the cleansing and comforting took much longer. I studied the way Janus worked, his manner nurturing and purposeful, soothing and resolute. Despite the fractures in his physical form, he maintained a fluidity of motion, a sense of being and consistency of effort which made the ease of his gestures seem organic.

I slid forward in my chair and watched while Janus helped the boy back through the waiting area, instructing the mother on the need to keep her son's foot clean and to apply the salve morning and night. He didn't seem to notice me at first, and approaching the older woman, bent down to say something close to her ear—his words brought a comforted smile to her face—before leading her into the examination room. At the doorway, and without turning around, he said, "Everything all right, Walter?"

"Yes. I'm fine."

He disappeared into the other room, closing the partition behind him this time. Fifteen minutes later, he returned and walked the older woman to the door. He then helped the frail girl to her feet. Another twenty minutes passed—there was a bit of commotion behind the screen, the girl having come to life, saying, "Shit, doc. Shit! What am I gonna do?" while something metal hit the floor—and following a short silence the two appeared together, Janus holding the girl's arm. He made a phone call and then came over to me. "Angel," he spoke in a soft, almost soporific tone, "this is Walter Brimm. Walter's a neighbor of mine. A cab's coming, Walter. Make sure Angel gets in it. Tell the driver 153 East Ninth and nowhere else. Can you do that?"

I assured him I could, and when Janus reached for his wallet, I said, "Don't worry. I got it."

I sat beside the girl, both of us silent, watching Janus as he tended to the man with the bandaged hand. The partition was opened again and I could see Janus cut away the gauze and expose the wounds to the air; the fingers burned and blistered, covered in a soggy ooze of pus and salve and decomposing skin. Even from a distance, the sight was ghastly and I had to look away while Angel said, "Damn." The cab came and I brought her outside as Janus instructed, pulling my own cap onto her head and wrapping her in my scarf. (The gesture was excessive, I realized, but I enjoyed it nonetheless.) I gave the driver twenty dollars for a six-block fare and told him to make sure Angel got up to her apartment. The idea of taking charge this way appealed to me and I returned inside the clinic with a sense of accomplishment.

Janus finished examining the man's hand, washing and scraping and re-medicating what remained of the outer tissue. I slipped off my coat and was called back into the second room, where I passed behind the partition and was told to "Wash up. Hold this here." One end of the gauze was set against the man's

wrist which I secured as Janus slowly rewrapped the bandage between each finger and around the burns. Up close, the wounds
were nearly overwhelming and emitted an odor of sharp decay. I
tried to control my queasiness by clenching my jaw in a frozen
half smile, and averted my eyes as best I could, but then Janus
wanted me to apply the tape. "Put it here. And here," he said.
The man was powerfully built, with huge shoulders, his round
head shaved and set beneath a black cap, his skin smooth and
brown, his eyes soft and welcoming. "Ugly thing, ain't it?" he re-
acted to my discomfort, and smiled, "Gonna be all right, though.
You just put the tape where the doc tells you and don't worry
about it."

I did as told, and afterward helped the man on with his coat,
zipping his injured hand inside against his chest. The other three
men had abandoned their station by the coffee machine and the
front room was empty. Janus poured himself a cup of coffee and
sat in one of the plastic chairs. The sun passed through the
window and over the tiles. A portable heater—its cables bright
red—did its best to warm the air. "I noticed you're limping,"
Janus said.

"It's nothing," I explained about my stepping oddly from the
curb, and insisted, "It's just sore."

"Better let me have a look."

"No, really," I pulled off my boot, lifted the cuff of my slacks,
and pushed down my sock. "See? Not even swollen."

Janus drank his coffee. To compensate for his bad eye, he
wore a pair of square, brown-framed glasses when examining
patients. The prescription helped ease the extra work of his right
eye, though sitting there with me, he put the glasses in his shirt
pocket and rubbed the back of his left hand across his brow. A car
alarm went off on the street as three boys rocked the hood of a
red Mustang then sprinted away. I put my boot back on, and leaving the buckles undone, said, "If I'm keeping you."

"Not at all. The evening rush will start soon enough. The rest
can wait," he glanced out the window, his fractured hand falling
into his lap, his head turned to me in profile. I waited for him to

look back at me—he seemed briefly lost in thought and I didn't wish to disturb him—and recalling how he appeared earlier as he treated his patients, how tranquil and content he seemed, I finally said, "Myrian tells me you've been here over fifteen years."

"That's right."

"On your own?"

"More or less."

"Fifteen years is a long time."

"I've been lucky."

"I mean that's quite a commitment."

"It's day to day, like anything else."

"You're being modest. It can't be easy."

"I'm a glutton."

"So I hear."

Janus smiled. His receptiveness pleased me—as usual, I felt oddly comforted in his presence—and shifting around in my chair, I asked him in terms of the clinic, "Do you ever have any help?"

"I get nurses to volunteer sometimes, and the occasional medical student."

"I don't see how you manage. It must be overwhelming."

"How are you feeling, Walter?" he changed the subject.

"I'm well enough."

"Sleeping better?"

"Yes. And exercising. My stamina's coming back."

"Good."

I pushed the heater away with my boot and glanced once more about the room. The light in the ceiling consisted of two long florescent bulbs which buzzed and blinked in unpredictable spasms. I felt the throbbing in my ankle but resisted reaching down to rub at the ache, and thinking again of the conversation Janus and I had a week ago when he came by my apartment, I recalled how in the middle of my struggle to explain my circumstance, he refused to indulge me and offered instead a more effective and firm compassion. ("How one arrives, Walter...") The memory still pleased me. (How often in his work at the clinic Janus must deal with frail and fallen men like me who promise to mend their ways if he'd only cure them of their latest affliction; defeated souls who rescind their pledge the moment their strength returns, and how did he maintain his faith through all the endless amount of bullshit and dissention?) I envied what I saw, the calm he created for himself in the eye of the storm, my own queer state so far removed from his world that I couldn't help but blurt out, "How do you keep from going crazy?"

Janus leaned toward me, his gaze fixed and reaching for the side of my chair, he tapped the surface of the plastic twice. "It's only too much if you stop and think about it."

"That's the trick?"

He smiled. "Exactly."

A new patient came into the clinic then, a heavyset man whose breathing was loud and rose out of his chest like puffs of wind pushed up from the hollow of a deep cave. I watched once more through the opened partition as Janus helped the man onto the examining table and listened to his heart and lungs. He initiated a breathing treatment of warmed air mixed with microcrystalline suspensions of albuterol and oleic acid blown through a tube into a plastic mask, and I noticed as before the ease with which Janus worked, the lyric of his movements, the trouble caused by the crushed bones in his left hand and right foot less pronounced, the grace of his motion even more remarkable when juxtaposed to my own fits and seizures these last several months. I stood there for several minutes, then buckled my boots and waved goodbye before the treatment was completed.

During his break for lunch at Great Mercantile Insurance, Martin made a habit of walking about the city with his camera, searching for sights which caught his eye. Today however, possessed of certain information, he decided to alter his routine and drove uptown. Myrian was on her hands and knees in the lower left corner, completing a final spate of grass growing between several large rocks when Martin came into the Pancake House. "Well, well. Small world," he called, and without looking up, Myrian sighed, "Have you been following me again, Martin?"

"Of course not. I was just passing by on my lunch," he walked within two feet of where she was kneeling, and staring at the spot of flesh exposed in the center of her lower back where her T-shirt parted from her pants, he cleared his throat and said, "That's quite a wall. Dinosaurs, is it?"

"Yes, Martin."

"You should have told me you were here. I could have come earlier and photographed you as you work."

"No thanks," she got up and moved to the other end of the wall.

"I could help you put a portfolio together. Or fliers, to attract business."

"Anyone who wants to see my murals can check them out on their own."

"But for convenience," he pressed on. "In case you ever decide to do something outside the city."

"In that case, I'll let you know."

Martin followed her down the wall, his camera already out of its case and held at his side. "Forget the murals then," he studied her bent over once more, imagined the curve of her hips fluted perfectly for the grip of his hands. "You must need shots of your other work. Your canvases and the paintings on the walls of your apartment. You can send the slides to galleries, to see if they want to show your stuff."

"Why would a gallery be interested in the work on my apartment walls?"

"Your other stuff then."

"We've had this conversation."

"I know, but I haven't given up. So?"

"No."

"Alright," he set his camera bag down on the floor. "Forget your paintings. Come pose for me. Let me take a few shots."

"How many times are you going to ask?"

"Until you say yes."

"And what do I always say?"

"Come on. You know you want to. I'll buy you dinner."

"No, Martin."

"Pose for me."

"Not a chance," Myrian stood darkening the tail of a tyrannosaurus, the right side of her face turned in profile as Martin inched closer, his right hand holding his camera out, his finger accidently clicking off a series of shots until Myrian jumped at the sound of the shutter's release, and cursed, "Goddamn you, Martin!" The manager—a middle-aged man in a shiny black bow tie, bright red vest, and thick-framed glasses—came hurrying over to see what was wrong. "No problem here," Martin assured everyone.

"There damn well is a problem!"

"Perhaps if I got you a table, sir, somewhere in the rear," the manager peered uncomfortably at Martin and pointed toward the far side of the restaurant.

"No, no. That's alright. I was just leaving." He regretted his impulse to snap off a shot and almost wished his finger hadn't slipped. He apologized to Myrian, but she had turned away by then and resumed her work. "I'm going," he said, though he took no more than a half step from the wall. "I only stopped by to say hello," he placed his camera in its case, rezipped his blue parka, moved slightly toward the door, then all the way out.

Sad, sad, sad. ("What bullshit!" Martin Kulpepper thought to himself and very nearly howled in disgust.) After a year and still she insisted on playing this game. He drove back to work, and later that night stopped at Edelbee Camera where he purchased a half gallon of ChemSeal, six roles of new film, and a photo sponge. His plan was to unwind a bit, have a drink and something to eat, and then head out toward First Avenue, Mandinger Park, and the Mission to see what sort of mischief there was for him to shoot. (If nothing significant caught his eye, he'd drive back to the Embassy Club and ask if any of the girls wanted to spend an hour posing at the Red Sky Motel.) Coming up the stairs to his apartment, he was still thinking about Myrian, annoyed by her resistance that afternoon, yet convinced from how she acted when he was around—her composure faltering, her eyes darting deliriously back and forth, all her false display of rage a tease— that the idea of being with him excited her a good deal. He took encouragement from this, the promise of her eventually giving in and what would happen then between them, and despite how exhausted he was by the repetition of their little dance, he knew there were still ways to win her over, whether she appreciated his resourcefulness or not.

I slept soundly for the first time in weeks, and following a breakfast of eggs and toast, went back to Janus's clinic where I remained until mid-evening. Dozens of patients arrived, each in their turn clamoring for help: mothers with sick children; boys and men with every sort of serious sore, wounds, and bumps and cuts; bouts of influenza and salmonella; girls complaining of discomfort in their bellies, with rashes and raw aches between their legs; others with varying degrees of injury, illness, and addiction, burns and bruises, dislocations and infections, one broken ankle, and a shattered nose.

By noon the waiting room began to overflow. I found a clipboard in the storage area and recorded names and assigned numbers to people, taking down symptoms and degrees of emergency which I reported back to Janus. I explored the storage area and brought up salves and wraps, medicines and ointments, crutches and splints, and whatever else was requested of me. Such work was arduous and once the last patient was seen, I returned to my apartment exhausted and well spent.

I woke again rested and restored, and after a warm shower and breakfast, went out and bought several of the day's newspapers and magazines that I read—the business sections only— bringing myself up to speed on current deals, facts and figures, and market trends I knew so well before my collapse. I took copious notes, cross-referenced information, and made a list of sources to survey and double check. Late that afternoon, I went back to the clinic, and the following morning I bused across town to the main library where I reviewed the most recent analyses while printing out information from the Internet on three separate corporations.

On my way home I stopped at Circuit World and bought a computer and printer which I paid extra to have delivered and set up the next day. My holdings at the time consisted of $80,000 in cash, a five percent interest in two small software companies, and a three percent share in a fiber-optics firm Jack Gorne took public last year. Although my broker's license was suspended and I was prohibited from handling any client's accounts, I was not barred from trading in the market, and such resources, while a minor percentage of what I once had, afforded me sufficient funds to start rebuilding a financial base. I had the computer set up on my writing table, and for another $100 fee paid a technician to load up my machine, connect me to the Internet, and show me how to open an account with Marketrac as a day trader. By noon, I'd put $10,000 into my Marketrac account and began trading on-line.

In a vacuum then, inside my tiny room, I purchased 300 shares of the textbook publisher Harcourt General, operating on a series of educated hunches strung together from my research. (I'd reason to believe Richard Smith, chairman of Harcourt whose family controlled seventy-eight percent of the company through Class B shares, was about to put the business up for sale despite its wave of recent growth.) My investment beat Smith's announcement by two days. The value of Harcourt stock soared thirty and one-half percent to over $54 a share.

I bought Oracle Corporation stock, and Nabisco—the target of takeover suitors—as well as Lycos, Inc.—one of the nation's biggest Internet portals—just before it was purchased by Telefonica of Spain, and Unilever Co., before it was bought by George Weston Inc., and rode the tide to a series of impressive gains. I acquired Apache Corporation as it prepared to buy up the gas production assets of Collins & Ware, and blocks of Kodak—the company's decision to escalate its stock repurchase program led values to rise more than nine percent—as well as TiVo Inc., a week before it announced its venture deal with AOL. Nortel Networks, Epicon, and ADC Tele-Communications stocks all earned a profit, and delighted by my initial success, I phoned my attorney in order to discuss the next stage of my plan.

Myrian applauded my new enterprise. Although I'd yet to tell her exactly what I was doing—"A few investments to pay the rent," I said whenever she asked—she was happy for me just the same. (Two weeks into my project, she chimed, "You look like a new man, Walter Brimm!") She was working then on her new canvas and we developed a routine of spending part of our day together. Instead of a single composition, Myrian now envisioned a series of eight—each five by six feet—with the position of the male figure altered slightly from one canvas to the next; his slumping form with its distinct mix of promise and gloom, at once writhing and turning in order to reach for the woman, gaining on her by degrees. She set up her easel in the center of my apartment, and arranging her paints, her palette, and brushes, took up her art. I offered to pay for the eight blank canvases she needed to complete her vision but she was hesitant. "Why would I let you do that?"

"As a friend."

"It isn't necessary."

"All the same," I persisted until she agreed in part. "Two canvases."

"And some brushes and paints."

"We'll see."

Our fraternity delighted me. My affection—faultless—was altogether platonic (though I envied Janus) and enabled me to discover in the clarity of my emotions a depth of unconditional joy and innocence otherwise reserved for Rea. (My daughter's presence was missed with the acuteness of flesh torn from bone.) However much I still suffered moments of dark regret, when Gee and Rea were all I could think of and the rest of the world vanished into a hoary abyss, I was encouraged by my progress, the hours of unflappability which came more frequently now and prompted me that March to confide my intentions.

Myrian had just finished a long stretch in front of her canvas in which I noticed her adding only a slight shadow to the image of the man, yet somehow the shading brought the figure to life. I waited until she went to the window—it was still morning and the sun glowed soft across her face—and asked if she was working that night and would she be walking with me to the clinic. (As part of my routine, I went each evening to assist Janus in whatever way I could.) "I'm scheduled for five," she said.

"Five it is."

Myrian smiled. I shifted around in my chair, and—without further preamble—told her how I recently transferred fifty percent of my interest in both Beletone Fiberoptics and Miveral Software, along with all the stock and profits made while trading on-line, plus an additional $30,000 cash into a Charitable Trust created in the name of the clinic. I explained how the papers were drafted, detailed the current status of the stocks and bonds, what cash was ready to be drawn upon, and how exactly a Charitable Trust operated, until Myrian interrupted, disbelieving, and asked, "What are you saying?"

"A Trust."

"But?"

"I realize money's a crude way to express my appreciation for all the kindness you and Janus have shown me. I also know the clinic's current financial situation is weak and certain creditors are again beating a path to the door. Under the circumstances, this is the best I could come up with."

Myrian looked at me, stunned, and bringing her hands to her mouth, stood for several seconds without moving. When finally she said my name, her voice was elated. "Walter!" (Walter Brimm!) and reaching for me, she exclaimed, "So this is what you've been up to! Why didn't you tell me?"

"I'm telling you now."

"But you've been working for weeks! And you haven't told Janus?"

"Not yet. I wanted to keep things a secret until all the pieces were in place."

"It's too much money. It's all you have."

"It isn't, really. I've quite enough otherwise."

"But you shouldn't. You can't."

"Why not? What else am I to do with myself?"

We laughed together then, and in my happiness I accepted a kiss. Myrian insisted I tell Janus, "This minute!" and pulled me from my chair. Two patients were remaining from the morning rush as we entered the clinic: a large woman in an ill-fitted jump-suit, a plaster cast covering her left forearm, and an older man suffering from serious bouts of angina; the beat of his heart wheezy and weathered by age, convulsing in painful spasms which Janus treated with distilled doses of Quinaglute. We waited back in the storage area until he was through. The room was cramped, with wooden shelves and a series of dark grey file cabinets. A bare light in the center of the ceiling shined down on the old desk Janus used to record his patients' notes. (During my first few nightly visits to the clinic, I organized the room by putting labels on the shelves, cross-filing patient records in chronological and alphabetical sequence, preparing an inventory of the supplies, and making a list of items ready to be reordered.) Janus came down the hall, concerned something was wrong—for what else could have drawn Myrian away from her paints?—and asked, "What's the matter?"

"Nothing," she grabbed hold of his arm.

I stood by the first shelf and removed the clipboard from its hook, reading the list from the night before. "You're low on Zithromax, hydrocortisone, and hydrochlorothiazide. You could also use more gauze, silicone dioxide, and Neosporin."

Janus went and leaned against his desk. "I'll see what I can do."

"If it's a matter of money," I couldn't resist, excited now about delivering my news.

Janus waved me off. "Medway's waiting on a check to clear."

"Perhaps I could help."

"It's alright. Someone's always waiting."

"You should let Walter finish," Myrian sat beside Janus on the desk. He turned and looked at her for a moment, then stared back at me.

I described again the whole of my plan, explained the details of the Trust, how the money would be used, and the way I'd oversee the statutory requirements and day-to-day maintenance of the funds. "From now on you only have to worry about running the clinic. The financial end will be taken care of."

Janus shifted his good eye against the light and continued to stare at me, obviously surprised by my offer. He took several seconds to weigh his response, and instead of gratitude, asked, "Why do you want to give the clinic all this money?"

"Because I respect what you're doing. Because you need the capital and making cash is the only thing I do well. Because it would please me a great deal if you'd accept. Someone should have done this for you a long time ago," I stopped then and offered no further explanation, tried not to think of Gee and what I hoped she would say when she learned of my philanthropy; how delighted she'd be to know I'd at last recovered my health, and eager then to invite me back home—oh yes!—she'd rejoice in the proof of my becoming a truly repentant and altogether enlightened fellow. "That's all," I said. "That's the only reason."

Janus looked around the room, at the narrowness of the space and the half-empty shelves. He folded his arms across his chest, his bad hand set atop his right wrist—the fingers bent at permanent curves, two of the knuckles crushed flat, the tips of the middle three digits drawn in as if ready to pierce the center of his palm—and staring at me, said, "It's too much."

"It isn't, really. You accept donations from public and private sources all the time."

"Nickels and dimes."

"Money nonetheless."

"This is different."

"In what way?"

"In every way," Janus referred then to the current principal of the Trust as an absurdly excessive sum.

"But it's already done," I made clear. "All you have to do is accept."

"And why are you doing this?"

"He already told you," Myrian came around to the front of the desk. "He wants to help. Isn't that a good enough reason? Isn't it possible someone else might want to offer up a bit of charity without expecting anything in return? If Walter wants to do this, and the clinic needs the money, who cares about anything else?"

The question proved a knotty point, exactly the sort of challenge Janus faced when people first attacked his decision to open the clinic. ("Why are you doing this?" They ignored his answers, convinced there had to be some underlying ambition weighted with personal gain.) Such a large sum of money was, of course, hard to turn down, and it was possible to argue he had no right to reject Walter's charity as the bequest belonged to the clinic and wasn't his to refuse. Still—the irony of his suspicion notwithstanding—there was the question of reciprocal obligations, his duty to make certain Walter's incentive wasn't ground in ulterior motives, for if Janus accepted the funds while Walter was thinking in terms of redemption and winning back his wife, what responsibility was he under then to take Walter aside and tell him the truth? He folded his arms tighter across his chest, paused a moment, then answered, "I don't know."

PART III

"My only fear is that I will not be worthy of my sufferings."
FYODOR DOSTOYEVSKY

CHAPTER 19

"So, what do you think?"

"About the house?"

"Yes."

"Do you want to sell?"

"I do."

"Then I think you should."

"What about your place?"

"I still want to keep it and rent it out. I've looked into transferring the title to the *Review* and writing off the costs."

"Can you?"

"I hope so, once we move."

"We don't need a big place."

"No, we don't."

"Just enough for the three of us."

"It's true."

Gee came around and got into bed as Tod slipped off his jeans and set them across the arm of the chair. The room was cool as they closed off the vent and liked to sleep wrapped together warm beneath the heavy beige comforter. Standing there, with his feet arched against the hardwood, bare-legged and unbuttoning his shirt, Tod stared at Geni under the covers. Being with her now, steadily so these last few months, still caught him by surprise at times; their affair both complicated and remarkable, promoting specific confusions as to whether their relationship was a plot hatched long ago or came about only after Walter's collapse. ("What can I possibly say when, after everything, here I am just as Walter predicted?") He looked at the empty space beside Gee on the bed and tried to imagine how often Walter stood in the same spot and stared down with equal wonder.

Leaving the bedroom, he walked across the hall to check on Rea. The gesture appealed to him, was something he enjoyed in the nights he slept over. The faint light from the hall entered the room, the soft sound of Rea's breathing as he stepped closer to the bed and brought the edge of her blue blanket up over her shoulder. On the dresser was a photograph of Walter. Unlike the master bedroom, in which Gee had shed every last physical reminder, there was something appropriate Tod believed in Rea having a photo of her father. He stood for a moment and tried to remember the last time he looked at a picture of his own father, Alfie Marcum, all querulous and thick-browed, with fat hands, a bulldog's face, and a drinker's unsteady distemper. Despite his homely mask, Alfie always seemed to have a girlfriend on the side, married women mostly, taken from the pool of coworkers in the many odd jobs he had over the years.

Tod closed Rea's door and walked back up the hall where he tried to forget about his father, but the memory of Alfie's infidelities and how his running around put Tod's mother in an early grave, led to a correlative recollection of the night Walter broke down and collapsed on the floor of the Imperial Hotel. Such a blurring of the two caused Tod to try and draw a distinction between his father's indiscretions and the consequence of his own affair with Gee, but somehow the difference was hard for him to define just then, and frustrated, he slipped into bed.

Propped up on three pillows, Gee lay reading a copy of Lyn Mikel Brown's *Raising Their Voices*, and as Tod got in beside her, she asked about Rea. ("Sound asleep?" "Deeply, yes.") She closed her book and turning toward him then, said, "Maybe it's too soon."

"What?"

"This weekend."

"She needs to see her father."

"At some point."

"It's been almost four months."

Gee sighed. No matter how committed she was to finalizing their divorce, the idea of seeing Walter again unnerved her. "Best case scenario, he comes and goes and we're cordial. And worst case," but she stopped, and forced herself to admit, "Rea is looking forward to seeing him." In the time since Walter's collapse she'd spoken honestly to Rea about what happened, had told her as much as she needed to know, was respectful of Walter's position as her father, but made perfectly clear that no, Daddy would not be moving back home. Last week, as they discussed the prospect of selling the house and buying a new place with Tod, Rea seemed receptive, though certain questions came up. "Do you promise to tell Daddy where we move?" she was concerned. "Will you let him know where I live?"

For the longest time, Gee had tried to define the breakdown of her marriage, how beyond the events of last year their separation was the culmination of a thousand different battles, each significant and unrelated to her feelings for Tod. ("Not Tod," she felt it was important to note, though the more she focused on removing him from the equation, the harder it was to be sure.) What reason then? She composed a list: The distance between us, the estrangement that entered my bones like a chill and made it impossible to recall a time I moved with any sense of joy or freedom when I was with you. How our love turned old, the incompatibility of our desires—not always this way. How your honesty (lost), your resourcefulness (narrowed), and faith (ignored) all faltered until everything which once appealed to me was no longer there. What reason? (Walter!) Because your approach to life turned rigid and wore me down. (It wore you down, too.) Because your love became constricting and rid itself of trust. Because you became harsh and cynical. Because you lied. (I know, you can accuse me too, but it's true.) Because you allowed the very worst within you to take over. Because I'm frightened when I think back. Because you were unjust and forced me to pity you at a time I should not have been made to do so. Because it takes too much energy for me to care the way I once did. Because it's over. That's all. There's nothing more to it really.

She reached across and found Tod's hand. The feel of him and the ability to touch his flesh was something she still was not completely used to, and yet the strain in her face gave way while rolling onto her side, she said, "Turn off the light." She shifted her hips then and lifted her left leg over his center. ("Here I am," she thought. "Here and now.") Her needs were not immediately sexual, although the proximity of Tod's body stirred her. She felt the length of him, the contour of his flesh and texture of his muscle, the weight of his arm, the width of his fingers, the size of his penis, even his smell all different from Walter's, and placing herself on top of him, she offered and received sweet kisses as she settled and set herself down. "It's you," she whispered then. "Everything," she confided, all deep and light and certain.

CHAPTER 20

In the end, after a period of high speculation, Janus agreed to accept the Trust, and delighted, I considered the moment a great triumph. Such a glorious feeling! What a magnificent confirmation! I cheered and spent the next three days finalizing the last details, reviewing the clinic's debts, and putting the first checks in the mail. New supplies were purchased and equipment ordered. As happy as I was for Janus, and my desire to help the clinic notwithstanding, my own expectations could not be discounted. I laid no claim to virtue being its own reward and waited eagerly for my beneficence to provide me with favor.

Signs that I was on the right track included the quick $9,000 I made acquiring Invensys P.L.C. stocks just before the company's planned spin-off into the United States. (I also made a significant profit buying and selling Corning, Inc., Juniper Networks, and JDS Uniphase.) My health continued to improve, and motivated, I added several dozen push-ups and sit-ups to my afternoon walk, tightening my chest, stomach, and arms. Myrian finished her series of canvases, which turned out wonderful. She said that I inspired her—"Absolutely, Walter Brimm!"—and as a gift, offered to paint a wall of my apartment. "It'll be fun. Tell me, what would you like?"

I dismissed the idea, then changed my mind and showed her again the photograph in my wallet of Gee and Rea. "Can you do this?"

Myrian studied the snapshot, and after a brief hesitation in which her gaze did not quite reach my eyes, she smiled and said, "Sure I can, Walter." and so she did.

Further proof of my good fortune came early in April as I learned that I'd passed all the tests put to me by the court-appointed doctors, and as my prize I was allowed a visit with Rea, "Saturday," the letter said. "Eight a.m. until five p.m." And there it was. Fantastic! ("Yes!") How remarkable the universe! How ultimately efficient and fair! Here was the reward I was after, the notion that one good turn deserved another. If I could be vanquished as a consequence of all I did to Tod, then certainly I should profit from the charity I performed. This was the principle upon which I hung my hat, a theorem of supreme sensibility which held that equity and rightfulness were mandated in such a grand and glorious world.

It was with high expectation then that I pulled up in front of my old house at eight in the morning, awake for hours, too excited to sleep, my thoughts leaping back and forth between Gee and Rea, Rea and Gee. Such a time as this—so long in coming!—warranted celebration, and twice on the way over I couldn't resist and rolled down my window to shout, "Hooray!"

The front of my house was bathed in morning light that swept out across the lawn, soft and gold. (Janus had loaned me his car, which I took yesterday and had the oil and filters changed, the brakes adjusted, and the carburetor cleaned, and in my exuberance, I also purchased four new tires, windshield wipers, muffler, pipe, and shocks; the total investment more than the car was currently worth. "A gesture is all," I laughed at Janus's surprise.) I parked in the drive and moved quickly up the walk. Rea answered the door and how pleased she was to see me! "Daddy!" Her reaction so pure of heart as to buckle my knees. "Look how tall! How tall!" I repeated over and over and almost wept as I scooped her up and held her in my arms, feeling her flesh and bones, the smell of peppermint and Ivory soap on her skin, the moment dream-like and as perfect as I imagined in the weeks before.

"Where's your mother?" I glanced about, anticipating Gee's entrance, picturing her coming into the hall, her hair freshly combed, in a new dress, her eyes wide and eager to see me. How I longed for her then, my excitement nearly too much to bear. "Mommy's upstairs," Rea said as I set her back on the floor. She went to the table by the door and retrieved a folded piece of paper and pen. I opened the note and recognized Gee's writing at once: "Rea is to be home no later than five. Please feed her a timely lunch, though not dinner, and list below where you plan to take her. In case of an emergency," she felt a need to add, and signed at the bottom with a simple scrawling of the letter G.

The note caught me by surprise. Such avoidance on her part seemed ill-suited. (At the very least, I thought she'd say hello, if for no other reason than to make sure I was, in fact, well.) I did as instructed nonetheless, and in the process tried to place a positive spin on why my wife chose to hide away upstairs. No doubt her reticence to appear reflected on her desire to not intrude on my reunion with Rea. Perhaps, too—I indulged further—the note was a sly way of enticing me to go upstairs, as maybe she wanted a moment alone with me and was using her absence as a lure. Despite the prospect, I decided to play things safe and instructed Rea to "Say goodbye to your mother."

"Goodbye, Ma," she yelled up the stairs.

"Goodbye, darling," Gee's voice thrilled me with its sweet proximity. "Have fun. Be a good girl." Her tone was tender, a gentleness in her delivery which was lilting and maternal, and yet her inflection was also oddly pitched, forced high, unnatural and nervously rehearsed. I considered again running up to her and taking her in my arms, if for no other reason than to soothe her, but the possibility was much too real, and frightened of making a fool of myself before the day even began, I turned and led Rea out the door.

I'd spent Thursday afternoon shopping with Myrian and the back seat of Janus's car was now filled with several wrapped

packages—two new schoolgirl outfits, dolls and books and computer games—which Rea delighted in finding and asked at once
as I buckled her in, "Are those for me?"

"Well, let's see," I teased, and handed her one before we
drove off. By the time we reached Fourth Avenue all five boxes
were opened, the wrapping paper tossed off, and the empty
cartons piled once more in the back seat. Rea's joy made me want
to sing. ("La-dee-dee!") Her features, while more handsome, were
similar to mine, with narrow chin and deep-set eyes, a roundness
to her cheeks, and sharp extension to her nose, though her air
was her mother's, the way she spoke—even so young—with a
conciseness and candor consistently aimed at striking the nail on
the head. "So many presents," she thanked me with an examining look.

Although we'd spoken several times of late by phone, I an-
ticipated our actual reunion requiring a period of adjustment, and
as such, I decided to keep to a specific itinerary; protecting
against any awkward moments when uncertainty might arise between us and in our sudden silence Rea would gaze at me and
wonder, "So where have you really been, Daddy, and what are you
doing back now?" I informed her of my plan for us to have breakfast, but Rea said she'd already eaten, so we went to Peterson's
Pancake House just for juice and to view Myrian's work. I hoped
the dinosaurs would impress her, and was pleased when she
walked enthusiastically up and down the length of the wall. She
was fascinated when I told her I knew the woman who painted
the mural, and asked me then, "Is she your girlfriend?"

The question threw me. "My what?" I was startled she could
even think in terms of my having a relationship with someone
other than her mother. "No, of course not. She's just a good
friend." and wondering where she'd gotten such an idea, I waited
until we were back in the car and driving toward the Museum of
Modern Art before bringing the subject up again. "So you liked
the dinosaurs?"

"Yes. Especially the brontosaurus."

"Are you studying dinosaurs at school?"

"Our teacher read us a book."

"I see. You know Myrian, the painter, is my neighbor."

"In your apartment?"

"That's right. We're friends. Does your mommy have any friends like that? The way Myrian is a friend to Daddy, I mean?"

"Like Uncle Tod?"

"That's right," I steadied my hand on the wheel and turned us into the lot. "Like Uncle Tod."

"She has him."

"I see."

I hadn't been to the museum for some time, and distracted now by my conversation with Rea could barely concentrate on the paintings. We wandered through the first floor with its abstract works, the colorful pieces by de Kooning, Mark Tobey, Patrick Heron, and Jasper Johns, and as we reached the third hall, I spotted Miró's "Person Throwing a Stone at a Bird." The sight of the lone Miró inspired me to tell Rea, "This is where your daddy met your mommy." I explained the story of Miró's "The Beautiful Bird Revealing the Unknown to a Couple in Love," and how I found Gee sitting in front of the canvas.

"You mean the one Mommy put in the basement?"

"I don't know." I hadn't noticed as much when I first entered the house as the wall where the Miró print usually hung was out of view. "Did she?"

"The big one we used to have? She asked Uncle Tod to take it down."

"I see," the news depressed me though I tried my best not to let on, even as Rea said, "She covered it with a bunch of old blankets."

I didn't reply, did what I could to convince myself Gee's reason for removing the painting was that she simply couldn't look at the print everyday without me there. (She didn't get rid of it, I told myself as a means of raising my spirits, didn't set it on fire or put it out with the trash, but stored it downstairs in anticipation of my return.) I refused to think further than this, and hurried Rea up to the second floor and the classics of Rubens and

Botticelli, of gentle, smiling madonnas, and Christ laid over a rock while the Virgin Mary washed the wounds in his feet. I hoped she'd like these paintings better than the abstracts, but she said they were "too eerie" and having seen enough, we left after forty minutes and got back in the car.

We followed the museum with a trip to the Woodberry Aquarium where Rea enjoyed the saltwater tanks, the animated faces of the puffers and large angels, the bright colors of the loaches and box fish. As we passed the enormous freshwater tank, I stared solemnly inside but said nothing about the muskellunge. Rea wasn't hungry for lunch, so we decided to stroll across Fourth Avenue and on through Mandinger Park.

The day was pleasant, sunny and crisp, and a number of children Rea seemed to know were playing in the grass. I allowed her to run off and took my place along the fence with a half dozen other fathers watching their kids in a makeshift game of tag. After a short while, a small boy with an affliction in his legs and hips, a degenerative condition that caused him to move stiffly and put him forever on the verge of falling forward, approached the group of children who kindly altered the speed of their game in order to invite the boy to join in. The gesture was sweet, and regarding the scene from a distance, watching Rea as she rose up on her toes and extended her hands high in the air as if to dance with the boy, I couldn't help but smile.

Focused on the revelry, I didn't notice in time an older boy charging across the grass in order to knock the crippled child to the ground, pushing him down again as he tried to get up. "Hey!" I shouted, and turned to look at the collection of other fathers, the six men standing with me in the half-shade. "Did you see that?" and when no one answered, I yelled again, "You there, cut it out! That's enough!"

Three of the girls, including Rea, ran over and tried to chase the older boy off, but he simply circled around a tree and came again and knocked the smaller boy back onto the cement path. I was already moving forward as the second series of blows were delivered, and could see the stricken boy's expression the moment he was hit; his face filled with an ancient sort of horror, his eyes opening wide as he let go a terrified gasp, pitched and fell again, his arms too slow in coming up so that he crashed down hard on his chest and chin. I rushed to where he fell and bent down beside him. There was a scrape on his cheek and a welt already visible above his left eye. The older boy skipped over to the swings, laughing and trying to impress the remaining children with chin-ups and wrestling. The reaction of the others was subdued, each child giving way to their own fears. (Those who weren't immediately cooperative with the older boy's taunts stood silently shaken.) No one ran off—afraid of being chased— and however upset by the brutality, no voice was raised in the fallen child's defense. Even the girls who assisted before were reluctant to challenge the older boy again, preferring to hang back, satisfied they'd done their best and hoping the worst was over.

On my knees, I tried to scoop the boy up in my arms, but as I touched him, he rolled onto his side, and straining to right himself, managed to climb to his feet, pushing me from him while shouting, "Get away from me! Get away!" and limping off. Rea stood just to my left, watching me now, the features of her face fragile with surprise. (Although she was still a young girl, the knowledge conveyed in her expression gave the impression she was no longer a child.) I thought at first she was imploring me for answers, wanting to know, "Is that it? Is that all? Is it over?" and to this end, I'd no idea what to tell her, no clear way of explaining what had happened or comforting her. But then I understood—a bit too late—this wasn't what she wanted at all, for suddenly she was turning from me, disappointed and rushing toward the swings; all four feet and sixty pounds of her shooting across the grass, wielding a sizeable stick she snatched up from the ground, and without the least hesitation, no warning shrieks nor angry howls, she struck the older boy hard on the knee, and when he yelped and spun around, she recocked and levelled him flat in the face.

The mayhem which followed was unfortunate. Fathers came running toward us now, all the men who otherwise stood silent and glum as they observed the initial assault on the crippled child, shrieked and howled and said, "Did you see what that girl did? Whose kid is that? Whose kid? She hit my son!" I decided it was best to beat a hasty retreat rather than stand our ground and try to explain, and taking Rea by the hand, we crossed the park on our way back to the car.

We drove east, stopping at Hamburger Haven for lunch where I ate my food with a nervous sort of hunger, thinking about what happened at the park and knowing I should discuss as much with Rea. "I'm proud of you, of course," I said. "But you understand there are better ways of handling things."

"He started it," she said this calmly and without the sort of emotional tumult otherwise expected in someone so young. "He hit him first. No one else was going to do anything."

I agreed with her, and tried once more to explain. "It's the hitting we object to however, so it makes no sense for us to turn around and hit him back."

"Why?"

"Well, because."

"But doesn't he deserve to be punished?"

"Of course."

"Then why did those men just stand there? Why weren't they going to do anything?"

These were hard questions to answer, issues of indifference and insensitivity, qualities inherited over time and otherwise impossible for children to understand. "Well," I began slowly, "sometimes people are insensitive. Sometimes men, and women, we—that is people—don't care as much about what happens to others and only react when something affects them directly. Do you see? The men, the other fathers, weren't inspired to help your friend because they didn't think enough of the situation, didn't appreciate how it should matter to them. That's why what you did was commendable. You showed compassion for someone and weren't acting for your own benefit. Still, you shouldn't have gone after the boy with a stick. Do you get what I mean?"

"A little."

"I'm not saying the boy shouldn't be punished," I now re-peated, "but there are rules we have to follow. Laws of conduct. Just because the boy acted badly doesn't give us the right to respond in kind. People get what they deserve. I'm sure that boy will get what's coming to him." I was being too abstract, and yet I couldn't think of any other way to resolve what had transpired. I waited as Rea processed my more salient points, wondering how she would respond to the notion of fallibility, antipathy, and even cruelty in a world she was just then maturing into. She was a smart child, and deserving of the truth, and still I was surprised when she replied, "Is that what happened to you, Daddy?"

"What do you mean?"

"Because of Uncle Tod? Is that why you're living downtown? Are you being punished for trying to hurt him?"

Christ! (Rea!) "Who told you that?"

"Mommy said you were mean to Uncle Tod."

"She said that?"

"Yes."

I cursed under my breath.

"Were you?"

"I was no meaner to Tod than he was to me."

"Then why are you living downtown?"

"It's a long story. It's hard to explain. What did your mother say?"

"She said you got mad at Uncle Tod for no good reason."

"I didn't," I responded quickly and in my own defense, trying to imagine the conversation between Gee and Rea and what was actually said. I refused to believe Gee would go so far to say anything seriously damning against me—at least not to our daughter—though how was I to undo the idea Rea now had? (How does one undo anything?) I considered telling her about love, to make sure at the very least she understood my motivation and could separate my misdeeds from the mindless cruelty intro-duced by the boy in the park, but each time I readied myself to deliver just such a claim and let her know that my transgressions were no arbitrary acts of indulgence, I faltered, incapable of forming the proper sentiment, and in the end could do no more than peer awkwardly back at her with a befuddled sort of gaze, and stammer, "It was not for no good reason, Rea. What I did might have been imprudent, but if nothing else the reason was sound."

I waited for her to ask me then what exactly I was talking about and to clarify the core of my babble, but to my great relief she didn't and for reasons I never insisted she explain, she let the subject drop.

We got back in the car after lunch and drove to see Janus at the clinic. A dozen people filled the waiting area when we arrived. (Janus was in the examination room, removing sutures from a young girl's head.) Two men called to me, "Waall-ter!" and "Wally B!" I went to the clipboard hanging beneath the sign which asked everyone to "Please Check In" and finding only four people on the list, sorted through the confusion and got everyone to record their name in the order they arrived.

"Is this where you work now, Daddy?" Rea was curious. I smiled, eager to give her a favorable impression of what I was doing downtown, hoping to provide the answers I failed to deliver at lunch and let her see that my banishment to the east side was not as terrible as she might think. I described my friendship with Janus and how I helped him out in the afternoons. "The clinic is where people who haven't enough money or insurance to visit a regular hospital come for assistance," I said. "It's part of the reason I live here now, although," I quickly added, "I'd still prefer to live at home with you and Mommy." If the issue of penance and redemption was too much for a six-year-old to comprehend—"Is this your punishment, Daddy?"—I set the stage nonetheless and allowed Rea time to reach her own conclusions.

I introduced her to the people waiting—"This child? No, she can't be yours. You're too ugly, Walter Brimm."—then had her follow me back to the storage area where I removed the necessary files and brought them in to Janus. "Well, well, well," he turned and bent down. He had an easy way with children, a relaxed manner, completely natural and spontaneous. We stayed for three different patients, the procedures all fascinating to Rea and with Janus gracious enough to explain what he was doing throughout. (She, in turn, made no mention of his physical imperfections, though later in the car she asked about his hand and limp. "It seems he had an accident several years ago," I answered as best I could.) As we got ready to leave, Janus walked us to the door where he commented on the charms of my daughter, and touching my shoulder—something he'd never done before—wondered, "So, you're having a good day?"

"Excellent." I mentioned nothing of Gee's absence that morning, how she removed the Miró print from the wall, or of the incident with Rea in the park.

"Good," he nodded, and turning away before I could comment on the odd expression crossing his face, he put the same question to Rea. "Yes, yes, yes!" she sang and tugged on her cap.

We reached my building just after three-thirty and parked across the street. Rea ran in front of me up the stairs, and watching her, I was overcome by such a powerful mix of melancholy and happiness, wishfulness and despair, I could not possibly imagine spending another day apart. Myrian heard us coming and opened her door before we could knock. "Well, hello," she dropped at once to her knees, right there in the hall. "My name's Myrian. I'm a friend of your dad."

"The Dinosaur Lady," Rea stopped a foot away and stared at the streaks of orange in Myrian's hair and the many silver and gold earrings she had on. "We went to Peterson's this morning," I explained. Myrian laughed. "I love it. Dinosaur Lady is great." She invited us inside, the front room tidied up—a nice gesture—and on the coffee table was a plate of ginger cookies and milk. Rea looked at the art on the walls, the many shapes and colors which converged and dominated the space, and turning her head from left to right, asked the same as everyone, "Did you paint these?"

"Do you like them?"

"Yeah, they're cool."

"Cool is good. Cool's the whole point."

I went into the kitchen and had a glass of water, then stood just inside the doorway where I watched Rea on the couch, her head turned toward Myrian who'd picked up a large white pad and box of pastels and sketched Rea in shades of gold and blue and viridescent. When she finished, Myrian came into the kitchen. "She's great, Walter. An awesome little girl. I can tell she loves you very much," her eyes settled onto mine, her face identical to Janus's a half hour before; the same notice and caution in her tone. ("She loves you, but don't expect too much. All things in moderation. Tread slowly. Take what you can get for now.") I didn't question her look, and instead, checked the time and said with apology, "We really have to go."

Myrian sprayed the surface of Rea's sketch with a clear silicon in order to keep the pastels from smearing, and promised to draw her another picture, "The next time you're here."

We stopped quickly in my apartment where Rea was delighted by the painting of herself and Gee on my front wall. (Myrian's handiwork turned out exceptionally well and as promised ran from ceiling to floor.) Still, the absence of material possessions in my flat surprised Rea and she stared about with a puzzled and slightly sad look on her face. "So this is how you live now, Dad," I could all but hear her say, and waving my arms in order to ease her concern, explained, "Not all my furniture has arrived yet, of course. I've been so busy, but I've ordered everything, including an extra bed and large TV."

We drove off in a rush to make it across town by five, passing along the freeway and up Pembrooke Boulevard, where I regretted the end of our day and how swiftly the hours vanished. Twice I stole sideways glances at my daughter, and despite a few odd moments and revelations which threatened to disrupt our momentum, considered our reunion a triumph. Rea's nearness was exhilarating—after so many months!—and turning onto Bakersfield Road, accelerating up the hill and down the other side, I indulged myself further and pictured Gee in a summer dress—a bit premature for the season yet lovely just the same— her red hair left free and flowing about her face, soft and close enough against her skin that I envied the good fortune of each loose strand. I imagined her anticipating my return, fixing us a glorious dinner, preparing for the evening together, eager to have her family reunited and ready then to celebrate the wonder of our healing. Distracted in this way, delirious and determined, I pulled into the drive, convinced the day held further bounty, and other-wise confused by what I saw on the porch where waiting to speak with me were both Tod and Gee.

CHAPTER 21

Sitting an hour later inside Chick's Bar & Grill, I drank my whiskey with two cubes of ice and wondered if there was a single word in the English language to describe what just happened. Ambushed seemed to fit, but then that only covered the kind of attack I came under and not the effect of the surprise. (Brutal, fierce, and cruel all came to mind. Cunning, too, for they caught me off guard and hoped this way to shock me into submission.) I tried to hide my devastation and prove—what?—that I was up to the challenge and could get through their assault unscathed, but I lacked the stamina—so much having already been expended in the weeks before—and seemed to have forgotten again how to behave.

Hoodwinked and bamboozled! (I thought of these words as well.) What a wicked way to spoil my day. The whole of their presentation took less than five minutes. Gee's hair was longer than I remembered, nearly down to her shoulders, and left un-attended to blow as it pleased. ("Hello, Walter," she said, her tone deliberate, detached, her gaze possessed of warning.) The sun overhead readied itself for setting. I waited, shifting my hands behind my back, like a prisoner whose final sentence was about to be issued, clenched my jaw, and listened to what my wife and her lover had to tell me.

Tod addressed me whenever Gee faltered. "I wanted this to come from me," he said in earnest, his voice heavy with his own surprise. ("Can you believe it, Walter?") "I wouldn't want there to be any misunderstandings later." I ignored what he had to say, could not have cared less about his opinions regarding forgiveness and water under the bridge—or was it over the dam?—and how things in life just seemed to happen. In the end Gee seemed to believe our conversation went well, though I barely said a word, and relieved, she watched me turn and walk back to the car. "Goodbye, then," she offered me this almost tenderly, though the expression on her face was one of closure. How glad she was to have the situation resolved without any last-second outbursts or cruel charges on my part, no final entreaties nor threats to cleave at old wounds, and while I didn't want to disappoint her, I realized as I opened the car door that I wasn't yet willing to be so accommodating.

"How long?" I shouted this as they turned to step inside, Tod with his hand on Gee's back and both eager to get away. "Did you even wait a week? A day? Or were you already sleeping together?"

Gee continued into the house, though Tod stopped, and after deliberating a moment, started down the steps. I was still calling out, pleading and angry, desirous and despairing, chanting in a pathetic sort of singsong—"Gee! Gee! Gee!"—until the futility of my own sound echoed overhead. Tod drew up halfway across the drive and said my name with such misgiving that we wound up harmonizing in a piteous and peculiar sort of lyric. ("Gee!" "Walter." "Gee!" "Walter." "Gee!" "Walter.") When I finally fell quiet, he told me—insisted and tried to convince me—"It was never what you thought," though something in his face suggested not even he was sure of what he was saying.

I got back in the car and drove off.

What now then? (What now?) Things weren't supposed to end this way. (Truly!) I pushed my drink to the side, my sadness bitter, all of my expectations dashed, I repeated the word "Ambushed" followed by "Screwed!" and "Fucked!" and "Shit!"

How could this happen? All my faith in the decency and fairness in the world now gone, I wondered where was the logic? The orderliness I expected? (Where was Gee?) What incentive was left and what in God's name was I to do next?

Somewhere around six-thirty, I drove to Janus's clinic, where the evening rush of patients filled the waiting room. People called out to me but I made no reply and went straight back to where Janus was examining the ears and throat of a feverish young man. "Why didn't you tell me?" I closed the partition and demanded to know.

Janus stopped what he was doing and turned to face me.

"They were waiting for me, for Christ's sake!"

"Walter, I'm sorry."

"Did you know?"

"Yes."

"How long?"

"Recently. A short time."

"You should have told me," I said again.

"Maybe so."

"But?"

"There was nothing my telling you could change," he turned back to the man on the table and continued placing warm drops from a small bottle into his ears. I paced inside the room, feeling caged, and repeating to Janus the same question I asked myself over and over again for the last hour. "What am I supposed to do now?"

"Exactly as you've been doing."

"And what's that?"

"If you don't know, I can't tell you."

The man left and rather than call in another patient, Janus leaned against the examining table. For a minute I thought he was going to remind me that Gee had thrown me out months ago and any delusion I continued to harbor was my fault and no one else's, but instead he stared at me in the same way he used to when I first came from Renton General, and said, "For what it's worth, and I wouldn't have told you this three months ago, but you're going to be all right."

"Will I?" For some reason the idea upset me all over again. "Is that it? Is that all there is, being all right and getting through the day?"

"No."

"Then what?"

Once more, "I can't answer for you."

"Try."

"I know you had certain expectations. Even so."

"Was I wrong?"

"Yes." His quick pronouncement was harsh, though typical Janus and not without sympathy. "You can't expect to undo what happened," he spoke in solemn tones, and when I asked, "Why? Why can't I undo all this? I mean, I know I fucked up. I just didn't think I'd have to pay for my mistakes the rest of my life," he brought his fractured hand up beside his bad eye, and rubbing at his temple, said, "What don't we pay for, Walter? We do the best we can and sometimes even then the things we love cost us."

Much as Walter before, Martin Kulpepper now had a plan. The incident at Peterson's Pancake House inspired him, and following a series of other more recent encounters where Myrian saw fit to run him off, he no longer believed good things came to those who wait.

Late in March then, a few weeks ago on a Sunday morning, Martin pulled into the empty parking lot of Great Mercantile Insurance and used his key to enter the lobby and take an elevator up to the ninth floor. The offices of GMI were spread throughout the Peck and Hyde Building, with the Department of Claims on the first floor, the Division of Adjustment and Fraud three flights up, Accounting and the Department of Records on nine and ten. Junior administrators, sales, and field agents occupied the twelfth through fifteenth floors, with all the senior executives two flights above.

Martin made his way to the Division of Records, where he sat in front of the main computer and logged on. As a trained professional he had reason to be suspicious of Janus Kelly from the start—what a queer old bird, what a wounded duck—and seeing him with Myrian only made him wonder more. (Not long after he moved into Myrian's building, he began asking questions and gathering information, collecting pieces to the puzzle until he was ready now to document the cold hard truth.) In his work at GMI he'd learned the depths to which people were capable of descending: intentional fires and break-ins, larcenies and thefts, accidents and injuries peculiarly staged, piracy and losses reported, the paper trail of companies bilking clients for payment on services never performed. What a constant bit of bullshit—intolerable and criminal, yes!—and what in this world could possibly be worse than fraud?

In a matter of minutes he pulled up the first of three files—the one covering the claim Dr. Janus Kelly settled several years ago when his right foot was accidently crushed. The second file was in an entirely different database that cross-referenced policy holders, benefactors, and claimants at GMI against claims paid out to like parties by other carriers. (Obviously, Janus had tried to distance one claim from another, using different agents and carriers—the history of his settlements and sequence of injuries, the medical reports, and detailed accounts of what transpired scattered throughout the system—but modern technology made it possible to link all such data at the press of a few buttons, retrievable if someone had reason and the wherewithal to look.) Martin copied what he found and moved on.

The third file contained information on the claim paid for damages to Janus's eye and was buried in yet another archive altogether. That there were three separate accidents to check—and not just one as Myrian would have him believe—was not a crime itself, of course, and yet, wasn't it something? A remarkable coincidence. (How things do happen.) Martin studied the material before downloading the three files, saving the information on a separate disk. He printed out the pages, placed everything in a

blue plastic folder, and delighted with the leverage he'd acquired—for all affairs demanded a certain degree of clout, the
impetus of one person to put their oars in the water and propel
the boat from shore—he sealed the folder shut and walked back
to his car.

On the same day Walter was thrown a hard curve by Gee,
Martin came into the Appetency Café and sat in Myrian's
section, ordering up coffee and a piece of key lime pie. "I'm afraid
I have some bad news," he said as she brought him his order.

"Don't tell me you're moving."

"Certain details have surfaced," he ignored her comment,
continued as if he couldn't possibly be more serious, and informed
her then how the computer at Great Mercantile Insurance was
programmed to run ongoing searches for particular types of
claims. "Smoking guns and red herrings and that sort of thing.
With so many filings each day, and the enormity of Great Mercantile, the computer looks for similarities and inconsistencies in
particular accounts, whether multiple claims were entered in a
short period of time, payouts to recurring beneficiaries, a pattern
of injury or damages. There are even listings of clients at Mercantile who have received benefits from other insurance companies on similar damages at different dates. Some information,
in fact, surfaces after being in the system for years," he paused and
pushed away his plate, glancing at Myrian to see if she was keeping up with him then.

The early evening crowd was just arriving. Myrian stood
beside Martin's table, startled and angry and wondering if she
shouldn't simply turn and walk back across the restaurant, but
afraid this would only validate Martin's suspicions, she held her
ground and insisted instead, "I've no idea what you're talking
about."

"It's only fortunate I found the printout before anyone else,"
he ignored her reply. "The powers that be at Great Mercantile

will shit if they find the same information I did," he waited once more for Myrian's response, to confirm the information he now had was something she already knew, and convinced by her silence, he lied again and explained how he'd altered the numbers on Janus's file. "This should confuse the computer briefly. That's the best I can do for now," he touched Myrian's wrist in order to emphasize the depth of his generosity, and maintaining his calm even as she pulled away, smiled as she asked, "What is it you want?"

"Are you thankful?"

"For what?"

"My helping you."

"Are you helping me, Martin?"

"That depends."

"I'm thankful."

"Pose for me then."

"And if I say no?"

"Do you really want to find out?"

She had only gotten to work at five, having visited with Walter and Rea that afternoon, but left work at seven under the excuse of being sick. Janus was keeping the clinic open late and would not be home for some time, and insisting to herself that she was doing the right thing—"To indulge him is to neutralize him. To react otherwise is to create risk."—she drank two shots of whiskey before Martin arrived, trancelike in her movements along the wall, pretending to paint and perform as he told her. At some point her clothes were lost, the click of the camera filling the apartment as she slipped between shadow and light, helpless in the same way Janus must have felt the first time his flesh and bones were crushed, unable to explain the way such an extreme and beautiful and terrible thing could happen as it did.

I drove the few blocks back to my apartment and parked across the street. The lights in front of the building were off though the sky was already dark. I sat a few minutes, then came slowly up the stairs, anxious to sit in my apartment and compose myself against the events of the day. Under the circumstances however, I didn't completely wish to be alone and decided to stop and knock on Myrian's door.

"It's me," I said, hoping she was in, knowing she was scheduled to work at some point but not sure when. Typically, upon hearing my voice, Myrian would shout, "It's open," or let me in with a quick release of the latch, but when she came tonight to the door, she parted it only a few inches and in such a way that I could barely see inside. With her face pushed up to the crack, her otherwise clear eyes appeared clouded, her expression pinched as if she'd just risen from a bad dream. "Walter," her look turned over on itself and for a brief moment her bottom lip drew in against her teeth. I started to ask if she was all right, but she stepped back suddenly then and decided to let me in.

The furniture was pushed away from the right side of the room, with several paints and brushes set out atop a half unfolded drop cloth, a fresh orange shade laid in between two pale blue stars so that it seemed at first Myrian was in the process of reworking one of her old murals. No sooner did I step inside however, than Martin Kulpepper greeted me from the opposite wall. "Walter Brimm!" he set his camera against his chest and tossed back his head.

I turned again and stared at Myrian who was wearing one of Janus's old shirts. This alone was not unusual, but as she unfolded her arms, I noticed the shirt was unbuttoned and that she'd nothing on beneath. Myrian pulled the front of her shirt together, the brief glimpse meant to provide me with a better sense of the situation, though I remained confused and watched her walk across the room and sink into the chair by the window where she lit a cigarette and stared outside.

"Why don't you sit here, Walter," Martin maneuvered the remaining chair from the collected knot of furniture and positioned it accordingly. The light in the room was bright, the tall lamp, unshaded, cast odd shadows across the floor. "Myrian's been posing for me," Martin boasted, his fallow face pinched with dark, excitable eyes. He raised his camera and spoke shamelessly about how extraordinary she looked. ("Delicious" was the word he used.) I stared at Myrian, then went to where Martin had placed the chair and dragged it back to the right side of the room. I slid the couch around, positioned it in the space where it normally stood, covered the paints and moved the brushes in order to refold the drop cloth, which I then pushed out of the way. I put the shade back on the lamp, and turning toward Martin who was carping at me the whole time, said, "I think you should go."

Martin's laugh was indecent and hung in the air several seconds too long. "What's that, Walt?"

"I'm asking you," I lowered my voice and said again, "I'd like you to leave." I hoped Martin would not make a scene, but Myrian's presence complicated matters, and all at once he was placing his free hand against my chest, and said, "Listen, I don't know why you're getting all bent out of shape. Myrian invited me. If she wants me to go she'll say so."

"I'm asking for her."

"Sorry, Walt."

"You need to get your hand off me."

"Walter, Walter, Walter."

"Shoot's over. Get out." In hindsight, I suppose I could have kept my cool another few seconds and Martin would have agreed to go, but the situation had gone on long enough, and with my mood already ruined from the day's earlier disaster, I slapped at Martin's hand and said, "I'm not going to ask you again."

For her part, Myrian showed no sign of noticing the struggle. She sat with her bare legs crossed at the ankle, her knees drawn tight, her shoulders turned at an angle which allowed her to glance out the window while the ash from her cigarette fell to the floor. I felt Martin push his arm harder against my chest, and in turn, I grabbed hold of his shirt, watching his grey mouse eyes shift back and forth before he surprised me and dropped his shoulder altogether and pushed me against the wall. (Though I was taller, I was also much older and still not completely fit, while Martin was wiry and had little trouble knocking me back.) "Listen, Brimm," he rose up on his toes, the sour smell of his breath—a mix of broccoli and beer and smoke—pouring into my face, his forearm pressing hard into my sternum. "I already told you, this is none of your business. This is between Myrian and me."

And then he was falling, suddenly, Martin's head snapped sideways in such a way that his body was sent in two directions at once. Myrian's blow—her arms outstretched as she rushed from the chair, all her earlier stillness transformed—landed square on Martin's cheek, knocking him away from me while causing him to drop his camera. "No!" his wail was loud and alarmed as he stretched and tried to keep his instrument from crashing. "Myrian!" he yelled from his knees, howling again as she took hold of his ear and dragged him into the hall where he cursed and cried and rubbed at the side of his face. "Myrian, god-damn! For Christ's sake!" he cradled his splintered camera in against his chest, his voice cracked, dissolving into a more plead-ing and pathetic tone, as from his knees he said, "Myrian" and "Myrian," again.

I went and closed the door, turning back into the center of the room where Myrian had gone to stand. It took several sec-onds before she looked at me, and when she did, it was to dis-courage me from asking her anything. I watched her go and sit again facing the window, and following her, I dropped onto the edge of the couch. (What a night it was!) Shaken, I felt sure if I went to the window I'd see the constellations imploding, the order of the moon and heavens knocked on their arterial behind. My struggle with Martin distracted me briefly from my own de-spair, though sitting alone with Myrian, my dispiritedness came back in swift, excruciating waves until the whole of my dark mood returned.

"You should get dressed," I said at last, trying not to think of Gee, determined to focus on the crisis at hand. I retrieved Myrian's jeans and socks from a corner of the room, which she slipped on, then buttoned Janus's shirt to the top, the sleeves rolled up and the tail untucked, her movements restrained as she reached for another cigarette and striking a blue-tipped kitchen match, said, "He's a son of a bitch."

"I know."

"I don't want to talk about it." She swore again, "Mother fucker," and getting up, walked to the kitchen, returning with whiskey and two glasses. I allowed her to pour a short shot into my glass, and as she sat back down, I asked, "Are you all right?"

"It isn't what you think."

"I don't think anything," I wished to reassure her that my support was unconditional.

"You see how he is," she said. "He's been after me for months. Pose for me, pose for me, pose for me. I'd had enough."

"And so you thought by giving in he'd go away?"

"Yes."

"That's not it," I responded softly.

"It is."

"If it was only Martin badgering you, you'd have ignored him forever."

"What are you saying?"

"Just that," I watched as she pulled on the ends of her shirt, the coloring in her face still off, the fullness of her lower lip drawn in as I asked her then, "So, what is it?"

"I can't tell you."

"Does it involve Janus?"

"You think I was posing for Martin because of Janus?"

"I don't know. Why don't you tell me."

"Walter. There's nothing to tell."

"I'd like to help."

"You can't."

"Not unless I know what's going on."

"Please."

"Do you trust me?"

"Of course."

"Then tell me."

And so she did.

CHAPTER 22

I left Myrian's just after nine o'clock and went straight back to my apartment where I walked into the bedroom and closed the door. Surprised? (Christ!) In a million years I would .not have guessed. I sat on the side of my bed, struggling to take in the whole of what Myrian told me. ("He did what?") Given my own arrant history, I should have been able to understand what led Janus to make the leap from theory to deed, and still I couldn't get past the shock. (Janus!) How was I supposed to respond to such news? Exactly how? What a world it was! What an incredibly unpredictable walk in the woods. In but a single night everything was again turned on its head. First Gee and Tod, then Martin and Myrian, and now Janus. I was stunned, my thoughts muddled. All of this was simply too much. What point was there in anything? (What logic?) How could I explain the madness which kept coming at me in wave after insuppressible wave no matter which way I turned?

I stared at the far wall, which was pale with yellow cracks and fissures where both shadow and light came together and disappeared. The window was covered with a sheet of cardboard and two white towels to keep out the draft. (Moisture settled into the towels and had to be replaced and defrosted each night.) I glanced at my own muted shadow, wishing I could disappear as well, wanting to somehow put distance between myself and the events of my day. I pictured Gee on the porch of my old house and how she managed to crush me with just her eyes, equating my desire to reconcile to the hopelessness of restoring a fallen fruit to the bough of its tree. I cursed, and thought of Martin whose harassment of Myrian and threats against Janus had crossed over into something dangerous and obscene, and trembling then, I wondered what to do.

I considered the three separate times Janus improvised against fate, and tried to decide if there was a numbing resignation which allowed him to stand and endure the blows that splintered his flesh and bone or did he actually feel the horror of his deed? Although my initial reaction was one of astonishment, I knew intuitively Janus's intention was selfless and prodigal—however extreme—his perfect grace and the way he conducted himself at his clinic impossible for me to ignore.

I thought next of Myrian and what she did for Janus tonight—and for me all these many weeks—and clearing my head with a purgative "Aaaarrggh!" I focused back on Martin, my indignation and contempt, outrage and fear of him, his abuse of Myrian and the threats he made against Janus swarming over me like a hive of bees all hostile and noxious. But what could I do? I got up and went to my closet, searching for my suitcase, thinking what I really needed was to get away for awhile, to separate myself from everything and escape. All of this insanity was simply too much and who could blame me if I decided it was time to leave?

I tossed my suitcase onto the bed and began stuffing my socks and T-shirts, underwear and slacks inside. The gun Jack gave me several weeks ago was also hidden in the closet and I stuck it in the pocket of my jacket as I continued to pack, carrying on this way until my effort to flee revealed itself as farce, and throwing up my hands, I cursed again and hurried toward the door.

Halfway into the hall however, intent on seeing Martin and making sure his threats against Janus went no further, I stopped and realized my decision here, too, was flawed, for other than to bark and bleat and plead with Martin to leave Janus be I had no plan at all. Why would he listen to me? Why should he care what

I asked when we just nearly came to blows? No, what I required was a more specific strategy, a faultless bit of leverage to keep Janus from harm, and finding the keys to Janus's car still in my pocket, I went downstairs and drove across town, along the Avenues and West Belmarke Boulevard on my way to see Jack.

Jack Gorne stood near his high wall of windows and stared out over the city, toward Pendelton Field and the Mitlankee River. "Baaaah!" (He was in a bad frame of mind.) His latest investment—into which he sank substantially more than a large sum of cash—had crashed and burned. (Moods such as this, when he felt the firmament of his being unravel and taunt his faith, turned him coarse and vengeful.) His plan to import and sell genetically modified soybean seeds developed in Argentina and Brazil had suffered a serious blow, victimized by circumstances beyond his control. Just last week, Garst Seed Company, manufacturer of genetically altered StarLink corn—FDA approved as livestock feed only—was accused of allowing its corn to wind up in taco shells distributed nationwide by Kraft. With testing for human consumption incomplete, the press had a field day running articles suggesting the food chain was now dangerously compromised. Immediate recalls and buybacks of every last kernel of StarLink corn was ordered, while politicians threatened a moratorium on all forms of genetic farming in the United States.

"Fuck!" and "Fuck!" again. A public relations nightmare to be sure—and worse!—for the press was now reporting that a protein spawned by StarLink, Cry9c, was toxic to corn bores and other beneficial insects. Although Jack's soybean seeds were completely safe, his deal fell victim to hysteria, the lobbyists he hired and officials he bribed all for naught, while everything—"Goddamn it to hell!"—blew up overnight. "Fuck, shit, and hell!" he was in the middle of chanting when Walter arrived and buzzed up from the street.

"If it isn't too late," I waited several seconds for Jack to buzz me up, and once inside, told him everything that happened tonight. The stars and moon outside the windows on the twenty-first floor of Fordum Towers shined in the distance, the sky otherwise ebony and aphotic. I noticed at once Jack's mood was off—instead of his usual irreverence and drollery he was brusque—and still he listened to what I had to say, and only afterward did he reply, "So let me get this straight, your friend smashed himself up in order to defraud the insurance companies, and now this Martin person's threatening to turn him in and you want my help?"

"That's right."

"What exactly do you want from me?"

"I don't know. The last time, I mean with Gee, you said I should have come to you first."

"That was then."

"But Janus," I felt a need to explain, only Jack interrupted and mocked me with, "Are you telling me the ever-righteous Walter Brimm condones what the good doctor did?"

"Janus had his reasons. He was trying to keep the clinic open. He did what he had to."

"As you tried when you first went after Marcum."

"That was different."

"How?"

"Because I was wrong."

"Ha!" Jack raised his right hand alternately with his left as if taking measure. "Let me get this straight, the good doctor fucks the insurance companies in the name of his clinic and that's OK, and you fuck Marcum because the man's stealing your wife and that isn't?"

Frustrated—what a day it had been!—I answered, "You can't compare the two."

"Why can't I?"

"Because Janus wasn't thinking about himself."

"Brimm, Brimm, Brimm," Jack waved me off. "Don't be such an innocent. There isn't a man alive who doesn't act with self interest. Your friend did precisely what he wanted. No one was holding a gun to his head. The only difference between you and him is that he had the balls to get what he wanted without moralizing over whether or not the means justified the end," Jack got up and walked to the southernmost side of the room and the gold spiral staircase. I watched him ascend, winding and stopping just shy of the ceiling—a good thirty feet above the floor—and turning, he sat on the top step with both legs dangling over the edge. From so far away I didn't expect his voice to reach me, but the absence of walls and further furnishings inside the apartment created a cavernous expanse, allowing his words to ring down, resonant and clear. "So what exactly do you want from me?" he asked again.

"I don't know. What do you think?"

"Do you want me to put the fear of God in this Martin person? Should I bribe him, scare him, what?"

"Anything."

Jack leaned forward on the top step until I thought he might fall, his hands extended like wings, a gauzy darkness settling across his face as he stared down at me. "You want me to do your dirty work, is that it?"

"No," I lied. "I just need your help."

I watched as Jack twisted his way back down the stairs, passing through the shadows and across the floor. (He moved with an absence of grace, his elbows arched, his right shoulder turned forcefully as if pushing against an invisible weight.) "I'll tell you what," he looked at me then, a bit oddly yet not altogether dismissive. "You get things started and I'll help you out. Show me you can handle this sort of undertaking this time and I'll make sure you see things through."

"But that's just it," I struggled again to make him understand. "I can't do it. I don't know what to do. That's why I came to see you, Jack."

His stare was now severe as he leaned forward and jabbed his right index finger in the air as if to inflict permanent holes in the space between us. "I thought you told me you learned your lesson the last time. I thought you understood the necessity of finishing what you start."

"But I don't know where to start. Martin won't listen to me and I'm no good at this sort of thing."

"Bullshit. If you want to help your friend, go ahead and do it. I'll be right behind you when the time comes."

I continued to argue, and rocking anxiously back and forth, I thought of what Jack just said about doing what had to be done, and what Janus said earlier in all but the same words, and how could two so dissimilar forces follow the same edict to such inconsonant ends? Confused, I grabbed at the front of my knees in order to quit rocking and pleaded with Jack, "Understand, please. I can't do things the way you can. Certain situations require more than I can handle and that's when I fall short."

I didn't stop there and insisted again, "I'm no good at rising to the occasion. In this sort of situation, I've no idea how to start," and then I told Jack about the dream I had when I first came down with my fever, the one where the man trained his soul to deal with both universal darkness and light by abandoning dogs out in the woods, and as I did so, Jack's look turned even more queer, and shaking his head he finally asked, "What are you talking about, Brimm? You think you made that up? You think that was a dream?"

I fell silent, puzzled and staring at Jack. I knew I dreamed the scene just as I said, only here was Jack laughing and waving his hands in the air, insisting, "If it's experience you're worried about, Brimm, I can take you into the woods right now and show you exactly how to train your soul," and then he was laughing again, and assuring me that I should just go ahead and get started—"Go ahead, Brimm. Go on. Go on."—and that he'd be right behind me, and how confident he was that I would get things right this time, and laughing still, louder and more corrupt, motivating me—by what I wasn't sure—until at last I did get up and walked out the door.

———————————————————

Driving then, a body brought from rest to motion in a spectacle of flight, terrified and eager.

Martin heard the knock and asked, "Who is it?"

Walter had taken the stairs quietly, moving to the third floor landing, past Myrian's apartment where he assumed she and Janus were not yet asleep. (It was just after midnight and the events of the evening held much to talk over.) He pressed his face into the crack of the door and half whispered his reply.

"Brimm?" Martin undid the lock, his eyes pinched, a bluish bruise on his left cheek where Myrian struck him centered by a darker purplish welt, his mouth twisted into a dissolute sort of sneer. "What do you want?" His voice—a sparrow's caw at even the best of times—was uninviting.

"I came to apologize," Walter said. "I'd like to talk. May I come in?"

"Go away."

"Please. It's important. I have something for you."

Dubious, Martin was also curious, and stepping back, he said, "I'll give you one minute," and let Walter in.

I walked toward the coffee table where pieces of Martin's broken camera were spread out in varying states of disrepair, a set of tiny tools used—without success—to fix the fractured parts. Martin sat in the chair near the end of the table, wearing only boxer shorts and a white T-shirt, sorting through the pile of knobs and screws. He had small, effeminate hands that seemed well suited to such delicate work, though his fingers were inexpert, the mechanics of his movements coarse and clumsy. I watched him for a moment, unsure how best to proceed, and taking two steps toward the center of the room said, "About your camera. I'd like to pay for the repairs."

"Would you now? And is that what you have for me, Walt?"

"For your camera," I repeated.

"And why do you want to do this?"

"For compensation, because I'm partly responsible for what happened. I can pay you."

"For my camera?"

"For your camera, yes."

Martin settled his shoulders against the back of his chair, his hands locked behind his head, his elbows flared out and his thin arms showing their slight lump of muscle. "I don't know, Walt. I've had her a long time. She's been around the world with me and then some. I'm not sure she can be repaired."

"I'll buy you a new one then."

"Is that right?"

"Yes."

"All this for my camera?" he asked again, to which I nodded, "Of course."

His mousy face broke into a grin. "You wouldn't be trying to bribe me here, would you, Walt?"

"I don't know what you're talking about."

"Come on."

"If you mean Janus."

"You want me to bury what I have on the good doctor, right?"

"If I was to pay you," I went ahead and addressed the possibility.

"A bribe?"

"A deal, between the two of us."

"But as I work for GMI, it would have to be construed as a bribe."

"As you work for GMI," I heard my voice grow tense, "your using work product to blackmail Myrian could get you fired."

"How much money are we talking about?" Martin was suddenly interested in specifics. I took another step forward and asked in turn, "How much would it take?"

"Who knows," he broadened his grin, more insolent now. "OK. I'm going to accept your offer, for my camera only," he cocked his head and quoted me a ridiculously high price for a new Mamiya, mocking me with, "A check will be fine there, Walt." I stood three feet from the end of the table, my arms dangling down at the sides of my jacket while Martin taunted me further. "Throw in another $5,000 and I won't sue you for assault."

I watched as he looked away, turning his attention back to the pile of screws spread out on the table, and when I didn't say anything in response, he lifted his head suddenly, scowling, "Is there something else?"

I struggled to hold onto what remained of my composure, concentrating on keeping my voice low so that I couldn't be heard through the wall. "I want you to leave Myrian and Janus alone."

"So you've said."

"I'm serious."

"I'll take the money for my camera, but that's all."

"If it's a matter of more money."

"It isn't."

"Because I can pay you. We can work something out."

"Sorry."

"Why not?"

"Because the jig's up."

"Why are you doing this?"

"It's my job, Walt."

"I'll get you fired then."

"No you won't. I have the facts. Any other story you come up with will sound desperate."

"Stop. Please."

"Can't do it, Walt."

I moved closer to the table, standing near enough to see the thinnest strands of whiskers in Martin's scant moustache. "Where's your proof?" I asked, my shoulders trembling again, though my shaking this time seemed different, more presupposing and generated from an altogether separate source. "Who's to say Janus's accidents aren't all a coincidence?"

"That's right. Maybe the good doctor just has bad luck."

"Your evidence is circumstantial."

"If that's the case, what are you worried about? I'll turn in my report and we'll see what my bosses say."

"You think Myrian won't hate you if you turn Janus in? You think she doesn't hate you now?"

"You let me worry about that."

"Why are you doing this?"

"That's the third time you've asked me, Walt."

"But I can pay you. Please. If you really care for Myrian, you'll leave Janus alone."

Martin laughed. "Noble gestures, is that it?"

"Yes!"

"Fuck you! If Myrian hates me, as you say, I've nothing to lose by turning the good doctor in. We all get what's coming to us, don't we, Walt?" his grin stretched with such menace that his reference struck me like a blow to the chest. I continued to plead, and begged him, "Think of what you're doing. Think of everyone who'll be hurt. Please. You don't understand. You don't want to do this. Leave Janus be!" only he'd have none of it, and laughing again, he mocked me by lifting his arms behind his head once more in order to demonstrate how helpless I was to stop him.

Frantic and unsure what else to do, I spotted the photograph of Myrian in the moonlight hanging on the far wall, and turning away from Martin, I paced to the window, then back across the room where I nearly sank to my knees and wept the way I had a few months before. I thought about all the many days and weeks that had passed, about action and inaction, love and charity and duty, of Gee and Rea and Tod, of Myrian and Janus, about my parents, Katherine and Charles, of redemption and disappointment, penitence and compunction, of humility and compassion, about the clinic and serenity and oblation, need and desire, sacrifice and grace, of infinite sorrow and loss, of frustration and fury, until all at once I was whirling back around, the weight in my side pocket banging against my hip as I flailed my arms in the air, and reaching down, I pulled out the gift from Jack. Martin jumped as I turned to face him, no longer laughing, surprised to see how calm I was, how utterly serene and persuaded that everything could be restored to order and permanently resolved.

CHAPTER 23

Ⅰ screw things up sometimes. Obviously it's true, though I'm not offended any longer by those who insist on pointing this out to me and go on about my business now as best I'm able.

Looking back, I remember a woman down the hall screaming just as Janus and Myrian burst through the door and another man charging in saying he'd called the police. Janus knelt beside Martin to make sure there was nothing to be done, while Myrian—remarkably cool in the midst of crisis—made a quick search of Martin's apartment for the pertinent folder, which she took back to her flat. I've tried often since then, but can't recall exactly what I felt in those first few hours, whether I grieved my error or excused my actions and viewed what happened as part of some unique circumstance triggered by the fragility of my mood. For the most part I was completely numb, and if there was a benefit that came from my being still in a state of shock, it was that I remained as yet too dazed to fall apart.

Janus suffered a different sort of confusion. Staggered by what happened, he came from his knees and grabbed hold of my arm, moving me into the hall and down to my apartment. The bones of his shattered foot were set unevenly down upon the cold flat surface of my floor, the ache that I knew to enter his hip and lower back at night evident in the stiffness of his posture as he stood before the wall where Myrian had painted both Gee and Rea. His bad eye watered white tears which he wiped clean, his splintered iris holding my image in its wound. The fingers on his left hand were bent as always and covered with a flesh once torn by the smashing of bone, regenerated in thickened patches of pasty scars and odd stretches of tissue. Myrian had already told him about Martin and the events of our night when the gun went off, and shifting his weight away from his bad leg, he raised his crippled hand, and softly asked, "Whatever were you thinking, Walter?"

There was no need to tell him, of course, and so I didn't.

After a minute, we went back next door. The police treated me well enough, my muddled state working to my advantage as I confessed nothing. With my one phone call I got hold of Jack who came through in the end—"You did what, Brimm? But god-damn!"—and immediately arranged a criminal attorney who presented to the police a story of self defense. The gun Jack provided was unregistered and impossible to trace, the fabrication suggesting the weapon belonged to Martin, that I had gone by his apartment to make amends for an earlier argument and he'd become violent. Jack pulled strings, used his clout, and twelve hours later I was released on bail. "Tell me our justice system isn't the best in the world!" Jack slapped his hand across my back. "Don't sweat it, Brimm. Goddamn! Brass balls! I've a new hero! You'll slide through this like warm jism on a hooker's ass!"

Action and reaction. (Who might have guessed?) Early Monday, Janus went downtown and met with the Board of Directors at GMI. The president, CEO, and several other officers were each astonished—for what could one possibly say after hearing such an improbable confession?—and together they spent some time in private consultation. Attorneys were contacted, along with officers at the other insurance carriers with whom Janus had filed a claim, and taking into consideration the reputation of the man with whom they were dealing and the extraordinariness of his story, they assessed the particulars of what could be done. Eventually—and conceding there was nothing to gain from pursuing the matter with any sort of vigilance—a deal was struck, a silent agreement from which everyone stood to benefit, money promised and secured from the Trust, and that was the end of that.

How things do happen.

Only a handful of people bothered to attend Martin's funeral. I stood hidden in the back, listening as a pastor in black robe and paisley pants offered a brief eulogy though he'd never met Martin and admitted as much not once but several times during the course of his encomium. Later, Gee phoned for the first time since I moved downtown, having heard about the shooting and wanting to know what happened and if I was all right. "Whatever were you thinking?" she, too, felt a need to ask, and here I very nearly told her, "I was thinking of you," but such would have been cruel—what's done is done—and so again I said nothing and let things go at that.

Ten minutes later the phone rang once more and it was Rea, having also learned about my incident the other night, alarmed by what she overheard between her mother and Tod and frightened for me, her voice breaking, she found my number and slipped upstairs. "Daddy? Daddy? Daddy?" she said over and over, and began to weep. I assured her I was OK, allayed her fears, and made clear I wasn't physically harmed. In my eagerness to put her mind at ease, I answered all her questions with more detail than I provided anyone else at the time. (There is a particular comfort which comes when speaking to a child, for in their presence one is able to cast aside the clutter of false excuse and cut more freely to the core.) She wanted to know about the man who died and I told her then that he was someone I barely knew who'd threatened to hurt a friend of mine. "Like the boy in the park?" she asked, and I answered, "Exactly like that."

I expected her to have me distinguish then how I found fault with her performance yet, not twelve hours later, I did worse, but rather than query me in terms of moral ambiguities—of Right and Wrong—and how my deed might be justified while hers was not, she surprised me with a more essential question, forcing me to reassess my position—my poltroonery as it were and reticence to review my deed in total—as she asked, "Did you mean to do it, Daddy?" and what could I tell her then but "Yes."

An hour later, I was back downtown speaking to the police, and by nightfall my bail was revoked. Those who came initially to my defense were surprised to hear that I confessed. Even the police did not know what to make of me—they'd all but decided the case against me was weak—and when they asked why I was changing my tune now, I shrugged and told them simply, "Because this is the way it was."

The food I'm served, the sounds I hear, access to newspapers and books, even the thinness of my mattress and coloring of my walls are much the same as always, and other than my inability to visit the clinic and see my daughter and friends, I follow a routine similar to the way I lived on the east side of Renton. The papers come to the library, and some I receive, a day or two late, in the mail. I have a portable computer and research material at my ready. (The stock market isn't difficult to track and I continue to manage the clinic's Trust with regular success.) I read the business sections scrupulously and other stories as well. Just last week, I read an article on Abu Shlomo Ami, a Palestinian, who saved the life of Ehud Shamir, an Israeli, by knocking him out of the way of a car driven through a crowded intersection in Azur. From his hospital bed, where Abu Shlomo was recovering from the amputation of his right leg and arm, he looked out dolefully, and in answer to the questions put to him, replied in a voice surprisingly firm, "What else was I to do?"

I stand at my window and stare out at a patchwork of fading stars and a pale half offering of moon. The air—as I imagine it— is warm now and no doubt hinting of spring. I think of my circumstance, and the way I came from there to here, and how in love and war, feast and famine, fair weather and foul, the distinction between one man's good fortune and another's ruin is not found in the arbitrary construct of the universe, but in the choices made day to day. This is the order found at the heart of all dense matter.

Last week was my birthday. Janus and Myrian came to visit, Jack phoned, as did Rea and briefly Gee. That morning, I read a piece in the *Renton Bugle* describing an incident that happened some forty-odd years ago today. A freighter carrying 6,000 sheep sank in Kuwait's largest harbor, threatening to contaminate the country's entire water supply if not recovered in time. Karl Kroyer, a Danish engineer, happened to remember a comic strip he read as a boy in which Donald Duck no less retrieved his own boat from the bottom of a lake by filling the hull with Ping-Pong balls, enabling the ship to float to the surface. Inspired, Kroyer had millions of hollow pellets pumped into the sunken freighter, hoping to effect a similar result, and how extraordinary but the plan worked! I think of this tale often now, in dark moments and times of potential crisis, and calculate what around me will float and what will sink me for certain.

ACKNOWLEDGMENTS

In the course of any prolonged project, one encounters many people to whom they become indebted. My experience has been no different and I would like to thank then first and foremost: my parents, Ilene and Stan, whose unwavering support was unconditional and for whom no words of thanks can ever be enough; my brother, Bob (Bobby), whose own endless support—and love—proves once again that sibling rivalry need never affect our relationship; my publisher, James Pannell, for his generosity, his faith and vision all but unheard of in this day and age; Debra Hudak, for innumerable suggestions on the manuscript and overseeing the entire production process; Martha and Jim, the dearest of friends; Barbara Ellis, for her own blind faith; my agents, Elizabeth Winick and Henry Williams of McIntosh and Otis; and last, but never least, my glorious family, my core and foundation, the everything on which I selfishly balance my madness, my daughter, Anna, son Zach, and eternal Mary. Thank you. Without you, I do not exist.